Shard at Bay

By the same author:

WHISTLE AND I'LL COME
THE KID
STORM SOUTH
HOPKINSON AND THE DEVIL OF HATE
LEAVE THE DEAD BEHIND US
MARLEY'S EMPIRE
BOWERING'S BREAKWATER
SLADD'S EVIL
A TIME FOR SURVIVAL
POULTER'S PASSAGE
THE DAY OF THE COASTWATCH
MAN, LET'S GO ON
HALF A BAG OF STRINGER
THE GERMAN HELMET
THE OIL BASTARDS
PULL MY STRING
COACH NORTH

Featuring *Commander Shaw:*

GIBRALTAR ROAD
REDCAP
BLUEBOLT ONE
THE MAN FROM MOSCOW
WARMASTER
MOSCOW COACH
THE DEAD LINE
SKYPROBE
THE SCREAMING DEAD BALLOONS
THE BRIGHT RED BUSINESSMEN
THE ALL-PURPOSE BODIES
HARTINGER'S MOUSE
THIS DRAKOTNY . . .
SUNSTRIKE
CORPSE
WEREWOLF
ROLLERBALL

Featuring *Simon Shard:*

CALL FOR SIMON SHARD

A VERY BIG BANG
BLOOD RUN EAST
THE EROS AFFAIR
BLACKMAIL NORTH
SHARD CALLS THE TUNE
THE HOOF

Featuring *Lieutenant St. Vincent Halfhyde, R.N.:*

BEWARE, BEWARE THE BIGHT OF BENIN
HALFHYDE'S ISLAND
THE GUNS OF ARREST
HALFHYDE TO THE NARROWS
HALFHYDE FOR THE QUEEN
HALFHYDE ORDERED SOUTH
HALFHYDE AND THE FLAG CAPTAIN
HALFHYDE ON THE YANGTZE
HALFHYDE ON ZANATU
HALFHYDE OUTWARD BOUND
THE HALFHYDE LINE

Featuring *Donald Cameron:*

CAMERON, ORDINARY SEAMAN
CAMERON COMES THROUGH
CAMERON OF THE CASTLE BAY
LIEUTENANT CAMERON, R.N.V.R.
CAMERON'S CONVOY
CAMERON IN THE GAP
ORDERS FOR CAMERON
CAMERON IN COMMAND
CAMERON AND THE *KAISERHOF*
CAMERON'S RAID

Non-Fiction:

TALL SHIPS: THE GOLDEN AGE OF SAIL
GREAT YACHTS

Shard at Bay

A 'Simon Shard' novel

Philip McCutchan

HODDER AND STOUGHTON

LONDON   SYDNEY   AUCKLAND   TORONTO

British Library Cataloguing in Publication Data

McCutchan, Philip
  Shard at bay.
  I. Title
  823'.914[F]   PR6063.A167

  ISBN 0 340 34445 8

Hodder and Stoughton Editorial Office: 47 Bedford Square, London WC1B 3DP.

1

Hedge had been annoyed when Tayside Police had thundered on his door in the exclusive Atholl Palace Hotel in Pitlochry. Thundered was his word, not theirs: they thought they were being discreet. They knew the importance of Hedge; it was because of his standing in the Foreign Office that plain clothes men had been sent to convey the message that couldn't come by the open telephone line.

"Mr Hedge?" one of them, a chunky man with big ears, said interrogatively.

"Yes, yes, why on earth – "

"May we come in, sir?" A card was palmed: Hedge studied it. CID, and the speaker appeared to be Detective Sergeant MacCrimmon.

"It's very early," Hedge said, sounding petulant.

"But a fine, grand morning," MacCrimmon said. It wasn't early for the police. "The matter's urgent, sir. May we come in, please?"

"Oh, very well." Hedge stood aside. MacCrimmon went in like a great bear. His companion was introduced as Detective Constable Campbell. He looked what he was: very new to the

5

CID, and uncertain of himself in a posh suite. "Well?" Hedge asked peremptorily, tightening the cord of his orange silk dressing-gown. "What's this all about?"

MacCrimmon told him. "A message to Perth HQ, sir. From London, the Foreign Office."

"Ah. From whom in particular?"

"The Permanent Under-Secretary of State, sir."

"I see." Hedge almost genuflected. His own immediate boss, the Head of Security, was a mere second-grade God. He felt honoured and managed to look gratified.

"The message, sir, is short. You're required at Faslane on the Gareloch. The Clyde submarine base – "

"Yes, yes, I'm aware of what it is. Why?"

MacCrimmon shrugged. "I don't know. You just are, sir."

Hedge gave him a quick look: impertinence, or not? It was unlikely, considering Hedge's rank. Just Scottish. Scots were a dour lot, often uncouth. MacCrimmon went on, "We have a car. It's at your disposal, Mr Hedge."

"Thank you, but no. I have my own and I've no intention of leaving it behind. Vandals, you know." Hedge noted that Detective Constable Campbell appeared to be stifling an involuntary laugh; it was perhaps unusual to speak of vandals entering the grounds of the Atholl Palace but Hedge never took chances if he could avoid them and policemen of all people should know that complacency was wrong, was irresponsible. Hedge had never thought much of the police; an arrogant lot on the whole, not what they had been in his younger days, touching their helmets to their superiors. Hedge was old enough to remember pre-war days, staying with his grand-parents in the country where there had been a solid, bicycle-mounted village bobby, slow, ponderous and respectful. When the young Hedge and Betts had met in the village street where Hedge's grandfather was the squire, a JP and a Deputy Lieutenant, it had been a case of touched helmets and "Good morning, Master Cyril," to which Hedge's response had been "Good morning, Betts." Nicer days; but Hedge was forced back to the present by Detective Sergeant MacCrimmon.

"Take you two, two-and-half hours, Mr Hedge. Twisty roads after Dunkeld. Know the route, do you?"

6

"Vaguely."

"I'll route you," MacCrimmon said, producing a folded road map.

*   *   *

"Stuffed shirt," Campbell said as they drove away from the Atholl Palace.

"Sassenach."

"Aye, that's true, Sarge. All the same, are Sassenachs. Think they're something special." Campbell ruminated as they took the M9 south. "Vandals, in the Atholl Palace!"

MacCrimmon nodded and grinned tightly. "Nevertheless, don't laugh next time, Detective Constable Campbell. They don't like it. And we have a job we're reasonably well paid to do . . . I'd like us to keep it. Mr Hedge ranks as a VIP and he's said to be a bastard – I told you that, did I not?"

"Sorry, Sarge."

"Another thing: the job he does is dangerous . . . God knows what he might catch from the peace women around Faslane!"

Campbell glanced sideways. "That a joke, Sarge?"

"Not entirely."

*   *   *

Irritation rather than danger was on the mind of Hedge as he followed MacCrimmon's route by the A822 from Dunkeld to Kinloch, Amulree and Corrymuckloch to Crieff where he picked up the A85 past Loch Earn and then turned right through Glen Ogle for Glen Dochart and Crianlarich. Never mind that Crianlarich consisted merely of a railway station and siding plus a hotel and a handful of nondescript houses: almost every road in Scotland carried a sign for Crianlarich. A few more miles beyond and Hedge was coming down to the head of Loch Lomond. As that policeman had said, it was a fine morning and the glimpses of Loch Lomond between the trees were certainly beautiful, though they scarcely compensated for an early start after a rushed breakfast and the thought that he might now have to spend longer in Scotland, a country he had

7

visited only by order of the Head of Security (now down with shingles, which could be why the Permanent Under-Secretary himself had sent the message. Security was security and the Head had always had direct access to the top.) In being sent to Scotland Hedge had felt side-tracked: the Head had dreamed up an anxiety concerning the security of the Loch Faskally dam, a vital part, of course, of the North of Scotland Hydro-Electric scheme. All sorts of people, the Head had said, could do diabolical things to it – blow it up, poison the waters . . . probably he had been already sickening for the shingles. Hedge had argued his corner without success: he'd been ordered north and the Secretary of State for Scotland, whose pigeon it surely was, had not even been informed. Now, being already in Scotland, Hedge was being made use of.

He arrived at Tarbet angrily, his mind switching back to policemen. His own senior policeman, Detective Chief Superintendent Shard on secondment from the Yard, was a case in point. Argumentative, stood by his own point of view and seemed to regard the Foreign Office as peopled largely by dunderheads and geriatrics. Shard . . . *he* should have done the Loch Faskally job! Hedge didn't at all like being used as a field man. He preferred the plushness of his office suite and the handiness of his secretary and staff. Damn Shard, who'd been in Wales rather conveniently, liaising with Cardiff police over a man, a foreigner of course, who'd disembarked from a ship in the docks . . . Hedge turned right for Arrochar, whence he took the road down Loch Long for Garelochhead and, some five twisting miles beyond, after passing a number of what looked like oil storage tanks and a fuelling pier, picked up the right-hand turn for HMS *Neptune*, the Clyde submarine base on the Gareloch where lived, when not on patrol, the great nuclear-powered and nuclear-armed underwater fleet, NATO's last hope. Just beyond the turn he saw the caravans and the slogans: SEND BACK THE MISSILES. WOMEN FOR PEACE. MAKE LOVE NOT WAR, how stupid and dated! YANKS OUT and all the rest. Hedge's lip curled. Vermin. The caravans were filthy: Hedge fancied he caught the stench swirling in through the car's windows. Sick-looking, apathetic children who ought to have been taken into care by the local council, knickers waving from a makeshift clothes-line, stink of cooking oil like a hamburger stall, a woman squatting unashamedly behind a thin tree that gave no cover at all, toilet paper blowing about and a long-haired so-called man stark naked in a caravan doorway – it was summer and the weather was mild – smoking what was probably a reefer.

It made one quite ill.

Thankfully, Hedge turned down for the base, approached the gates and was stopped by a policeman and a policewoman, a pretty girl, and young. Hedge liked young girls, and the look on his face, as she asked for identification, was almost a smirk.

"Hedge of the Foreign Office." It sounded important, given added weight by Hedge's pompous voice and never mind the smirk; but all the WPC saw was a fattish man, soft white hands on the steering wheel, a man not far off being elderly, balding, jowly, and puffy round the eyes. She said, "Your identification, please, sir."

"I've already said."

She was patient: very often the old didn't take it in first time. "An identity card . . . "

The smirk vanished. "I never carry one. You should know that, young woman. Surely you've been warned?"

The policeman was coming up, the male one. There was a conference, and a sergeant was called out from a sort of guard room, outside which stood a naval rating on sentry duty, with a gun. They had not been warned; Hedge was shunted into a recess beside the guard room, looking daggers.

"I've never been treated like this before. I shall report this to the Commodore of the base. I'm being waited for, I suppose you realise?"

"We're ringing through – "

"It's scandalous. Absolutely scandalous! Utter inefficiency and I shall say so in the proper quarter."

"I'm sorry, sir. Security is – "

"I know all about that, thank you." Hedge, red-faced, sat stiffly holding his steering-wheel. The WPC went away, rudely Hedge thought. The naval rating watched Hedge, holding his weapon in a more pointed manner in case a spy made a dash for it. The girl was speaking again to the male policeman;

9

Hedge believed he had worried them, and serve them right. Later, they could stew in the juice of a reprimand. In a low voice the WPC was saying, "He doesn't look all that high powered, Alec."

"Daft old bastard. All the same, if he's genuine we should have been told."

Within half a minute they were and Hedge got a salute and an apology, plus directions as to how to find the Commanding Officer, Commodore Rushcroft. Hedge drove into the base proper, fuming. There was a good deal of activity, a number of busy people, naval personnel plus civilians, and an obvious police presence – Ministry of Defence police patrolling alertly, no doubt as much because of the peace women as because of possible spies or saboteurs. Hedge had never been very impressed with military or naval security – certainly as regards the military there was virtually none: any fool could get into a barracks and plant bombs and such, the whole thing was wide open. And take Portsmouth: you were supposed to be watched and convoyed when, for instance, you visited the *Victory* as a tourist, but in fact, once in, the dockyard was wide open to those of ill-intent.

However, it was different here at Faslane. They were taking security seriously and Hedge was relieved to note it. He decided not, after all, to make too much of the attitude of the police on the gate. If he did he could be made to look a fool, since he of all people should be applauding conscientiousness. He would, however, make a strong complaint about his arrival not being notified to the main gate. Really, he should have been met by a senior officer.

* * *

Rushcroft, who held the appointment of Commodore Clyde, was a small man, thin and bird-like and very sharp in speech, manner and intelligence. He seemed to be summing Hedge up, which Hedge disliked. Hedge had stated his complaint but had received no apology. Rushcroft had waved a hand airily and said, "We're busy, you know. Busy. Important matters." That was all.

10

"But surely – "

"Yes." Commodore Rushcroft had something in that sharp manner that said he didn't like civilians, of which there was already another present, a mousy man from the Defence Ministry whom Hedge knew of as a confounded nuisance and didn't like. He didn't expect this man to contribute much to the proceedings and he was proved right. The little wretch always reserved his comments for his own bosses. Hedge was introduced without further delay to a vice-admiral – Flag Officer Submarines, who had come up from Fort Blockhouse, the Portsmouth submarine base; and to an American captain named Rubinovitch, who came from the Poseidon base on the Holy Loch and in response to Hedge's muttered how-d'you-do, said, "Hi." He was a shambling man and wore gold-rimmed spectacles perched on a broad nose. He was big, bigger even than Detective-Sergeant MacCrimmon, and looked too gross to fit down a submarine's conning-tower hatch. The introductions made, Rushcroft lost no time in coming to the point.

"There was a penetration during the night, Mr Hedge. I've already informed the admiral and Captain Rubinovitch."

Rubinovitch said, "Sure have," and looked through his spectacles, enquiringly, at Hedge.

Hedge asked, "Of the base, do you mean?"

"What else?"

"The peace women?" Hedge asked gropingly.

"The intruder was male, and not peaceful. He was armed, and he was shot by a security guard."

"Oh dear." Hedge sucked in his cheeks and sat down with a thump: there would be trouble about this. There had been that continuing fuss about the Greenham missile base, the awful possibility that someone might get shot by an American. It was good that it wasn't a peace woman but it was serious enough even so. "Badly?" Hedge asked.

"Dead."

Hedge gasped. "Goodness gracious me!"

"I'm not asking for veiled comment, Mr Hedge. I am *informing* you, that's all. The thing's done. Of course, I'd have wished it otherwise – questioning might have been useful had

11

he lived. However, I lay no blame on the man who shot him. That's what security guards are for. The man did his duty.''

Hedge was still gasping. "Has this been released?''

"Certainly not. And won't be – from this base at all events. In the wider sense, it's up to the Ministry. And you, I gather.''

"Yes, yes.'' Hedge had his handkerchief out and was mopping a sweating face. "I agree with you. The press should be held off, at least until I've had a chance to consult with – with my Under-Secretary – ''

"Pippin.''

Hedge stared. "What?''

"Pippin.''

"Ah, yes. But in the Foreign Office we don't call Sir Edmund that. You know him?''

"At Dartmouth with his younger brother.''

Hedge cleared his throat, feeling on unsafe ground. Sir Edmund was known as a capricious man, and now it seemed that Rushcroft had a direct line to him. Rushcroft, however, was not plugging it – yet. He went on, "A thorough search was made of the body but there's no identification. You'd better take a look at it – what?''

"There's just a chance – ''

"That you might have come across him, have him on file – slim, but can't be neglected. He's on ice.''

"Yes, I see. Tell me, how did he get in?''

"Swam,'' Rushcroft said. He walked to a window, beckoning Hedge to join him. He pointed across the Gareloch, across placid blue water, almost the blue of the Mediterranean. A heat haze hung over it, but the farther shore was clear enough. Rushcroft said, "Weak point – the road that runs down the other side of the loch, from Garelochhead to Clynder, Rosneath, Kilcreggan. We're wide open, for one thing, to tourists' cameras – every Tom, Dick and Harry's equipped like a film cameraman these days. I've no doubt there's many a blown-up shot of us in the Kremlin.''

"And a swimmer . . . ''

"It's not all that far. A mile. Of course, he could have gone over from a boat – we don't know. Anyway, he was wearing a wet suit. And he was wet.''

"He wasn't seen to - to emerge?"

Rushcroft scowled. "Black mark and I accept it. No, he wasn't. But I don't think it was long before he was spotted or he would have dried out more than he was - the wet suit I mean."

"There was an exchange of fire?"

"Yes."

"And the peace women?"

Rushcroft glanced at the Vice-Admiral, then away again. He said shortly, "They began howling. That's how I'd describe it. Like a lot of banshees - horrible."

"But they've not reacted, apart from that?"

Rushcroft said, "They besieged the gates within minutes of the howling. Both gates. They went on howling, yelling obscenities. The guard was called out . . . and they dispersed soon after dawn. They could be back."

"Do you see a connexion, Commodore? I mean, could they have thought one of their number - "

"I can't say what they thought, they just heard shots and made the most of it. As I said, I'm definite the man was not from the peace camp - "

"Those women!" Hedge said viciously. "Quite appalling, so *unfeminine*. We should build concentration camps."

2

Hedge was taken to see the body; Rushcroft went with him, Captain Rubinovitch and the Vice-Admiral remaining behind. Hedge was ruffled: most surprisingly in his view, the remark about concentration camps hadn't gone down very well with the Vice-Admiral, who held no brief for the peace women but did stress their right to a point of view, their right to express it however confounded a nuisance they might be in the process. They as well as everyone else had to live in Britain. All that had taken the wind from Hedge's sails. Deflated, he had made vague noises of a non-committal nature until he had been rescued by Commodore Rushcroft, who produced from a drawer in his desk a square of plastic about three millimetres thick with a couple of screw-holes bored through it.

"Found by the body," he said, handing it to Hedge.

There was black lettering on white. Hedge gaped at it. It read:

Detachment
Ex
Against
The
Holocaust

14

Hedge said, "I don't follow." He read the words aloud, then repeated, "Detachment Ex against . . . It makes no sense."

Rushcroft said, "The initial letters form the word death."

"Ah, yes – yes, I see. But – "

"The e of 'ex' is put in to complete the word. Now do you see, Mr Hedge?"

Hedge nodded. "Yes. I think I do. What it really means to convey is Detachment X?"

"Yes. Convey anything to you?"

"Not a thing."

"Pity."

"I thought you said," Hedge stated accusingly, "that the intruder had nothing to do with the peace women?"

"Correct. But I never said he mightn't be CND – or with CND sympathies, that is. Probably as unwelcome to CND as to us, since CND doesn't carry weapons."

Hedge was staring at the notice again. "I suppose he meant to attach it somewhere. How childish – like graffiti. And so stupid – the wording itself."

"Somewhat contrived," Rushcroft agreed, and both the Vice-Admiral and Captain Rubinovitch nodded simultaneously. "But it's fairly graphic, and it's an obvious threat."

"And that's why – "

"That," Rushcroft said, seeming to have some power to take over Hedge's unuttered words, "is why the Defence Ministry contacted the Foreign Office, Pippin in person. Hence you."

Hedge nodded, wishing he could himself see the Permanent Under-Secretary of State as simple Pippin; it would make such a difference to his daily life. He said, "Yes, I was wondering really. I suppose this is thought likely to come from outside the country. Do I take it the man was a foreigner?"

"Middle East in appearance," Rushcroft said. "But I say again, no identification."

"So it's mere supposition?"

Rushcroft said, "I know an Arab when I see one."

And then the viewing of the body, packed in its ice. In its

15

vicinity there were the scarlet-and-gold stripes of a surgeon commander RN; the doctor pointed to the wounds. Head and chest. Death, he said, had been instantaneous. He gestured to a sick-berth attendant and the body was drawn a little way clear of the packed ice and Hedge saw the features. Decidedly Arab. Hooked nose, dark skin, big, bad teeth. Black hair, black moustache across the upper lip and down the sides of the mouth.

"Well?" Rushcroft asked.

Hedge said, "I don't recognise him."

Rushcroft shrugged. "I said it would be a long shot, but worth a try."

"Yes, indeed. Anyway, there's no doubt he's from where you said, Commodore."

"So what are you going to do about it?"

Hedge started. The tone was peremptory, naval. Almost as if he were being given an order to get the answers at the double. He dabbed at his lips with his handkerchief and said coldly, "There will be many formalities. Many avenues to be explored. In the Foreign Office one *never* rushes to conclusions. Consultation, advice from many quarters, so many aspects that need well thinking about . . . you know the sort of thing, I'm sure."

"Yes. Well, I won't detain you, Mr. Hedge. I shall be in touch with Whitehall again shortly."

That was all. Hedge went straight from the ice and the corpse to his car, and went in dudgeon. Not a glass of sherry, not a suggestion that he might be given lunch. Really! He would complain to – to Pippin? Probably better not. And Whitehall . . . what had Rushcroft meant by his reference to Whitehall? Defence Ministry, or Pippin?

*　　*　　*

The peace women and their male attendants were coming back to the base. They came just after Hedge had driven away from the main gate, intending to head for Helensburgh and lunch, which would go down on expenses but might, thanks to

Mrs Thatcher's probes into Civil Service habits, be queried if he indulged too much. He met the advancing peace persons on a bend and was nearly sent into a wall in attempting to avoid them. As he slammed on his brakes they howled at him, no doubt the same sound as Rushcroft had described. It was eerie and frightening, as were the cadaverous faces, with teeth like fangs, as the women grimaced at him through the windscreen. Lank hair and stringy breasts, all of them bra-less. All of them probably Ms. One woman made a long nose at him, both hands, fingers waggling. She looked not far off ninety and vaguely aristocratic.

He sat fuming, edged the car forward a foot. The howling increased and a filthy baby wearing napkins was dumped on his bonnet. Almost immediately a damp patch formed, turning the dust to thin mud. That was clever: Hedge was trapped and knew it. Only a thoroughly evil man would put a baby in jeopardy by moving farther, and if he did then he would be lynched. He quaked and a thin cry, a sound of incipient panic, left his lips. What harridans, what harpies – what bitches. But he mustn't yell any of that aloud. They must be humoured. He went into a routine for fighting down panic: deep breaths in and out, fear escaping on the outward breath. Drain the mind of thought, relax, let the tautened muscles fall slack. If the draining didn't work, and it didn't, then think of *nice* things. The approval of the Permanent Under-Secretary if he kept his head, the gratitude of the Foreign Service mandarins if he bowled out Detachment X, even the approval of the Sovereign expressed through the next Honours List . . . things like that. And machine-guns, turned on the peace women.

Placate them and they would go away.

He managed a smile, an ingratiating one through trembling lips. They didn't go away but after what seemed to be a century the police and navy arrived from the rear. As they did so, the peace women went into their own routine. They lay down on the road in front of Hedge's wheels, first removing the dirty baby just in case. One by one they were lifted and carried away for dumping, and a policeman thumped on the side of the car and shouted at Hedge to get moving pronto.

He was bathed in sweat. Goodness gracious, what an

17

experience! He felt hardly fit to drive, but drive he did, and took the right-hand turn for Helensburgh with a screech of tyres, only just surviving a coach that hurtled down upon him from the direction óf Garelochhead. Farther along he turned into a lay-by and sat with his engine switched off and his whole body shaking. Those women . . . they might have murdered him! God alone knew what it must be like to be a policeman at Greenham Common, where there were vastly more peace women than here at Faslane. Or an American serviceman, out on a limb in a strange country, not knowing when it was safe to use his gun, facing a charge if he used it on the wrong person, facing a charge if he didn't and let in a saboteur. Like Northern Ireland. Tied hands . . . at least one knew more or less where one was in the Foreign Office. Hedge thought of good things again: soon he would be back in London with his cosy life, and Shard detailed to take over in the field. *Where was Shard, for God's sake?* Oh, yes, of course, Wales. Well, he wouldn't be for much longer.

Calmer after a few minutes, Hedge drove on. Coming into the outskirts of Helensburgh he saw to his right a large black shape coming round a promontory opposite Greenock. One of the big nuclear-powered submarines, back from patrol. It had a very threatening look, a huge whale out to swallow a number of Jonahs. Behind him, the peace women would no doubt be in full cry again. That sub would have a full load of missiles . . . Hedge thought again about the dead Arab. There could be no doubt that the Arab and his confederates held a wider significance than the mere putting up of notices about holocausts. They wouldn't be above creating a holocaust of their own if it suited them and if anybody should tamper with the innards of the nuclear-powered submarines, well, it didn't bear thinking about. There were plenty of fanatics about these days, men and no doubt women who wouldn't mind being fragmented for their cause. But of course the Faslane base was very well guarded.

Or was it?

That Arab had penetrated. Admittedly he hadn't got far, but others might. And these days there were so many enemies, not just the Russians. So many weird sects and never mind that they were all lunatics. Sometimes Hedge thought that the very fact they were lunatics gave them a head start. You really had to be a lunatic yourself to get inside their minds and understand their mental processes and forecast what they might do. All those sets of initials: PLO, INLA, SNLA, Black June and Baader-Meinhof which were not initials but came to the same thing . . . all of them out to *destroy*.

Hedge drove into Helensburgh and found a hotel for lunch. He sat in the bar with a whisky-and-soda, looking out across the Tail o' the Bank towards Greenock. He'd last been on the Clyde during the war, as a young Foreign Office gentleman at the tail end of hostilities. He still remembered the great concourse of shipping, merchantmen and naval escorts, at anchor off the Tail o' the Bank. The *Queen Mary* and *Queen Elizabeth*, too fast to sail in convoy, liners of the Orient Line and P. & O., Furness Withy, Clan Line, Canadian Pacific, trooping or carrying war materials, and the great grey warships, the old battleships – *Rodney, Nelson, Warspite* and others plus cruisers and destroyers. It had been an inspiring sight but the young Hedge – the old Hedge now remembered – had been glad not to be part of it. The sea was a rough life, often wet and uncomfortable and very dangerous, from both nature and the Nazis.

But Greenock and its anchorage looked peaceful enough now, the waters standing empty beneath hot sunshine.

Long may it last, Hedge thought, drinking his whisky-and-soda. He didn't think much of the lunch that followed: rather tough lamb. The Scots were inclined to be primitive, and the potatoes had come out of a tin. Lunch was followed by a touch of indigestion and after the meal Hedge, feeling sour in the stomach and ill tempered, rang the police in Cardiff and left a message for Detective Chief Superintendent Shard. Shard was to return to London the following day without fail. By that time, via Pitlochry where he would have to return to pack, Hedge would be in his office. He detested the thought of driving through the afternoon and most of the night. At his age, it wasn't funny. His return journey was made the longer timewise by a spread of recumbent peace women across the road by the turndown for the Faslane base. Fuming, Hedge was forced to wait in a long line of traffic while they were carried away like so many sacks of potatoes.

*   *   *

Shard got the message when he reported to police HQ in Cardiff just after lunch. As it happened, he'd cleared up his business in South Wales, but he cursed nevertheless. A summons from Hedge could well mean cancellation of his leave, due to start when the South Wales job had been tied up. Hedge, of course, wouldn't consider leave as anything important, but Shard had made his arrangements some while ahead. Just too bad: you had to be philosophical if you were a policeman in his particular job and had a boss like Hedge. Shard took out some of his frustration next day, belting up the M4 for London, just inside the limit most of the way, largely in the fast lane. He reached Whitehall not long behind Hedge and was kept kicking his heels while Hedge was brought up to date on various matters by his secretary. Hedge had reached London in the early hours, had gone to bed and overslept.

When he was sent for, Hedge said, "Ah, Shard. I understand you were due for leave."

"Yes."

"Well, I'm sorry, but a difficulty has come up. A man's been killed at the nuclear submarine base on the Clyde. An Arab. It's down to us."

"The killing?"

Hedge glared. "I've told you before, Shard. I don't like flippancy."

"If you'd just explain the circumstances, Hedge. Do I take it it's being hushed?"

"Yes, of course. For as long as we can hold it from those damn peace women, which won't be long. The Press has been warned off, but it'll be all over Greenham Common and so on any minute now I shouldn't wonder."

Unbidden, Shard sat. "Just tell me about it, Hedge. From the beginning."

Fuming, since he was tired from a dreadful drive - tourism really ought to be controlled and holidaymaking drivers who in the summer season drove right through the night given police instruction - Hedge told his tale, exaggerating the way the peace women had attacked him at Faslane.

"Do you know, they really *smelled*."

Shard grinned, "You got that close, did you?"

"Willy nilly, yes. Well, what are you going to do about it?" He then told Shard about the DEATH message.

"Found near the body, on a square of plastic. Ready to be nailed up, I imagine. Do we know anything about Detachment X, Shard?"

Shard said, "It doesn't come to mind."

"Find out, then."

"Yes, Hedge. In the meantime, are you asking my opinion?"

Hedge fidgeted: all policemen were thick. "*Yes!*"

Shard shrugged and said, "Another example of the lunatic fringe - "

"Oh, for God's sake, Shard - "

"But none the less to be taken seriously, I agree."

"Oh, good." Hedge dabbed angrily at his cheeks with a handkerchief. He was very tired, feeling his age. He was suffering from the blasted economies forced on all departments by the PM: no chauffeur for such as Hedge. In many ways, oddly, life had been happier under Labour.

Shard said, "So we have a dead man, an Arab, and this message as I take it to be. That square of plastic. There could be prints. Where is it, Hedge?"

"Oh. Yes. Oh dear. I - "

"You left it in Scotland."

"Yes, I did. I thought it best, don't you know. Scene of the - the crime and so on - "

Shard said, "There's not much to go on really, is there? A dead Arab and a message on a piece of plastic board. Did *anybody* take prints? Fingerprints I mean."

"The body was in a wet suit."

"There could still be other prints, Hedge." Shard got to his feet. "I take it my leave's cancelled?"

"Yes, of course it is. National security - "

"All right, Hedge."

21

"What are you going to do?"

Shard said, "I'm going to Scotland. There's no other starting point that I can see."

*   *   *

Shard, cursing about his cancelled leave, went home by tube to Ealing. He would take the night express north from Euston and in Glasgow would get himself police transport to the Faslane base. The police would have been called in by now, although according to Hedge they'd not been notified up to the time he'd left for Helensburgh: both the Commodore commanding the base, and Vice-Admiral Submarines, had wanted the Foreign Office and Defence Ministry to have the first untrammelled picture and then to authorise a report to the civil power. Frankly Shard was wondering just why there was so much alarm about a dead Arab accompanied by graffiti. But he had to admit the facts were unusual.

Beth was out when he got home; he'd rung from Cardiff to say he would be back but hadn't been able to give a time and he hadn't rung again after leaving Hedge. He pottered around the house: one day, when he got some leave for sure, there would be jobs to be done, painting and papering and so on. Aside from actual leave, there was never time in a copper's life to get down to much except catch up on lost sleep, which made things hard for Beth. She came in, with shopping, after half an hour; and he had to break the news about the cancelled leave. After the phone call from Cardiff she'd half expected it but the confirmation was cruel and she sat down on the sofa in tears.

"Oh, Simon . . ."

Shard brought out a handkerchief. He always felt inadequate when Beth wept, the more so as he or his job was usually the cause of it. Ideally, coppers shouldn't get married, especially ambitious ones. Even those who were not attached to the Foreign Office and the whims of Hedge had their crosses to bear in the way of uncertain off-duty: crowd control, football matches, demos, marches, unlawful picketing, there was ever-lastingly something on in addition to risking their lives chasing armed villains. Everybody had a march now: anti-abortionists, anti-blood sports, anti-vivisection, anti-unemployment – it was always anti, never anything positive. Shard, thinking anti-Hedge thoughts, sat beside Beth and gave her a hug.

"Sorry, darling," he said, still inadequate. "Can't be helped. It's only postponed."

"Till when?"

He shrugged. "I don't know, do I? Depends . . . ."

"Where are you going?"

"North. Tonight."

She nodded but didn't probe: she'd been Shard's wife for long enough to know you didn't ask too many questions. Some might tell, but not Simon. He had a strong sense of duty, of loyalty. Besides, she knew, of course, what his particular appointment was, knew it was way beyond even the official Special Branch. Its operatives had to be dependable and had been very heavily screened. Beth herself had been investigated before Shard's secondment from the Yard had come through; and tucked away somewhere in the files was the information that Detective Chief Superintendent Shard suffered from mother-in-law trouble. This was not considered a security risk. It was a purely personal Shard risk, the risk being to his blood pressure when Mrs Micklem visited.

And Beth was not without guile. There was one way of gauging the likely length of Simon's absences. She used it now. She said, "I'll get mummy over."

Shard stood up, went across to a cabinet beneath a television and brought out a decanter, whisky, and a soda-water siphon. He looked round at Beth. "You?"

"No. About mummy . . . "

Shard poured himself a stiff one. He looked down at his hands. Big ones, capable ones . . . but top coppers didn't strangle their mothers-in-law. He said without emotion, "By all means – it's your home as well as mine."

It was non-committal. This time, Beth hadn't got what she wanted. And she knew it would be no use trying to get out of him any firm commitment about the holiday plans. She would simply do what she'd done before: cancel and take the loss of money involved.

*   *   *

Shard caught the 2330 Inter-City from Euston, which would arrive at Glasgow soon after 0600. He'd been too late for a sleeper; it would be a long night, as long a night as Hedge had had driving down from Scotland. Shard thought about Scotland, a place that beckoned when you had the time and opportunity to appreciate it. The glens and hills, the sharp, clear air, the distant sound of the pipes, the single malt whiskies, the Scots accents . . . the lochs, which when the sun shone from a cloudless sky could surpass the Mediterranean in their deep, almost purple blue. The heather in its season, the snow-capped summits around Loch Tay and Crianlarich and Glencoe, the latter with its enduring memories of treachery and murder so long ago. The Clyde, the steamers ploughing down to the Cumbraes beyond which the waters opened out into the Firth and the great peak of Goat Fell rose above Aran and Inchmarnock Water and the Sound of Bute. And back up the Clyde again to the Gareloch and Faslane, and the brooding threat of the submerged nuclear fleet, some of it in port, some of it restlessly at sea in its ordained positions deep below, the missiles ever-ready for when the order came. And the people who were out to sabotage Britain's defence, and dead Arabs bearing stencilled threats . . .

Shard dozed uncomfortably as the Inter-City hurried beneath its electric cables towards its first stop at Carlisle. Way behind in London, a man had walked away from Euston station after he'd seen Shard board the train and the train pull out. This man, tall and thin and with a dark jowl and the beginnings of a stomach that would weigh him down when he reached his forties, descended into the subway and took a tube, Northern Line southbound, and got out at Tottenham Court Road. From there, precautionwise, although he had no reason to suspect a tail, he twisted and turned on his somewhat lengthy route and eventually pressed a bellpush beside a sex shop in a side street between Tottenham Court Road and Portland Place. His ring was quickly answered and he was admitted by a small man who looked like a jockey. Behind this man, he climbed a narrow staircase with wallpaper curling down from damp plaster and surrounded by a pervasive smell of leaking gas.

The two men reached a sitting-room. In it a girl sat with outstretched legs in dirty jeans, her top half covered with a sweatshirt bearing a CND stencil. The jockey-like man said, in an accent straight from the bogs of Connemara, "Well now, Tack."

"Gone north," Tack said. "Glasgow train from Euston. I don't reckon he'll get off before Glasgow." He gave a snigger. "All right, Tim?"

"Spot you?"

"Course not!" Tack was indignant; he was good at his job, very professional in his approach. He said so. "So what now?" he asked.

"Telephone. Box on the corner. I'll not be long." Tim went down the sleazy stairs to call a Glasgow number.

3

Shard was awake when the Inter-City pulled out of Carlisle, past the Castle to head for the hills of the Southern Uplands of Scotland. He couldn't get back to sleep; and anyway the scenery was splendid in the early summer dawn's light. He eased away the cramps, yawned, stretched and thought of Hedge in London. Hedge had been critical of Vice-Admiral Submarines, who in Hedge's view had had no right to speak up for the wretched peace women who again in Hedge's view were a menace, a national threat that should be lanced like a boil. CND, Hedge had said, was obscuring any amount of real issues and paving the way for the actual saboteurs. There could, of course, be truth in that. But time would tell what was involved this time. Much would depend on the identity of the dead Arab, if such could ever be established.

Detachment X. That was certainly a new one. But over the years there had been so many terrorist organisations. There wasn't anything very remarkable in the setting up of a new one. Shard grinned to himself as the Inter-City ran through a deep cutting in a hillside. It was somewhat akin to the BBC: when some comedian or other TV personality began to run down, the BBC gave him a show of his own, maybe as a sop, maybe as a way of introducing fresh personalities to keep up the endless belt of mindless drug-substitute. It could be the same with international terrorism: when one of the practitioners grew stale, someone dreamed up a new organisation for him and off he went with a fresh image and some nice new initials. It didn't lessen the danger, though.

Shard was met on arrival, an arrival that did not go unnoticed by a man waiting anonymously by the bookstall on the main concourse of Glasgow Central. The officer who met Shard was CID. The Foreign Office had been in touch and a car was waiting to take him straight to the Gareloch. When he had been driven away the anonymous man left the station and like Tim the night before, made a call from a telephone kiosk. He had recognised Shard from information passed by Tim; and he happened to know the CID man by sight. It was part of his job to memorise police faces.

The call went to a terraced house in Liverpool, near the docks on the Birkenhead side of the Mersey. "Shard," he said. "On his way. Any orders?"

A voice rattled in his ear, passing the orders. The man assimilated them and rang off.

*   *   *

Vice-Admiral Submarines had gone back south to Fort Blockhouse. He had other matters to worry about, he'd said. Shard learnt this when he had passed through the peace women who were now forming a more or less permanent body-barrier outside the gates, just as though a missile-carrying submarine might attempt to leave by road. The man from the Defence Ministry, Hocking, remained. By now the plastic notice had been dusted for prints and those of the dead man had also been taken. Photocopies had been rushed to the Defence Ministry in London and after these had been checked both by the Ministry and Scotland Yard a nil report had come back. Shard was given copies in case the FO had them on file. There were in fact three sets of prints on the plastic board, one of them being those of the dead Arab.

27

Shard had a look at the man. He didn't know him and hadn't really expected to. The face was a nasty one and the expression in death was not peaceful. Possibly he had anticipated a tough time with Allah.

Commodore Rushcroft had accompanied Shard on his mortuary visit. He said, "I'd rather not keep him here, Shard."

Shard lifted an eyebrow. "The peace women, sir?"

"Well, it doesn't help. But it's more a question of morale. Seamen don't like corpses aboard."

"Even in the nuclear age?"

Rushcroft gave a short laugh. "Time doesn't change what used to be called Jolly Jack very much. The old superstitions linger on. Besides, we're all living under a certain amount of strain."

"Yes," Shard said. "I appreciate that, of course."

"So get him moved." Rushcroft added, "Please."

Shard said, "I'll call Glasgow. Have there been any other developments? Press, for instance? I saw some press-like faces outside – "

"Yes, and cameras of course. Oh, they're laying siege all right, but they've not been admitted. It's those women, obviously they've talked. I've had word through from Greenham Common, unofficially. They're restive down there too. These things spread, you'll agree."

Shard nodded. "You'll not stop the press speculating or printing what the women tell them."

"I realise that. There's something else that's worrying me more, though." Rushcroft stood sparrow-like and perky, hands behind his back, bright eyes staring at Shard. "Those women. They've been chanting, on and off. *Navy murderers.*"

Shard said, "I saw a placard to that effect."

"That's not good for morale either."

"Are the men jittery, sir?"

Rushcroft frowned. "Not jittery. We don't have jittery men in the submarine service. First sign of that, out they go, back to general service. But it creates an atmosphere that's not conducive to concentration and efficiency in what's becoming our first and last lines of defence. No-one's job is easy at

28

Faslane, Shard. Every time my chaps go ashore they run the gauntlet of those damn women. That tells, after a time, though I'm not proposing to bother you with my own problems in that direction.'' This was a long speech for Commodore Rushcroft; Shard waited, guessing that more was to come. It was. Rushcroft went on, ''There's something else. I suppose it was to be expected. The women are howling for blood now - ''

''So I was told by the detective sergeant,'' Shard said in reference to the CID man who had met him. ''They want charges brought.''

''Yes. Charges of murder. Well, until my authority inside the base is superseded by the civil power, no charges will be brought. I've confirmed that with the Ministry of Defence.''

''You'll have held an enquiry, sir?''

''Of course. I have all the facts, not that there are many, and they're all perfectly clear. The man who fired was within his duty.''

''May I see a transcript of the enquiry, sir?''

''Yes, certainly.'' They left the mortuary, walked through bright sunshine towards the administrative block that housed the Commodore's office. To their right a big black shape loomed, darkly silhouetted against the blue of the Gareloch, the blue slashed here and there by the white wakes of small boats crossing the loch. That black shape looked immensely sinister, immensely powerful. The sheer size . . . once, submarines had been small stuff. Not any longer. That black shape's displacement tonnage when submerged, Rushcroft said as he noted Shard's look, was equal to that of a wartime cruiser.

''And the punch - well, I needn't elaborate of course. I just hope I don't see the day the button's pressed.'' Rushcroft laughed suddenly. ''I'm a peace man, Shard. I know what can happen. But we'd be naked without it. I only wish we could persuade the peace women.''

''That's what we'd all like.''

''Yes.'' Rushcroft walked on, thoughtfully. ''That Mr Hedge of yours. Chairbound, I imagine?''

''Yes, sir. Mostly. Why d'you ask?''

Rushcroft shrugged. ''Just curiosity. Chairbound warrior - so are most of us, come to that. Perhaps it was just those women that had got under his skin and I can't blame him for that.'' He said no more but Shard got the idea Hedge had done some skin burrowing of his own. It would be all in character. It was time Hedge sought early retirement, but he'd never reconcile himself to having no-one to pomp at. In Rushcroft's office Shard was shown the transcript of the inquiry. As Rushcroft had said, it was straightforward enough. An unauthorised entry had been made and challenged, the challenge had not been answered but the intruder had produced a gun and aimed it and the security guard had fired. When Shard had read the transcript he was shown round the base, together with the Defence Ministry man, Hosking, who had already been taken round once. The security, Hosking said, was very tight and the Arab had been lucky – at any rate till he'd been spotted, and Hosking was confident that anyone else who managed to penetrate would also be spotted before harm could be done. It was the fact of Detachment X itself that was worrying Hosking more than the actual penetration.

"I'll be digging,'' Shard said. That was his worry. Hosking should be literally mending his fences. "What do you think is behind it?''

"I've really no idea.''

"But not just the posting of notices?''

"I doubt if it stops there, certainly.''

Shard asked, "What can they do, though?''

"Do?'' Hosking stared through pebble-lensed spectacles.

"Yes, do. From what I've seen, no-one would ever get aboard the submarines themselves, or into the armament stores or silos. Presumably that would be the aim of any saboteur – to cause damage at least if not – ''

"Ah, but there's also the question of morale, not just here in the base but nationwide. We don't want the whole country getting an attack of nerves, you know. If there were too many penetrations, here and Greenham and other places – well, think about it for yourself.''

Shard had. And he didn't believe Detachment X was in business just to get the country rattled, not that he had anything specific to go on yet. It was just a hunch, based on experience. Arabs were killers, it was second nature. But, of

30

course, this didn't have to be an Arab organisation. The dead man was no more than an operative, a hired hand maybe. The tour of the base was just about finished when a messenger approached from the direction of the admin block. There was a telephone call for Mr Shard, on the closed line from London. At the other end of it was Hedge.

Shard went to the Commodore's office and took the call.

"Yes, Hedge?"

A rattle and a thin voice. "Is that Shard?"

"Yes."

"What a terrible line, all crackles."

"It's manageable. Go on, Hedge. I'm listening."

"Very well." Hedge paused. "Something's come up. How are you getting on, Shard?"

"I've – "

"Because I want you back here, soonest possible."

Shard asked, "Is this urgent, Hedge?"

"Yes, it is, of course it is or I wouldn't have . . . get a car to Glasgow airport, Shard, and fly." Hedge sounded agitated. Shard asked if he could be more informative; after all, this was a security line. But Hedge couldn't. Or not very; he said, "I've had the Yard on the line, that man Hesseltine. That's all I can tell you." Then he rang off. Shard grinned at the instrument. 'That man Hesseltine', Assistant Commissioner Crime at Scotland Yard and Shard's boss in the Metropolitan Police, was a red rag to poor Hedge, who resented Shard's split loyalties. Hedge was a jealous man and knew Shard had an immense respect for Hesseltine. Hedge had sounded very disagreeable on the phone.

But orders were orders.

*   *   *

Trade union members were often no respecters of anyone's orders: the news came through from Strathclyde Police on the car's radio. An unofficial strike, one of lightning suddenness, of air traffic controllers at Glasgow airport and at Prestwick. Nothing would move until that had been sorted out and it looked like taking time, far too much time.

"Back to British Rail," Shard said. "Will you call Mr Hedge in London, please. Tell him I'll be there soonest possible."

Police HQ would do that. Shard cursed the delay, knowing it would have a poor effect on Hedge. But it couldn't be helped and in any case the something that had come up might not in fact be all that urgent. Hedge had been known to go off at half cock before now. The police car was now not far off Glasgow. The detective sergeant, who was driving, was glancing constantly into his rear view mirror. He said, "I think we have a tail maybe. A blue Volvo, keeping about two cars behind."

"Right," Shard said. "I'm not going to look round – we haven't spotted him. See if you can get the registration, just in case."

The DS could, when the intervening cars handily turned left. He read it off. Shard made a note. "We won't try to shake him off," he said. "We'll see what happens. Or I will, in due course."

The DS glanced sideways. "Watch yourself, sir."

Shard grinned. Strathclyde Police wouldn't want to lose a senior officer from the Met and the Foreign Office, but he would soon be outside their territory. He said, "Nice of you to be concerned, Sergeant."

"All part of the service, sir."

Twenty minutes later Shard was dropped by Glasgow Central. The blue Volvo, still with them, went on past. A glimpse of two men in it, neither appearing to take an interest. The car vanished into the traffic. Shard walked into the concourse, bought a newspaper. He went for a drink. The train wasn't in yet, wouldn't leave for another forty-five minutes. Shard sat with a large whisky, smoked a couple of cigarettes in succession: he couldn't kick the habit and didn't really want to. You had to die of something in the end and his was a dangerous way of life in any case and a cigarette often kept tension at bay, which was important. The do-gooders could aim their propaganda elsewhere and ruin someone else's pleasure. Shard was immune from being got at by propaganda, though never immune from villains . . . he looked through windows onto the station. Fairly crowded though not overly so, people coming and going, buying tickets. A man drifted up to stand near the ticket office, reading a newspaper. If he wanted, he had a view of the window where Shard sat and of the door through which he would come out. But, apart from the fact that he didn't shift, there was nothing to say he *did* want. Shard studied him as far as was possible through the passing Glaswegians. Ordinary enough; but tails usually were. Dressed in a business suit, medium grey with a dark blue shirt, age about thirty-five and very interested in his newspaper. Shard finished his whisky slowly, stubbed out the second cigarette, and went out onto the station. The Euston train was in now, gate number one, and he made for it, not looking round as he offered his travel pass. The train was more crowded, he suspected, than it would have been normally, BR profiting from BA; but half-way along Shard found a number of vacant seats in a coach not far behind the restaurant car, which by some miracle had a crew aboard. He sat down facing the engine, and waited. He didn't see the grey-suited man and had made a point of not looking down the departure platform for him. As if by another miracle, or as if drawn by the important will of Hedge, the train pulled out dead on time.

*   *   *

Hedge said to his secretary, Miss Fleece, "What a blasted nuisance Shard is sometimes!" The call had just come through from Glasgow and Hedge was very annoyed.

"Yes, Mr Hedge." Miss Fleece always agreed with Hedge; but she had a soft spot for Simon Shard and this time she came tentatively to his defence. "He can't help being strike-bound . . . "

"Oh, rubbish."

There was no sensible response to this. Miss Fleece sat, pad and biro ready still, but Hedge had nothing further to dictate. The day's memos were over and he said she could go. He would like some coffee, however. Waiting for it, Hedge reflected bitterly on Shard and the wretched Hesseltine who always made him feel inadequate, as though his mental

33

processes were not fast enough for the Yard, which was arrant nonsense since the Yard was never exactly speedy and had access to very many more men than had Hedge: Mrs Thatcher had had a bad effect on the Foreign Office, Hedge thought once again. In any case, the Foreign Office didn't speed; it was a dignified establishment and moved with measured tread - like the old-fashioned bobby on the beat - in the best traditions of diplomacy. All modern policemen were quite impossible and mostly brash. Insensitive was perhaps the best word - used to dealing with a low sort of person and not understanding the higher echelons of Whitehall. This morning Hesseltine had been rude, by telephone.

The coffee came, Miss Fleece retreated again, and Hedge went on thinking about Hesseltine. Hesseltine had virtually reprimanded Hedge for not having kept him informed. Hesseltine had learned about the visit of Detective Chief Superintendent Shard to the Clyde Submarine Base from Strathclyde Police, more or less by accident.

Hedge had said snappishly, "He's my man. Not yours."

"On secondment, I agree. But - "

"And as such, nothing to do with you, Hesseltine."

Hesseltine's patience had sounded very forced; the gritted teeth could almost be seen. "I should have been kept informed of the course of events, Mr Hedge. We have - or we may have - to work together on this. I've been contacted by Defence Ministry . . . this thing could become nationwide, all the defence establishments. And that includes London."

"Yes, yes, yes. Don't try to teach me my job, Hesseltine, I don't like it. And I think you're seeing Reds under the bed, frankly. Just a dead Arab!"

"And a dead Irishman," Hesseltine said in a flat tone.

Hedge started. "What? What was that, Hesseltine?"

"I think you heard."

"Where?"

"Here in London."

Hedge said aggrievedly, "I'm sure there are plenty of dead Irishmen in London at any given moment. What's special about this one?"

"The body bore gunshot wounds and it was found, still alive

but bleeding to death, in a cul-de-sac behind the RAMC HQ at Millbank – ''

''Army! That's Defence Ministry – ''

''*Outside* the military establishment, Hedge. So it's ours. But I thought you ought to know. There's a connexion with Detachment X. The DEATH slogan had been tattooed on the body, on the chest. And there's something concerning Shard personally . . . ''

Hedge listened with his mouth hanging open, a pudgy hand using his handkerchief to wipe away sweat. The moment Hesseltine had finished he had put through the call to Faslane, demanding Shard.

*   *   *

The Inter-City swung easily through the Southern Uplands, Glasgow and Motherwell left behind, gliding almost soundlessly on welded rails towards the Carlisle stop. Shard was hungry for lunch, not yet being served. Soon the stewards would be coming through. No-one else had joined his particular coach after he had taken his seat; the train seemed in fact to be far from full. One or two people had walked past, probably heading for the lavatory or maybe, hungry like himself, chasing up the restaurant car's possibilities. The train's gliding motion was sleep-making and from time to time Shard dozed, his jacket removed and rolled up on the rack. While awake his mind was busy, probing around the puzzle of Detachment X, tending to see it as no more than yet another manifestation of the lunatic fringe, the ever-lasting protesters, but protesters didn't normally get shot in service establishments and Whitehall's immediate reaction was natural . . .

With Carlisle still some way ahead nature asserted itself in another way: Shard got up and walked through to the lavatory. That was when he became aware of the grey-suited man. Something made him turn and look over his shoulder. The man was coming through from the next coach in rear, almost as though he had been waiting for some movement on Shard's part. Shard went on through to the toilet compartment, aware of the man coming up close behind. He hadn't got the door

35

shut when it burst in upon him with the man's weight behind it. There was little room for manoeuvre: the wash-basin, the toilet seat, took up almost the whole space, and Shard was held helpless behind the door as the grey-suited man squeezed it hard against him. The man had something in his hand now . . . Shard heaved against the door, but the man had his back against the frame and was immoveable. Shard aimed a fist at the face but found his wrist gripped and held and then, through his jacketless shirt sleeve, he felt the sharp penetration of a needle into the fleshy part of his upper arm. A hypodermic: and at once there was a coldness, a freezing coldness that seemed to take the strength from his arm and then from the rest of his body.

He staggered, slumped, collapsed across the toilet seat. He was unable to speak but he was conscious. He was not in control of his limbs. He lolled stupidly, like a rag doll.

The grey-suited man looked down at him, not saying anything. There was a push at the half-open door and an elderly man looked in, questioningly, eyebrows raised.

The grey-suited man said, "A friend – taken ill."

"Oh, dear. I'm sorry."

"Not to worry – "

"I'll get the guard. There may be a doctor on the train."

The old man was gone before he could be stopped; the grey-suited man shrugged. The guard turned up inside two or three minutes.

"Could be a stroke," he said.

"No. He's liable to these attacks. I'm used to this – "

"I'll call for a doctor," the guard said.

"No use – not without the right drugs which a doctor wouldn't have with him. How far off Carlisle?"

"Thirty-eight minutes . . . "

The grey-suited man said, "We're getting off at Carlisle. Being met. I'll get him to hospital and he'll be okay. No need for a doctor meantime."

"Well, if you're sure." The guard acquiesced. He didn't want any responsibility, just the friend's assurance. Shard was lifted from the toilet compartment and laid out on two empty seats and his jacket retrieved from the rack and put over him.

Carlisle came up and the train glided to a stop; the guard held the journey up while the grey-suited man ran for the barrier and spoke to his waiting friend. They both came back at the rush and Shard, with the guard's assistance, was lifted down to the platform, watched by a gawping crowd, and carried through the station to a waiting estate car. This vehicle, once Shard was in, drove off fast, heading for propaganda purposes in the direction of the hospital initially but then making for the M6 motorway southbound.

*   *   *

"No Shard," Hedge said savagely. "He should have been here by now, surely?" The train notified by Strathclyde Police would have reached Euston an hour and a half earlier and Hedge was livid, waving fat hands at Miss Fleece and at Detective Sergeant Kenwood from Shard's security section. "Check with Euston," he said to Kenwood. "Use my phone."

"Yes, sir." Kenwood did so. Yes, the Inter-City ex Glasgow had arrived, five minutes late. There had been a delay at Carlisle, ten minutes, and only five had been made up. Kenwood was about to ring off and tell Hedge when the man at the other end, a chatty man, said something else and Kenwood's expression changed.

"What *is* it?" Hedge asked plaintively.

Kenwood put a hand over the mouthpiece. "A passenger taken ill at Carlisle, sir. A man, accompanied by a friend."

"Well?"

"Could possibly be Mr Shard, I suppose, sir."

"You mean he didn't arrive in London?"

"The sick passenger didn't, sir, no. He was taken off by this friend, said to be being taken to hospital."

Hedge shook. "Give me that phone, Kenwood." Kenwood handed over and Hedge spoke pompously. "This is an important matter, whoever-you-are. I want the name of the passenger removed at Carlisle." There was a pause. "You don't know? Damn it all, I would have thought . . . " Hedge's voice tailed away and his face went red; he disliked being

37

addressed as mate. He banged down the handset angrily and drummed fat fingers on his desk. "Where's Mr Orwin?"

Detective Inspector Orwin was not yet back from Millbank, Kenwood said.

"He's to report as soon as he is. Thank you, Kenwood, that's all for now."

Harry Kenwood went down to the security section. Hedge glared across his room at Miss Fleece. "I'll have to speak to Hesseltine again. Get him, will you." Then he changed his mind. "Get the police at Carlisle first."

The call went through; Carlisle nick knew nothing of the removal of a sick passenger but at the behest of the Foreign Office would pull out all the stops in a search for Detective Chief Superintendent Shard until such time as they were called off by Hedge, who was unable to say for certain that the passenger *was* Shard. Shard could at times be unpredictable, even insubordinate in subtle ways, seeming to think that Hedge was a congenital idiot or something. Hedge rang off simmering. It was going to be a long day, and he had a dinner party. *Had* something happened to Shard? Hedge recalled that he himself had once been hooked off a train by villains, but not from a toilet compartment. How in heaven's name had Shard come to be in a toilet compartment with another man? Hedge got back on the phone again, this time to Assistant Commissioner Hesseltine.

"I am reporting facts, Hesseltine. Or rather, what may become facts. Shard seems to have disappeared." He gave Hesseltine the details, adding that Carlisle had been alerted and he was awaiting information. In the meantime, this would be handled by the Foreign Office though the co-operation of all northern police forces, co-ordinated by the Yard, would be appreciated. Having said this Hedge rang off and at once regretted having given Hesseltine a loophole through which he might well contrive to take over. But it was too late now and of course Shard had to be found. Hedge was now totally convinced that Shard had been the sick passenger, the only doubt being the sick part.

On the heels of his call to the Yard, his internal line burred and he was informed that he was required by the Permanent

38

Under-Secretary. Yet again; Sir Edmund had been demanding him all day, ever since a personal call had come through from Commodore Rushcroft and even more since Hedge had been forced to report his earlier conversation with Hesseltine, the personal matter, a nasty one to be sure but obviously false, about Shard. Once again Hedge left his office suite and ascended on high to report progress or the lack of it to Pippin, an ill-chosen nickname for a rock of a man with a face like a bull and heavy eyebrows hanging over eyes that pierced like bayonets. Or marline-spikes; Sir Edmund looked more like a retired admiral than a diplomat. Hedge reported Shard's apparent disappearance and soon after he had gone back to his own room Detective Inspector Orwin reported back from Millbank, where he had joined the team from the Yard. He was able to satisfy Hedge on a point that had occurred to him only while he'd been with Sir Edmund and had caused him to miss a heart-beat, since Sir Edmund might well have asked the question, how was the Millbank body's nationality known? It hadn't occurred to Hedge to ask Hesseltine. Orwin said the man had spoken before he died and the accent had been heavily Southern Ireland. And he had uttered Mr Shard's name, apparently.

"Yes," Hedge said. "I want to talk to you about that, but first the actual details of the – the affray. Did no-one react?"

Orwin said, "The guardroom at the RAMC depot did, sir, and saw two men beating it in the direction of the subway – Pimlico, sir. But they made their getaway – ".

"By tube, surely not?"

"No, sir. The army used its loaf – and the telephone to Pimlico underground station. The villains didn't go down the subway."

"No clues?" Hedge asked despairingly, though strictly it *was* Hesseltine's job to catch the killers.

"None, sir. It's like Belfast – they always get away with it. Makes one think maybe they came from there."

"Yes," Hedge said, frowning in thought. "Yes, it does. An IRA gunman . . . pursued by Ulster loyalists, the *illegal* sort? Do you know what the Assistant Commissioner's doing about this, Orwin?"

39

"Not really, sir. All I know is, the body's being finger-printed. We might learn something from that."

"Yes." Hedge placed his fingers steeple-wise beneath his chin and closed his eyes for a moment, looking like a parson in prayer. He was beginning to feel his age; that awful night drive down from Scotland was with him yet, he was still tired even after a full night's sleep last night. So many things battered at his brain, decisions, decisions and the need to think things through so that he got it right before the decisions were made, and got it right at conferences too. And always the press waiting to pounce and catch the establishment out. It was too bad; everything moved so fast these days . . .

"Are you all right, sir?" Detective Inspector Orwin was solicitous, sounded worried. He hadn't been as long as Shard in the Foreign Office, under Hedge. "A glass of water – "

"Oh, I'm perfectly all right!" Hedge snapped. "Don't fuss."

"I'm sorry, sir."

One had to keep going and never show the strain so far that people asked if you were all right and offered water. That way lay premature retirement and Hedge was not a wealthy man nor a retiring one. He made an effort and sat up straight. "Tell me, Orwin. Was any mention made by the Yard people of a connexion between – this Irishman and Mr Shard?"

"Not to me, sir."

"I see." Another decision. "Well, I shall confide in you, Orwin, as my senior man in Mr Shard's absence. I shall pass on what the Assistant Commissioner told me. In the strictest confidence, of course, that's understood?"

"Yes, sir."

"I'm telling you only because it's relevant to our, er, investigations, and I'm telling you what was told to me – without prejudice. That's to say, neither I nor Assistant Commissioner Hesseltine place any credence in it. Neither does the Permanent Under-Secretary." Hedge took a deep breath and there was a glitter in his eyes, almost as though he were taking perverse pleasure in what he was about to say. "What the Irishman said before he died amounted to this: Mr Shard was taking bribes from the Irish National Liberation Army –

40

INLA. I have to add this: the Assistant Commissioner, acting under instructions from the Metropolitan Police Commissioner himself, immediately put an investigation on Mr Shard's bank account and discovered a large sum of money credited by means of a draft paid in through a bank in Liverpool.''

4

Detective Inspector Orwin didn't believe a word of it either, and said so in plain language. It had to be an attempt to frame Shard. There was no dirt in Shard's life. The whole thing was too obvious to be taken seriously; and it would take the Irish to imagine it could stick. Hedge stressed the fact, the incontrovertible fact, of the money in Shard's account. Oh yes, he might be able to account for it if he *was* guilty – though of course he wasn't – but it would be hard for even a top police officer to account for a sudden inflow of a hundred thousand pounds sterling. And there was more to come: Shard's house had been done over by C6, the Fraud Squad, and a sum of money, five thousand in used fives and tens, had been found hidden in his garage, wrapped up in an oily cloth at the bottom of a large Tesco's carton used for the stowage of aerosol cans of de-icer, damp start, car polish, old rags, cloths and so on. Shard's wife was very upset. There was the mother-in-law staying in the house, Mrs Micklem, whose reaction had been different and this had been noted by the investigating officers. Mrs Shard had said she often took the car out in Shard's absence and usually left the garage open. This, said Hedge,

42

was incredibly stupid for a policeman's wife but was probably true.

"It is, sir."

"Oh?" Hedge's eyebrows went up. "You know, do you?"

"They're good friends of mine, sir. I've often been to the house. I've heard Mr Shard telling Beth off about it - "

"Beth?"

"Mrs Shard, sir."

"Oh." The details of Shard's domestic life, except when garages and such obtruded into duty, were of no concern to Hedge. Nevertheless, sleuthlike now, he asked a relevant question. "And the mother-in-law? Have you met her?"

"Once, sir."

"And?"

Detective Inspector Orwin grinned. "A tough old nut."

"H'm." Hedge fiddled with things on his desk. "Pending further information in regard to Mr Shard's whereabouts - "

Orwin interrupted. "It's not being suggested, is it, that there's any connexion between Mr Shard's disappearance and the clap-trap about the bribe?"

"By no means," Hedge said. "Certainly not! I told you, the story's not being believed. However, as a policeman, you'll know the routines have to be gone through."

Orwin nodded reluctantly. This was true enough; but was one of the aspects of police work that made a man wonder why he'd ever joined the force. If you couldn't trust Shard, who *could* you trust? But being fair, he knew it was in Shard's own interest to have all suspicions cleared away. Now he made a suggestion. "How'd it be, sir, if I went along to have a word with Beth - Mrs Shard, set her mind at rest?"

"She'll not have been told he's missing yet. That's not to leak, Orwin. The press is being held off. We want to keep these people in the dark. That having been said - and marked well by you, Orwin - I've no objection to your going round." Hedge paused, dabbing at his cheeks with his handkerchief. It was a very hot day and his air conditioning didn't seem to be working as well as it should. More blasted economies forced on VIPs by the Treasury and its First Lord. "Er . . . eyes and ears open, you understand?"

Orwin didn't like that. Leaving Hedge's room he began to appreciate the difficulties under which Shard worked. Hedge was a right old bastard.

*   *   *

Hedge had gone to his club for a drink before his dinner party when Assistant Commissioner Hesseltine rang through and asked the Permanent Under-Secretary if he could drop round for a chat. Sir Edmund made himself available, courteously. He had a lot of time for Hesseltine. Shard was on both their minds: a good man in trouble of two sorts currently. You couldn't sweep accusations of bribery under the carpet. One thing above all that was worrying both Hesseltine and Sir Edmund was why. Why the alleged bribery - why the frame?

"Just to throw dirt, d'you suppose?" Sir Edmund asked.

Hesseltine shrugged. "We can't say yet. Pressure of one kind or another . . . I've an idea we'll be informed before long."

"By INLA?"

"Presumably, sir, yes."

"That's another thing." The Permanent Under-Secretary lifted himself from his chair. "Whisky?"

"Thank you, sir."

Sir Edmund crossed the room to a corner cupboard and brought out a decanter and a jug of water. Neither he nor Hesseltine used soda, an insult to good whisky. He brought the glass across, frowning. "As I said, there's another thing: another why, if you like. Why, all of a sudden, an *Irish* involvement? We've been thinking in terms of Arab terrorists until now, Hesseltine."

"Yes, we have. Simply because it happened to be an Arab at Faslane. In cold blood as it were, there's no real reason to think the Middle East is particularly concerned with our nuclear defence - "

"The Irish are more likely, d'you suggest?"

Hesseltine side-stepped the question. "I'm suggesting the Arab was just a minnow, sir. All terrorism works hand-in-glove and it's often hard to draw lines. I see no reason why that's not the case this time.''

"So the Arab was a red herring - of a sort?"

Hesseltine grinned. "I don't know about herring. But *red* may well be the link, the common ground. Probably - almost certainly - is. INLA's red enough, anyway."

Sir Edmund went to a window and stood looking out at London. He said, "Yes. So the bribery - perhaps it *is* the throwing of dirt. Show up the British police before the world, show what the Irish are up against in the fight for freedom!" He swung round again. "That'd be Irish enough for anyone!"

Hesseltine gave a bleak smile. "The stage Irishman - he's a joke, of course, even a stale one. But he exists. We in the force know that for a fact. Look at some of the damn stupid crimes - small ones, burglary. Total ineptitude very often. The Irishman who breaks in, falls asleep on the job and gets caught - that sort of thing. But not this time."

Sir Edmund raised an eyebrow.

Hesseltine said, "I've had the report from the fingerprint section. The man outside Millbank was McMahon."

"McMahon? Not the - "

"Yes, sir. Some of the London bombings, and others in Ulster. He's wanted, or was wanted, here and both sides of the border. Well, we've got him - a little late."

"Have you been in touch with the Garda?"

"Yes. Unofficially. I've some good friends over there. We all have the same objective: to stop terrorism."

"And what's the objective of Detachment X?"

"In basis, terrorism pure and simple. I'm not in the least conned by their professed dislike of holocausts."

"Can you be more specific, Hesseltine?"

"Not yet, sir. Early days . . . but there's an obvious connection between Faslane and what happened at Millbank - McMahon's DEATH tattoo - "

"And the Shard connection."

"Yes. I don't want to see Shard suffer. It's a filthy thing to have to fight, and you know what they say about mud. We have to clear this for good and all."

45

"Without forgetting our principal commitment - Detachment X."

Hesseltine said, "I don't forget it. It's part and parcel, after all. Bowl out one and you bowl out the other."

"I hope so," the Permanent Under-Secretary said drily. "I hope so indeed."

Hesseltine looked up sharply. "Do you mean you think - "

"It doesn't really matter what I think. But let's clear the air, shall we? I believe in Shard - I flatter myself I know the men who work for me, and Shard's always been as straight as a die. But good men can be got at, have been got at in the past, and money talks, to use a cliché. To use another: every man, it's said, has his price."

"Are you by any chance backtracking?" Hesseltine asked.

"No." Sir Edmund's tone was crisp. "Just facing facts and keeping an open mind. And that's something I'm bound to do. I hope you understand."

*   *   *

"There's absolutely nothing for you to worry about, Beth," Orwin said. Beth was suffering a bad attack of the shakes and her face was white, pinched-looking, with deep circles under the eyes. "No-one believes it, obviously - "

"They found money, Bob!"

"I know. Planted. Good God, Beth, it wouldn't be the first time!"

"Yes," she said. "I know all that. But you weren't here when C6 turned up. You'd never think Simon was a senior officer of - "

"Beth! It's their job, *our* job. They wouldn't have been liking it any more than you, but you can't let sentiment, or - or feeling or any of that stand in the way when you're on a job. You must know that. Simon would be the first to understand."

"If he'd been here . . . where is he, Bob, do you know?"

Orwin shook his head, hating himself for obeying Hedge. He took refuge in the use of language. "Can't say. Just that he's away on a job, but you'll know that, of course."

"He hasn't been in touch?"

"Not that I know of." Orwin turned as someone came into the room: Mrs Micklem. "Hullo, Mrs Micklem."

"Good afternoon, Mr Orwin. Another of you?" Mrs Micklem sat down with a bag of knitting. Orwin guessed she would soon begin counting stitches to bring the drawing-room to uneasy silence.

He said, "A friendly visit. No more than that."

Mrs Micklem glanced across at her daughter, a shrewd look. "Beth's very upset. The whole thing has been very upsetting for us both. I hope Scotland Yard realises that."

"Of course they do."

"You'd never have thought so."

"Well, I'm sorry," Orwin said shortly. Shard's mother-in-law was a real bag and Orwin guessed she hadn't been much comfort to Beth. He also knew she had never liked Shard from the start. Currently there was a somewhat odd look on her face. She glanced about the room, lips pursed. She said ominously, "They even asked about the furniture. Such impertinence."

Orwin noticed it then for the first time: a brand new suite, sofa and two chairs, expensive – very. The last time he'd been here . . . more than a month, six weeks . . . the old suite hadn't really looked in need of replacement. That was the sort of thing they would look for, as Shard would very well know. In Orwin's view that was a guarantee of innocence. No policeman would be such a fool. He said as much, but Mrs Micklem just shrugged. She had an expressive face and Orwin didn't like what he saw. Like the glitter in Hedge's eyes, which Orwin had interpreted correctly. She wouldn't want Shard to be guilty, it would rub off on her daughter, but if the worst happened she would find a lot of comfort in a string of I-told-you-sos.

Orwin spoke to Beth. "They'll have taken the money, of course."

"Yes. And the box of car things."

"And dusted for prints, all round?"

She nodded. "It was horrible."

"I know. But do try not to worry. The absence of – "

Mrs Micklem interrupted. "If you're about to say that the absence of my son-in-law's fingerprints on the notes will prove he's innocent, well, I wouldn't be too sure, Mr Orwin. He

47

could've made sure he wore gloves – couldn't he? After all, he's a policeman." Her fingers moved lightning-like, the steel knitting needles flashing back a ray of afternoon sun.

Orwin couldn't hold back. He said bitterly, "Whose side are you on, Mrs Micklem?"

She wasn't ruffled. She said, "Oh, I'm not saying I think he did, certainly not. But facts have to be faced. We mustn't be ostriches. That's what they're going to say, isn't it – that my son-in-law could have worn gloves? None of this is very nice. It'll be a relief to hear what my son-in-law has to say to it all himself." Then she asked the question direct. "Has he been arrested, Mr Orwin?"

Orwin felt like committing an act of GBH. He said, "No, he hasn't," and left it at that. Neither Mrs Micklem nor Beth asked any more questions, probably because they knew he wouldn't answer them. He was thankful for that.

*　　　*　　　*

From Carlisle station the estate car, a fairly elderly Volkswagen, having laid the red herring towards the hospital and subsequently left the M6 at the Penrith exit, drove fast along the A66 towards Scotch Corner. Shard, fully conscious but still unable to move or speak, had been blindfolded and handcuffed and covered with a car rug soon after the vehicle had left the built-up area and he had no idea where he was, except that the easing of the speed and the swaying as the Volkswagen took the turn off the exit road told him they had left the motorway. An estimation of the time elapsed and the speed led to a guess that they'd left by the first exit after Carlisle, north or south, he didn't know which. That was so far as he could go. Now he was lost. There was a curious feeling throughout his whole body, a sort of jitteriness, with everything tingling and feeling as if he was about to drop apart, but otherwise he felt all right, no feeling of sickness or anything of that sort. From time to time the men in front spoke, but in low voices and monosyllabically. Shard gleaned nothing except that he believed there was an Irish accent from one of them. He couldn't be sure even of that. The car was being driven very fast and was swaying as the driver overtook from time to time and swung back in again. It seemed an eternity before the speed eased for a sharp right-hand turn. After that the driver took it slower and there were many bends and turns and after another seemingly interminable drive the Volkswagen slowed further and finally stopped with a wrench of the handbrake and the engine died.

The front doors opened, then the back was lifted. Shard was dragged out and carried a little way. He heard a door being opened, then another, after which he was dumped down on something hard. The floor. So far neither of the men had spoken, but now one of them did, the one with the Irish accent.

He said, "Journey's end, Mr Shard. You'll be able to talk soon. In the meantime, be assured the injection'll have no lasting effect." A moment later the blindfold was untied. He saw that he was in a small, square room with a dirty window covered by the open slats of a decrepit Venetian blind. The light was dim but he could see the two men, one of them a thickset man with a beard, the other the grey-suited man from Glasgow Central and the train. They were looking down at him but nothing more was said until they both turned away, when the bearded man said, "We'll be back."

Then they left the room and the door was locked on him. He thought: why bother? The handcuffs were still on his wrists and he still couldn't move. But of course he would move soon by the sound of what had been said. When he did, there was the window. That, however, was out. Beyond the Venetian blind and the dirt of the pane, Shard saw close-set bars.

*   *   *

The first report that had gone through to the Yard from Carlisle nick had been an early one to say that nothing was known at the hospital of anyone brought in off a train. It had taken time to establish this, hospital routines and medical red tape being what they were, and after this nothing at all had been picked up. The police were working in the dark, nothing to go on, a trail without a starting point. Not even the estate car's registration number was known. No-one at Carlisle railway station had thought about that. Indeed, why should they? A CID man from the Yard had already tried to contact the guard from the Glasgow express but this too had taken a long time. The guard was not at home and because he wasn't at home he was going to face trouble from his wife. His wife was on the simple side and it turned out he'd pulled wool over her eyes about his schedules; as a result of some questioning of his mates he was discovered much later that day in bed with another woman. When at last this discovery had been made the guard was able to give a description of the grey-suited man and of the sick passenger and the latter description fitted with that of Detective Chief Superintendent Shard. This was reported to Hesseltine after his return to the Yard from the FO. Hesseltine now had something but it was fairly negative. Shard had been kidnapped. His captors were not known. He could be alive or dead.

It was a blank, and frustrating. Hesseltine paced his office, deep in thought, getting nowhere. How did this link with the alleged bribery? Were Shard's captors the ones who'd paid in that draft or were they some other outfit? Were they Detachment X? The prints from the train toilet compartment had proved nothing, and hadn't really been expected to. So many passengers used lavatories. But the routines had been gone through, and all the prints had been checked with CRO, Shard's own FO files, and with Defence Ministry. Result, nil. Many of them had been uncheckable, too smeared and blurred and superimposed. So nothing had been proved either way. Even Shard's couldn't be identified.

Hesseltine was about to call the Foreign Office and leave a useless report for the Permanent Under-Secretary in Hedge's absence when one of his telephones burred and he answered.

It was Dublin, his contact in the Garda.

5

Hesseltine put down the telephone thoughtfully then took it up again and dialled the Foreign Office security section direct. He got Harry Kenwood, who recognised the voice straight off.

"Yes, sir. Kenwood here."

Hesseltine asked the question routinely, though he would have been informed if the answer had been affirmative. "No word of Mr Shard?"

"Not a thing, sir."

"I want to contact Mr Hedge, Kenwood. Where's this dinner, do you know?"

Kenwood said, "Yes, sir. Athenaeum."

"Call him, please. Have him rooted out – as discreetly as possible. I'm coming over."

"Here, sir?"

"Yes." Hesseltine cut the call and sat for a few moments staring at the handset. Hedge wasn't going to like being dragged back from a convivial occasion and would very likely be already a little tight, but he was going to have to concentrate. Not so far away in Whitehall Harry Kenwood was calling the Athenaeum and having similar thoughts about his boss. Hedge came bad-temperedly to the telephone and

51

grumbled that if it was really important he would walk across to his office. This he did and reached the Foreign Office shortly after Hesseltine, whom Kenwood had taken up to wait in Hedge's room.

"What's this all about, Hesseltine? In the middle of - "

"I apologise for the necessity. I've had a call from Dublin."

"Oh. Oh, very well." Hedge moved towards his desk and sat heavily in the swivel chair, motioning Hesseltine to sit as well. "You'd better tell me, then. I assume it's important."

"I think it could be. It won't take long. The Garda's got two friends, associates, of McMahon's."

"Associates?"

"INLA. They were arrested only about an hour ago - largely a matter of luck for the Garda. An incident similar to what goes on in Belfast, a fast car and some shots and a man killed, an Englishman normally domiciled in Northern Ireland - "

"Known?"

Hesseltine said, "Yes. Not important, not to us anyway. He was a member of the UDA, hence the shooting. Anyway, the killers were unlucky this time. An unmarked police car happened to be passing and the killers' car was rammed and there was a shoot-out. The Garda came out on top. The two men are damaged but alive." He paused, staring at Hedge, who was dribbling a little from one corner of his mouth. There was quite an aroma, mainly whisky. "One of them had a briefcase. In it was - literature. Three guesses, Hedge."

"Detachment X?"

"Spot on. And the men are known, as I think I said, to be friends of McMahon."

"Anything about Shard, the bribery?"

"Not so far as I was told. I think those men could do with questioning, Hedge. By us. The Garda's willing to co-operate."

Hedge asked, "They'll send them over?"

"No, of course not. But they'll make them available in Dublin. I can send a man over. It's up to you, though - your pigeon, Hedge."

Hedge gaped. He was surprised at Hesseltine. He had been

52

all ready to stake his personal claim, believing Hesseltine would want to hog the show. He said, "Er – yes, quite. Yes, it's in our hands. Pity about Shard. *He* could have gone. I'll have to send Orwin, I suppose, but he's not terribly experienced in our particular aims as yet."

"I say again, I can send a man."

"Totally unnecessary." Hedge wasn't going to let go if he could help it. He could be tenacious in his own interest and had always wished to end his career when the time came with something better than a CBE. What better way to that end than by frustrating some dastardly assault on Britain's military and naval establishments? As Hesseltine waited impatiently for him to make some further pronouncement he said importantly, "I think I should refer this to the Permanent Under-Secretary, Hesseltine. He's been taking a personal interest."

This, Hesseltine had expected. It was seldom Hedge took decisions upon himself. He waited while Hedge used his scramble line to Sir Edmund's private address. Sir Edmund answered himself and quickly. Hedge passed the report and there was some talk about Detective Inspector Orwin followed by a number of yesses and noes, obsequiously uttered, and then obvious consternation on Hedge's face and some spluttering. Hedge hung up rather abruptly. Hesseltine believed he had in fact been hung up on.

Hedge said unbelievingly, "Sir Edmund's also doubtful about Orwin's lack of FO experience. He said I must go."

Hesseltine repressed, with difficulty, his desire to laugh.

*   *   *

Hedge had once been a field man, for quite a long time too, but hadn't liked it. He had withdrawn with immense pleasure into the safe decorum of the Foreign Office itself, where he could sit like a fat spider in his web and manipulate things, manipulate other people. There had been occasions since when he had gone willy-nilly into the field again and he congratulated himself on having achieved some quite considerable success – he was easily able to disregard a certain element of sheer luck – and this no doubt was why the Permanent Under-

Secretary wanted him to go this time, it wasn't just Orwin's lack of experience. Sir Edmund had made much of the need to show Dublin how importantly the intrusion of Detachment X was being treated in Whitehall. The diplomatic approach and all that. Well, naturally, Hedge saw the point about the ham hands and big feet of Scotland Yard, which accorded with his own view – not that Sir Edmund had said all that in so many words, but the inference had been obvious. It must remain within the Foreign Office and Hedge was the only man available, though Hedge didn't dwell more than a fraction of a moment on *that* aspect.

He made his arrangements. He caught the 2255 BA flight from Heathrow and settled down with a brandy. Nice air hostess . . . she fussed over him, even though she didn't appreciate his importance, the importance of his flight. He didn't hear her remark to the rest of the cabin staff, that he looked the sort who'd complain at the drop of a hat. Hedge touched down at Dublin airport at one minute to midnight, right on time. He was met by an unmarked car that whisked him to Garda headquarters. The driver was a cheery, round-faced Irishman with fair hair, not the lugubrious, dark Irishman that filled so much of Ireland, and he talked a lot. Hedge answered monosyllabically. The Irish accent, he found, grated; and he didn't like the Irish anyway, British people basically who thought they were foreigners, though why anybody should want to be a foreigner was beyond Hedge's comprehension. When the questioning was over, and he hoped it wasn't going to take too long, he would pass the rest of the night in the luxury of the Shelburne Hotel, where accommodation overnight had been booked for him, and in the morning he would take a walk along O'Connell Street which once in better days had been Grafton Street, after the Duke of Grafton – shocking to think Nelson was no longer there, his pillar blown to smithereens by order of what called itself a responsible government – and then he would fly thankfully back to London.

On arrival at headquarters Hedge was welcomed genuinely enough but nevertheless received a shock. Hesseltine, it seemed had got things wrong – or hadn't been honest with him.

54

He was not to be permitted to interview the friends of McMahon at all. That had never been the idea, he was told firmly. He would be allowed to listen in, by means of bugs, from a room adjoining the interrogation room, and afterwards he could put any further questions through the medium of the Irish interrogating officer. He protested but to no avail.

"Scandalous. To bring me all this way!"

"But think now, Mr Hedge." That Irish accent again. "It'd do no good at all, now would it? An Englishman to do the questioning, of men like these two? Sure it's not a word they'd utter in your hearing, if they knew."

Well, perhaps they had a point. In any case they were adamant. Hedge was forced to make the best of it. He was given a large whisky, Irish. It was surprisingly good - Old Bushmills, Black Bush. The best, they said. The Irish always boasted.

* * *

The men had come back as promised, the grey-suited man and the one with the heavy beard. The grey-suited man was armed with a small automatic. By this time Shard was normal; speech and movement had returned, but the handcuffs were still in place and his arms behind him. The day was darkening; a little earlier he had got to his feet and looked out of the window. All he saw was a blank wall, the stone wall of a building. He was probably still somewhere in the north, but that was all he could say. Scotland, England - he didn't know.

The bearded man said, "Well, now, Mr Shard." Shard saw that he held his jacket over his arm, the jacket he'd taken off aboard the train from Glasgow and which had been placed over him after his removal from the toilet compartment. Now the bearded man produced Shard's notebook, in which - or on which to be precise, on the paper cover - Shard had jotted down the number of the tail's car in Glasgow.

"So you knew," the man said. "You spotted the tail."

"Yes."

"And your driver would have reported it, of course. Well, no matter. That car was abandoned soon after - "

"And had been stolen, of course."

"Of course. And carried new number plates. We're not fools, Mr Shard. Nor, I think, are you."

Shard didn't comment. The bearded man scratched reflectively beneath his chin and said, "Money, now. We're all in need of it. Do you take bribes by any chance, Mr Shard?"

"I do not."

There was a smile from both men. "You're wrong, you know," the bearded man said. "Very wrong. Your bank account is now one hundred thousand pounds the fatter. And then there is the fact that your wife leaves your garage door open when she goes out."

Shard's mouth set. "What do you mean?"

The man explained fully. Shard felt murderous, knowing what Beth would be suffering, knowing too that Mrs Micklem was currently part of the scene, part of what would look like disgrace. But no-one would believe, surely, not even Hedge. This was crazy, and he said so.

The man shook his head. "Many respected people have taken bribes as you well know. No-one is above suspicion, and the notes in your garage are very real. There will be more payments to follow – "

"Anyone trying to make a payment will find himself in the bag."

"Yes, perhaps. Yes. That doesn't worry us."

"Why not?"

The man shrugged. "You'll see, Mr Shard."

"What's the point of this. What do you gain from it?"

"If you think about it, perhaps you'll see for yourself. A discredited policeman is not a happy thing to be, Mr Shard."

"I told you. They won't believe it." Shard spoke through clenched teeth, wishful to get his hands round the man's throat, squeeze, shake him like a rat. Both men were laughing at him now and he took a step forward, a useless step with his hands held behind his back but it was a reflex action and it was stopped dead by the grey-suited man's gun, which moved like lightning and came down on his temple. He staggered and fell, and the men laughed again and then left him, presumably to think about it as suggested. There was blood on his head,

56

running down his face, and his head ached. He thought of the men as rats. They had involved Beth. But he had experience enough not to be surprised. In the force you got used to all kinds of dirt and families were never sacrosanct. He also had experience enough to know that the bearded man had been truthful insofar as plenty of police officers had been sentenced for taking bribes, and this would be regarded seriously until such time as he could present himself in London. And that was another point: he had disappeared. That wouldn't look good. Of course, the train guard would make a report and two and two could quickly be put together. But of itself it didn't prove anything, and he had to accept that the dirty money in his garage would be real.

Or would it?

There could be bluff around. He could only hope so. But he didn't believe it. They knew about the garage, knew that Beth so often left it unlocked. They'd cased the joint, and they would scarcely go to the trouble of doing that without following up. And why were they unworried about the prospect of another payment leading to an arrest?

It didn't make sense. And he still couldn't see where the gain lay for them. He racked his brains, endlessly, as night came on. That next in-payment to his account: it could be made by post, presumably. That was why they weren't bothered. But it hadn't sounded quite like that. And there was still the query, *why*?

Just after the light had gone, largely because of that close stone wall, food was brought, both men again. The grey-suited man stood by with his automatic while the other man fed Shard, like a nurse, with bread and soup and a glass of water. The blood had dried now and his face felt stiff, his head still aching. When fed, he was left alone again and a half-hour or so later the men came back and a mattress and pillow were thrown in through the door.

*　　　*　　　*

In the early hours of next morning Hedge in Dublin was easing away cramp in his neck as he concentrated on an earpiece, the receiving end of the wretched bug. It didn't seem to be working properly; in Ireland, nothing did. There were crackles, and every now and again it faded and then came back with increased sound which Hedge found tiresome. It was all tiresome; the voices were mainly those of the interrogators; the accused men spoke but seldom and then not very usefully. They admitted the shooting since they couldn't very well do anything else. But they were giving nothing away, not yet anyhow. It was going to be a lengthy process; Hedge thought wistfully of the comfortable bed in the Shelburne Hotel, all the luxury and then an ample breakfast with nice strong coffee – not that he hadn't been brought coffee from time to time, he had, but it was terrible stuff from a canteen, wishy-washy in a cheap cup bearing some sort of crest and insignia in case it got stolen, like British Rail. It made Hedge hiccup at one point, loudly and painfully, and he hoped to goodness the bug wasn't two-way or something. He searched in his pockets for a Rennie and found he was out of them. He clicked his tongue: Miss Fleece again. He would have to tell her . . . he came back to the present when a loud voice in the bug said, "Ah, get stuffed," and then the thing went into one of its fade periods, and he missed the rest.

Then something more germane came across, loudly again. A man said, "Fuck England." That was more like it, and Hedge listened intently for more heresy. He got it. "Fuck the bloody British. Fuck the Royal Navy." Ah! Faslane? The voice veered off the mainland of Britain, however, though the pejorative remained the same. "Fuck Paisley, fuck the bloody Northern Ireland Secretary, and begod fuck Cardinal O'Fiaich too if that's what the bugger says."

Hedge sucked in disapproving lips at the constant use of the four-letter word. But he believed there was a sound of incipient hysteria . . . not quite the word, these men were tough. But something of the sort, and there might come a crack. After a few more moments and a few more expletives there was a sound like a slap followed by a yell of pained surprise. The Garda seemed to be getting tough as well. Soon after that an officer came in to see Hedge.

"We've been interrogating them together, you'll realise, Mr Hedge – "

"Yes! You said you were going to. If you recall, *I* said they should have been done individually."

"We have our methods, Mr Hedge."

"Yes, yes. Do I take it you're now going to separate them?"

"That's the idea," the officer said briskly. "One one side, one the other."

"Of me? Rooms either side of here? Goodness gracious, I can't listen to two separate interrogations at once, I'm not superhuman!"

"You have a point, Mr Hedge. Take your choice, right or left."

Hedge fumed. "Which offers the better prospect? Which do you advise?"

"Garrity. Room to your right. We're going to crack him. The other's impervious, waste of time."

"Is Garrity the one who kept on using – er – "

"Yes." The tone was disparaging. The Garda officer was a good Catholic, a devout man who hadn't liked the reference to Cardinal O'Fiaich. Garrity was going to pay for that and a good deal else beside. Hedge had already been told that Garrity's companion, the man in the other interrogation room, had been wanted for a good long while, both sides of the border and in England. His name was Phelan. Hedge had never heard of him so far as he could recall; no doubt he was known to the Yard – Hesseltine hadn't said so, but Hesseltine often kept things to himself and then had the impertinence to suggest that he, Hedge, was unforthcoming.

There was a tapping sound from the bug and Hedge started listening again. The book was being thrown at Garrity now; there were a few more fucking this and thats and then there was a squealing sound followed by threats, quickly cut off. The Garda was nicely on top now, Hedge believed. Garrity was in for murder and was going to get a rough ride. In past years a number of Garda men had lost their lives, and prison officers in Mountjoy Gaol had been beaten up by Garrity's friends from time to time, and the prison service wasn't going to love Garrity when they got him inside. They wouldn't go outside the law, not much, oh no, but there were ways as Garrity well knew. Hedge believed he heard the sound of sobbing; Garrity

59

was young, had very likely been bulldozed by threats into Detachment X, and hadn't toughened up fully yet. When the Garda officer resumed, he could be heard reciting all the crimes that were going to be pinned on Garrity, who wouldn't see freedom again maybe till he was an old, old man, if then. Then he changed his tack, the usual routine, hinting at how Garrity could benefit by co-operation. There were some crimes that just might not be put down to Garrity and life inside could be made happier by words dropped in the right quarter.

Then the more matey scene was dissolved: Hedge's bug told him the interrogators were being changed round. There was silence for perhaps ten minutes: Hedge looked again at his watch and thought of bed, but perhaps he would get there soon now. After the ten minutes were up, another voice came through the bug, sharper, hoarse, hectoring – the man from the other interrogation room taking his turn and keeping to the routine.

"It's no use, Garrity. Phelan's talked."

"He'd never do that."

"Well, now, he just has, d'you see. Begod, he's shopped you good and proper, so he has, Garrity. Do you want to hear?"

Silence. Again the intent Hedge eased the cramps in his neck. The interrogator went on again. "The Stephen's Green killing – "

"I never!"

"Phelan says you did so. Phelan's very positive – dates, times, names, you know what I mean. The killing of a priest in Belfast, the shooting from a car in the Falls Road that got the wrong man, but the wrong man was as dead as if he'd been the right one. Now, the holy father's not going to like that any more than we do, Garrity. And Phelan's against you now, d'you see." There was a pause, then a familiar name came through to Hedge. "He's talked about McMahon, Garrity."

McMahon in London, dead outside the RAMC headquarters in Millbank. McMahon who'd talked of bribery. Hedge knew, or was pretty sure he knew, that Phelan hadn't in fact mentioned the name at all, but it was possible Garrity would fall for it, for how else would the Garda know?

Garrity asked hoarsely, "What about McMahon, then?"

"You tell me," the other voice said.

"You don't know, do you?" Garrity sounded a shade happier, just a shade. Hedge listened to the Garda interrogator demolishing the happiness, inventing a lot more that Phelan hadn't said, stressing the fact of the DEATH hand-outs in Phelan's briefcase, of the murder of McMahon, himself a member of Detachment X as well as INLA. Phelan, the Garda officer said, had talked about a civil bombing campaign in England. Did Garrity dispute what Phelan had said? If he did, it would be foolish, and bad for him when he went inside. But co-operation would bring full protection against the IRA and INLA and any other ill-disposed persons in the Irish gaols. Hedge heard that far but no farther: the bug went on the blink and there was nothing but fizzes and crackles and a high whine cutting through them. Hedge seethed, took out the earpiece and shook it, but it was no use. He wrenched it out again and sat for a long while in total frustration. So typically Irish.

The Garda officer came in and Hedge ranted at him. The officer listened patiently: in this, they were both on the same side and Hedge was considered important in London. Then he said that his assessment of what Garrity had come across with, taking that together with Garrity's silences and omissions, was that Detachment X was after civil rather than military targets in Britain. Hedge stared blankly and said, "Oh, rubbish, my dear fellow! So far these people have *clearly* been concerned with military, or anyway naval, targets and I – "

"Ah – so far, Mr Hedge. Yes. But I say again, my assessment is that in the future they will not be – "

Hedge said pettishly, "It's a large assumption on what sounds like thin evidence."

The Garda man disagreed; there had been, he said, a strongly positive reaction from Garrity and he knew his own people better than did Hedge. Detachment X, he insisted, was in his view not interested in stopping holocausts. "I think it's all a blind, Mr Hedge. There's going to be something big, sure enough . . . but I doubt if it's to be military. Or naval." He paused, looking down at Hedge. "We're not done with Garrity yet, or Phelan either. Phelan may talk in time, since he knows

61

Garrity's a weak man and likely enough to have talked. Are there any questions you'd like put, Mr Hedge?''

Hedge said, "Yes, there are – "

"Listen now," the Garda man interrupted, sharp and sudden. The bug, placed by Hedge on a table, had come back to life. Just audible came sobbing, the sounds of panic and hysteria, and a number of faint fucks applied largely to the Garda. But not only the Garda: Phelan too.

"There," the interrogator said. "Now what do you think of that?"

* * *

Hedge had put his wishes to the Garda: he wanted them to ask Garrity about Detective Chief Superintendent Shard and the deposited cash. He wanted Garrity questioned closely about targets to be attacked by Detachment X and when they were scheduled for. It had to be asked; he didn't really expect results. Garrity and Phelan might not know in any case, they must be the small fry, the left hands who wouldn't be told what the right hands were doing. Not unless something was imminent, anyway.

Hedge was right about the nil result. Garrity had nothing to offer. Phelan hadn't uttered. It was four a.m. by the time Hedge had been driven in another unmarked car to the Shelburne, where he retired to bed weary and cross. He was up late for breakfast but had some sent to his room. It was an excellent breakfast. After it he took his self-promised walk along O'Connell Street in a masochistic frame of mind, thinking again about Lord Nelson. An act of ingratitude – after all, Nelson had fought for the Irish as much as for the rest of the British Isles. British Isles! Sick joke now, with Southern Ireland so long defected and all its inhabitants waiting their chance to blow London up.

Hedge went back to his room at the Shelburne to pay his bill and collect his overnight bag and he was on the point of leaving by taxi for the airport when he was approached by a man, an Englishman whom he vaguely remembered having seen before in London. In the Foreign Office . . . the man introduced himself as Harcourt-Fanning, he must be Foreign Office. He was, now, of the Embassy in Dublin. He was plainly in a state of suppressed nerves. There had been an explosion, he said. Word had just come through. Fifty estimated pounds of explosive had gone off in a car in the New Forest.

"*New Forest!*"

"We doubt if it was meant to, Mr Hedge. The Irish . . . it went off prematurely. There's nothing left of the men, of course, and not much of the car."

"Detachment X?"

Harcourt-Fanning nodded. "There were charred pamphlets and a plastic notice up a tree. There's a huge crater – "

"Casualties?" Hedge mopped at his face. This wasn't going to look too good: him in Ireland, and the thing blew behind his back. The target had very likely been Southampton, he supposed. *God damn Shard* . . . oh, but of course he'd disappeared, obviously by *force majeure*. Or was it? That bribery . . .

"No human casualties at all," Harcourt-Fanning said. "New Forest ponies, that's all."

"All," Hedge said bitterly. The world was a madhouse these days, full of lunatics, do-gooders, fringe groups . . . at any moment now he would have the animal rights people howling for blood.

6

When Hedge reached Whitehall the Head of Security was back, in obvious pain from the shingles.

"You should be in bed," Hedge said.

"I will be again, soon. This explosion - "

"I can cope, Head."

"Yes. I wanted to be here in your absence, that's all. Did you have any success?"

Hedge made his report in full. The Head of Security said nothing had come through from the Garda while Hedge had been on his way back. Presumably neither Phelan nor Garrity had said anything more. Hedge said, "The Garda seemed convinced it was a case of renewed bombings - they had very thin evidence, I must say, but now it seems they may have been right. The New Forest, you see."

"Exactly."

"Southampton, d'you suppose?"

"Or Portsmouth - "

"Navy again! *That* doesn't support the theory."

"Not entirely, no. But a bombing's a bombing, my dear Hedge, and Portsmouth's only a theory. Besides, I don't suggest positively the dockyard." The Head of Security's face was drawn and pale, and the mouth seemed pulled down at one corner. "I've always had the feeling that terrorism wouldn't stick wholly to London. London's London – big, large concentration of population, yes. Prestigious. But there's a damn sight more people in the rest of the country, and they all feel safe because they're not in London. Attack the provinces and you get a hell of a lot more widespread alarm, right?"

Hedge nodded. The Head went off at a tangent: he didn't appear to be concentrating fully. "That Arab, at Faslane. No identification, I gather?"

"None, up to the time I left for Dublin, Head."

"H'm. Arabs and Irish, an explosive mixture. And there's Shard – a nasty business, that. There's a toothcomb in progress – "

"I initiated it," Hedge said, sounding unctuous.

"But a nil result still."

*   *   *

Word went to all police authorities in England, Scotland and Wales: a new bombing campaign against mainland Britain appeared likely and there was to be full alertness without in any way alarming the general public. The press was not to be informed and if they dug anything up it was to be denied. At the same time the usual exhortations, such as around Christmas time, could be made once again: report anything suspicious such as unattended packages or furtive men with Irish accents. The public was used to that by now; it wouldn't arouse any particular alarm. Nor, Hedge guessed, would it really arouse many reports or any extra alertness on the part of the populace. The British always minded their own business.

At 12.20 that morning, the morning of Hedge's return from Dublin, a Korean girl named Ho Suzy was arrested at a branch of Barclays Bank in Eastleigh near Southampton. A cashier had been right on the ball when Ho Suzy paid a cheque for ten thousand pounds into the account of one S. Shard, for crediting his account at his own branch. The police had been informed immediately; Ho Suzy, soft-eyed, pretty, and pregnant, had

65

been detained in the bank meanwhile and was duly arrested. On orders from Whitehall, she was not questioned locally but taken in a police car under escort to Scotland Yard. At this stage the Foreign Office did not want to be seen to be involved; but it was Hedge who did the questioning, with a senior police officer present.

Ho Suzy was fully co-operative even if what she said to Hedge was lies. The father of her unborn child, she said, was Simon Shard, who had disowned her when she became pregnant. It was because of this that she had agreed to act as paying agent for certain persons known to her as having given bribes to Shard in the past. She understood the risk involved but she wanted Shard shown up.

"You realise you'll be charged?" Hedge asked.

"For bribery? It was not me."

"I don't say it was. With being an accessory. That's serious in its own right." Hedge got up from his hard chair and paced the room, frowning. She was certainly attractive . . . *could* Shard have been suborned by her charms? Of course, that didn't prove he'd taken bribes, but senior police officers attached to the Foreign Office didn't fornicate. He went back to Ho Suzy and stared down at her, his face full like a moon. "Of course, if you'll tell me who these people are, the ones who offered bribes . . . a word might well be put in."

"I do not know their names."

"Oh, nonsense, of course you do, since you took orders from them! Come now, Miss Ho."

"No, I shall not say. I do not know. It was done through . . . what is it you say, intermediaries?"

"Yes, intermediaries. Then tell me who *they* were."

Ho Suzy smiled, taunting him with her looks, her sexiness. "More intermediaries," she said. "You wish to know *their* names?"

"Yes," Hedge said shortly.

"Robin Hood. Arthur Scargill. Bernard Shaw."

You couldn't give women the rough treatment. Especially off-white pregnant ones. The anti-racialists would make a meal of him. Hedge tried and tried but in the end had to admit defeat. Ho Suzy just sat there and smiled placidly, hugging her very pregnant stomach. The baby . . . *was* it Shard's? Perish the thought! Such a scandal – but no, Hedge simply wouldn't believe it. It was all part of the frame. He left the room with the police officer and went along to talk to Hesseltine, much as he disliked having to seek advice from the man. Hesseltine, however, had a solution to offer.

"The charge *per se* needn't necessarily be regarded as particularly important – "

"Goodness gracious – "

Hesseltine held up a hand. "I said needn't necessarily. That allows scope. And once she's charged . . . I suggest she be released on police bail."

"H'm." Hedge pondered, cheeks wobbling. "Unusual, in a case like this, surely?"

"It's results that count, Hedge."

"Ah! Put her under observation, you mean?"

"I can arrange that easily enough."

"Yes, a good idea," Hedge said. There was no knowing where Ho Suzy might lead them. Hedge didn't believe she had much intelligence, it was even possible she believed in Robin Hood, Arthur Scargill and Bernard Shaw. She might cast all caution to the winds and lead them right to the source. Hesseltine wasn't so sanguine but said he had some very good men and she would find it hard to shake them off. Hedge went back to the Foreign Office, hoping he would soon know who Ho Suzy's paymasters were. The big boys, presumably. Ho Suzy had taken a risk and no-one sacrificed their liberty for nothing.

*　　　*　　　*

There had happened to be a reporter from a national newspaper in the Eastleigh branch of Barclays at the time Ho Suzy had been detained and then arrested. This reporter, in Eastleigh not on duty but to visit a sick aunt, had heard the mention of the name Shard, a name known to him in his professional crime-reporting capacity. He had been much intrigued by all the circumstances and had rung his newspaper as soon as possible. Certain enquiries were then set in train:

67

moles abounded everywhere. It was not difficult to unearth a few pointers and the newspaper managed to dig up Detective Chief Superintendent Shard's extra directory home address. A reporter was despatched in the hopes of talking to Shard's wife. Nothing had leaked about the bribery aspect, but the reporter who had been in the Eastleigh bank had immediately jumped to that conclusion, perhaps naturally. Senior police officers juxtaposed with sexy eastern women depositing money had that sort of ring about it. Another matter that had not so far leaked was the fact of Shard's disappearance; so the newspapermen didn't have that on their minds at all. However, the time when Shard was likely to be at work was obviously the best time to catch his wife on her own, and there was always a better story to be got out of a wife, the more so this time since Shard would definitely not be talking to the press.

The reporter arrived in Shard's road just after Beth had driven off in the car, having this time made sure the garage was locked. In the small garden there was an elderly woman pottering about. The reporter approached.

"Excuse me," he said over the gate.

"Yes, what is it, who are you?"

"I was wondering if Mr Shard was in."

"No, he isn't. Nor Mrs Shard. What did you want, Mr – er – ?"

"Press." The reporter named his newspaper.

"Well, I've nothing to say to the press, thank you very much." Mrs Micklem sniffed, felt inclined to say, especially *that* rag. "What cheek, sending you round here!"

It was an indiscreet remark: the reporter was a very experienced man with an excellent nose for news, and he believed the elderly woman, probably a mother or mother-in-law, was in possession of some since her reaction had been one of annoyance rather than of surprise. Why? What was it she thought he had been sent round for? The Eastleigh man had mentioned possible bribery, and where there was smoke there was fire more often than not.

Mrs Micklem asked, "How did you get my son-in-law's address?"

Mother-in-law established. She had a tiresome look about

68

her, a complainer, a nagger. The reporter took a chance and told more-or-less the truth. "The Foreign Office gave it, Mrs - ?"

"Micklem."

"I wonder if I might come inside for a moment, Mrs Micklem?" He took another chance. "We might be able to . . . to help. The press often does, and my newspaper likes to, well, see that people aren't - "

"I know all about your paper," Mrs Micklem said with asperity, "but you may as well come in rather than talk out here in front of the neighbours." She swung away and marched up the short path to the front door and went in ahead of the reporter, who had scented victory and a good story. Mrs Micklem showed him into the sitting-room and stood with her back to the empty grate, staring at her visitor. "Well? What is it you want to talk about?"

The reporter, still guessing as to the facts, still in the total dark really except for the report from Eastleigh, plunged in at the deep end. He said, with a touch of phoney embarrassment, "There's a girl. She could be Chinese. Ho Suzy."

*   *   *

Next day a newspaper was brought to Shard and laid on the floor of the room, opened where he was intended to read. There was a headline: MOTHER-IN-LAW TELLS ALL. The shock was immense: the old bitch. What the hell had she thought she was up to?

She was certain her son-in-law was innocent, that he would have an explanation when he returned, that he had obviously been framed. Scotland Yard had taken the money away - the report made much of the fact that actual cash had been found on the premises. Credit where credit was due, however: Mrs Micklem seemed genuinely to believe in Shard's innocence and resentful of the distress caused to Beth. But it was different when it came to the girl. Shard ground his teeth. Who in God's name was Ho Suzy?

Mrs Micklem had been scandalised. Shard could appreciate her feelings well enough. But that was where the fiction began,

69

the reporter's imagination in the interest of a good selling story. The muck-raking – muck-inventing rather. The moment Shard was free he would start an action for libel. Mrs Micklem, the report stated, had been distraught, the betrayed mother-in-law. If it was true that a girl, obviously pregnant, had paid money into his account, then perhaps her son-in-law wasn't innocent after all. It all hung together. Loose women and bribes. And he was away an awful lot . . . Mrs Micklem, the paper said, had broken down in tears. And a query had been left in the air: where was Detective Chief Superintendent Shard? Out of the country already?

*   *   *

Hedge was beside himself. Immediately on his early arrival at the Foreign Office next morning, keenly anticipating a report from the Yard that Ho Suzy had been successfully tailed, he was sent for by the Head of Security, who was looking worse than ever. The newspaper was flourished at Hedge, who paled as he read.

"Scandalous! A writ must be issued at once, Head."

"Not so fast, not so fast. First, an internal investigation to establish who made the leak. We must have our facts at our fingertips – "

"Of course. I shall see to that immediately."

"Then the newspaper editor. This is serious, Hedge – I need hardly say. We're going to be thoroughly discredited throughout the country. And that Korean woman!"

"I agree entirely. But she may yet help."

"She hasn't yet." The Head of Security had been put in the picture about the surveillance. He didn't seem hopeful. Perhaps it *was* too much to hope for. But it was all they'd got. The Head flourished the newspaper once again, his face a threat. "This. Get on with it – priority. And this Mrs. Micklem. I'm going to talk to her, and Shard's wife. Have them brought, Hedge – send a car."

Hedge went back down to his office, shaking like a leaf. The Permanent Under-Secretary wasn't in yet but soon would be. Hedge tried hard to think of him as kind old Pippin, but failed.

Within minutes of Hedge reaching his office, Miss Fleece and the whole security section was in uproar.

Moles, such hard things to find.

*   *   *

The bearded Irishman had come back soon after Shard had taken in the newspaper report. He said, "Well now. I suppose you're getting there, Mr Shard."

"Where?"

"The reason for the bribery."

"The alleged bribery. I – "

"The money's there. That's a fact. And now this." The man bent and lifted the newspaper. "The whole country will know now," he said, unconsciously paraphrasing Hedge's boss. "At a time when things are about to happen, both the Foreign Office and Scotland Yard have a nasty scandal on their hands, a very nasty one. That will pre-occupy them and will not be good for their efficiency or for the British people, as you will see. Such things never help, Mr Shard. And there is something that is not in the papers, but soon will be."

"What's that?"

The man smiled. "Your child, Mr Shard." He tapped the paper. "It says Ho Suzy is pregnant – and it is a fact that she is. Soon there will be headlines naming you as the – "

"Get out," Shard said through his teeth.

"Of course. So you can think about it by yourself. I shall be back later. Enjoy your morning. It's a nice day, plenty of sunshine."

He left Shard alone. Shard's mind went in circles. Somewhere a bird was singing, close to the window, a sound of peace and tranquillity. Shard was just aware of it; lucky bird! There was no peace in his mind and no tranquillity. His first thought was for Beth. What would she be thinking, what would she be feeling, what would Mrs Micklem be saying to her – and she to Mrs Micklem come to that. Beth was a loyal wife. The atmosphere would be fraught. Mrs Micklem might take off for home. On the other hand, Hedge was going to see her as lethal to what was left of security and might insist on her remaining

71

where Beth could put some sort of clamp on her tongue. And now this business of paternity. When that broke, his name would be mud, and he was currently in no position to wash it off.

If he'd been able to get his hands on Mrs Micklem he'd have been done for homicide.

Down south in Whitehall Hedge was also feeling homicidal. He had made Mrs Micklem blench: he could be tough. Mrs Micklem, he said, was a threat to national security and he had a good mind to have her arrested and charged – he didn't say what with and she didn't ask. Beth sat silent, glad enough to see her mother being bollocked. She had already said similar things herself, but Mrs Micklem had simply said, "Hoity-toity," and tried to justify herself. With Hedge, it was different. Hedge, in the sanctity and dignity of the Foreign Office, was impressive to the lay person. Mrs Micklem had begun to weep. When that started Hedge coughed, rang through to Miss Fleece, and had Mrs Micklem removed from his office for a cup of strong tea. He retained Beth.

"Now, Mrs Shard. Naturally, you're anxious about your husband – as to his whereabouts, perhaps."

"Yes," Beth said, fists clenched in her lap.

"So are we, Mrs Shard, so are we."

"You mean – "

"I mean only this: we don't know where he is." Hedge stared into her face, into haunted eyes. "This is for your ears only, certainly not for your mother's, you understand?"

She nodded.

"We believe he's in the hands of – undesirable persons. No doubt you'll have read in the papers of a sick passenger removed at Carlisle from – "

"Yes! Was that Simon, Mr Hedge?"

He nodded. "We believe so – no proof, but a description . . . yes, we think so. We don't, as I said, know where he is. But soon the press is going to get hold of it. They'll add the alleged bribery to the sick passenger and they'll put two and two together. And I've no idea what they'll make of it . . . except that certain sections may well make innuendos. I expect you know what I mean."

"But surely, if they connect Simon with that passenger, it'll be obvious he didn't leave the train of his own accord? That he wasn't disappearing because – because he'd taken bribes?"

"That," Hedge said pontifically, "is of course how *we* see it. I'm only warning you. You know what the press can be like, some of it. I don't say they will, mind you. But you've got to be ready for dirt and you've got to take it in silence."

"Yes, I see that."

A finger was wagged at her. "Not a word – not one word – to any newspaperman. I shall arrange for you to be given protection, a plain clothes man who will be very discreet but may be called upon if you're under pressure. And for heaven's sake, my dear girl, keep your mother under control."

*   *   *

The CID officers tailing Ho Suzy had been efficient. Longish hair, dirty jeans and sweat shirts bearing slogans of up-to-date appeal – the various ways of doing it, standing up, under water, up a mountain – had blended them nicely with the crowds as Ho Suzy made her way along Victoria Street to the subway at Westminster. She had caught a Circle Line westbound and had got out at Gloucester Road but only to change trains onto one bound for Ealing. She had got out finally at West Kensington, had crossed the North End Road to the west side and walked along it into the Hammersmith Road, swinging a handbag from her left shoulder, never once looking round. Perhaps it was too good to be true.

She crossed to the north side of the Hammersmith Road, walked westerly, then turned off right towards Brook Green. She was walking purposefully; she had to be dumb, not to suspect. Once in Brook Green she twisted and turned a bit, so many streets, but the tail had no difficulty in seeing her enter a three-storey house, somewhat sleazy, in Downton Street. She went up some steps, opened the front door, went in and slammed it behind her.

From a telephone kiosk some distance off, while one of the CID men kept obbo on the house, the word went through to the Yard and Hesseltine was informed. His orders, watch it and

73

report all comings and goings, were just routine. It could prove a long slog. One of the men went round the back, checked his bearings, isolated the house, lit a cigarette, and drifted to the end of the service alley onto which the house backed. He had noted that all the windows at the back of the house were heavily curtained, the curtains themselves of a thick, dreary material and very dirty. All one house, not flats as such as had been established from the lack of duplicated bell-pushes by the front door. Not flats as such, but maybe rooms used by prozzies. Ho Suzy could be one. If so, it was going to be quite a job, reporting back to Scotland Yard on the comings and going of the punters, none of whom were likely to be of interest anyway. But it was a complication that didn't, in the event, arise. There were no callers, and no-one left the house. Not, that was, until after dark that night when a small man with yellow skin, visible in the street lamps, left by the front door which he shut behind him. He walked briskly north, a CID man keeping his distance behind. The second CID man used his walkie-talkie and called the Yard. He was told to stay on obbo and await his relief. The Yard called the Assistant Commissioner Crime, who had gone home to bed leaving orders that he was to be kept informed.

Hesseltine decided the time had come to investigate the house in Downton Street. The man on obbo was called and told to expect reinforcements, armed. More or less as an after-thought, Hesseltine called Hedge, told him what he proposed to do.

Hedge concurred. Better to carry on using the Yard. He still didn't want to involve the Foreign Office overtly.

Within the next half hour, something resembling the Heavy Mob, the Flying Squad, though in fact it wasn't them, turned up in Downton Street.

The CID man approached them and reported to the Detective Inspector in charge. "No movement, sir."

"All quiet on the Western Front, eh?"

"Yes, sir."

"Won't be for much longer," the DI said cheerfully. "Door locked, I take it?"

"I don't think so, sir."

The DI nodded, moved towards his two cars, gave quiet orders. There was another vehicle round the back and officers were moving up the service alley, disturbing cats and dustbins. The DI went fast up the steps, taking the lead, and shoved the front door open. He was met by total silence, like the grave, eerie. A stench of dirt and decay. His torch – he hadn't yet found the light switch – showed peeling wallpaper and a lack of stair carpet. The stairs reached up a long way and were steep. Still nothing stirred as the torch beam travelled up the stairs.

"Right," the DI said, and his voice seemed to echo. "Room by room, basement and ground floor first."

Empty. So were all the rooms on the first floor. And the third. They found Ho Suzy on the fourth floor, in a bathroom or what passed for one – cracked handbasin, lavatory pan, bare floor, brown-stained bidet of all things, no bath, but a good deal of blood. Ho Suzy was slumped on the pan with her head down. The dripping had stopped, but the ends of the hair were matted. The DI's face was pale; he'd never seen anything quite like it. From the girl's right ear a hatpin, old-fashioned, long, thin, made of steel, protruded. It had gone through the eardrum into the brain.

7

The press got onto it: more trouble for Hedge, though it was scarcely his fault. The Head of Security was really bad now, should never have returned to duty and was confined again by doctor's orders. The Permanent Under-Secretary was seriously alarmed and ticked off the incidents on his fingers: Faslane, Millbank, Shard's disappearance, the explosion in the New Forest, Ho Suzy dead and no clue at all to the killer. It could be assumed that the killer had been the yellow-skinned man who had left Downton Street but the Yard's tail had lost him after not very far. He had, the report said, kind of merged with the dark and vanished. And, as already foreshadowed by Hedge, the press had got hold of something else: Shard's disappearance. The speculation had already started. There was the bribery, and there was the cash, as admitted by Mrs Micklem. It was all a pressman's dream of heaven.

"Do you see any links, any leads?" Sir Edmund asked, after his enumeration of events.

"I'm afraid not, Under-Secretary."

"What about those men in Dublin?"

"Garrity and Phelan? There's been nothing fresh so far."

"Red herring?"

"The Garda didn't seem to think so, Under-Secretary. And the New Forest explosion tends to support their theory of a simple bombing campaign."

"Yes. What we need to know is, where next?"

Hedge said helplessly, "There's no knowing."

"Find out," Pippin said.

"Yes, Under-Secretary." Dismissed, Hedge went back to his office. It wasn't really fair, half a Yard job, half his. Split command, but he was determined to remain on top. Sitting at his desk, attended by the conscientious Miss Fleece, Hedge felt somehow unclean. The press again: remarks about the paternity of Ho Suzy's baby, which now might or might not be born. That depended on the medics, but certainly she had looked very far gone and it could yet, Hedge supposed, be born by caesarian section or whatever. It was horrible to think that the Foreign Office had become involved in anything so distasteful as fornication, even if only by innuendo . . .

*   *   *

Almost concurrently with Hedge's thoughts in London, something happened up north. There was a loud explosion and a bright flash of flame that seemed to come over the stone wall and into the room occupied by Shard. The building rocked. Then there was silence broken only by the distant reaction from the grey-suited man and the bearded Irishman. They had become excited; and after a while one of them came to Shard – this time the grey-suited man.

"RAF plane," he said. "Probably on a training flight, a Tornado."

Shard had heard them from time to time, another indication that he was still in the north. Flying at speed over the hills, down the glens – if this was Scotland – between the crests, tricky work. He asked, "Anyone eject?"

"Don't know."

"You haven't bothered to look, give a hand to – "

The man laughed edgily. "Would you, in our place? Grow up, Mr Shard. We've moving out, fast. Any time now, the

77

district'll be swarming." After that they didn't lose any time. Shard was given another injection. Once again he remained conscious but without speech or movement. The blindfold was replaced and he was carried out to the estate car and concealed beneath the rug, the handcuffs still on his wrists. The car was started up, lurched back to the road, and then driven fast. Around ten minutes later it slowed and stopped and a window was wound down and Shard heard voices. The new accent was Yorkshire. Someone, probably a police officer, talking to the driver, the grey-suited man this time. They might not want to reveal the bearded man's Irish accent. Yes, they'd seen the crash and were driving to report it. They had tried to render assistance but it had proved impossible and they thought the best thing to do was to get a report in as fast as possible. There was a word of approval and then they got on the move again.

So near and yet so far. Shard felt throttled with frustration. There was no more stopping after that. Traffic passed, going fast as the sounds told him, no doubt ambulances and RAF vehicles and more police. They were taking a number of bends, some sharp, giving an uncomfortable time to Shard. No doubt the Pennines and a normally lonely road through the dales, beneath the high fells. There were RAF airfields on the fringe of the dales – Leeming, Dishforth, Linton-on-Ouse. Shard heard the men talking now, as though they had only just got around to thinking about the crash *per se*. Someone, it appeared, only one, *had* ejected and had been seen. His parachute, as he came down very close to a craggy peak, had caught on a rock projection and his body had swung in hard against the rock itself, and then the parachute material had split further and the airman had fallen a long way. That was what Shard gathered from fragments of conversation. The man might still be alive, might certainly have had a better chance if help had come earlier. Shard heard the bearded man say, "It's a risk the bastards take, that's all. Don't expect me to have any sorrow for them."

The drive went on. The bends seemed to straighten out after a little over an hour and the speed increased. They stopped for petrol, stopped for more petrol later on, a matter of hours later, and soon after this the speed came right down and they were obviously in traffic.

*　　　*　　　*

Disturbing reports reached Hedge. Harry Kenwood, Shard's DS, had been keeping his ears open in pubs where he was not known. He had heard many a conversation.

"Bloody fuzz, feather their own nests all right, eh."

"A young girl like that, and got knocked off because of it more than likely."

"Discrimination against the coloureds – " This was in the London Borough of Camden.

"Racism, do what you like if they aren't white."

"Fuzz always takes bribes, stands to reason."

It was all quite unreasoning, but as had been remarked in Kenwood's hearing more than once, where there was smoke there was fire.

"A damn stupid thing to say," Hedge said furiously.

"I quite agree, sir, but people say it. And they're saying it all right. We can't win, sir, we never can."

"Any other sort of talk . . . personal, say, to Mr Shard?"

"Only what I've reported, sir."

Hedge nodded. "All right, Kenwood, thank you." He sat on in thought after Kenwood had gone. The pubs – the common people. It would be a nine-days' wonder unless it was stirred up again. (That was what Hedge hoped, anyway. If there were more explosions there might be a reaction, confidence lost in the authorities.) But in the corridors of power other things were being said, certainly not by responsible people such as the Permanent Under-Secretary and his ilk, but by members of parliament, some of whom could have axes to grind. Some of them had talked to Hedge and asked questions: was it the fact that Shard had, as it were, defected? Were secrets being passed? And again the hint: where there was smoke . . . mothers-in-law might be very ill advised to talk to the press, but they were often in possession of secrets themselves. If Shard was really in cahoots . . . . Hedge reacted angrily and in defence of his department, but he had been

79

forced to advise the Permanent Under-Secretary that there was a very restive air around Westminster. And the clubs were seething with rumours. Perhaps it was time a statement was issued?

"Not at this stage," Sir Edmund had said.

"But really, I think – "

"No, Hedge. We've far too few facts to go on. Also, I don't want to play into the hands of these people. I don't want authority to be seen to be rattled. And another thing: we still have no idea as to who our adversaries really are. We have one Arab, one Korean girl, and three Irishmen if you count the two in Dublin. So, for now, the less said the better. We must wait upon events for a while, Hedge. We must see which way the cat jumps."

But the cat seemed to be in no hurry, or if it was then its jump was being made under excellent cover. Hedge felt as though he were on the brink of a precipice, or moving about on an earthquake that might suddenly swallow him up. All those blocked avenues! The dead couldn't talk, and Hedge would so much have liked to know more about the bribery of Shard, the *alleged* bribery that was. If only he could get at the reason for it . . . he was beginning to think it could even in some twisted way be aimed at himself via his department. Discredit one of his top men and you discredited him as well. There was a saying that rot began at the top and worked down. If that should prove to be so, then there loomed the threat of premature retirement, honourless and with an inadequate pension.

Hedge cast about in his mind for enemies. He had made a number during his time in the Foreign Office but apart from the mutual dislike he had to concede that they were very decent people – gentlemen, not the sort who would do anything dastardly behind his back.

*   *   *

In his new location, Shard still had no idea where he was other than that, because they had been in traffic, it was a certain enough guess that he was in a town and probably a large one. The traffic crawl had lasted right through to their final stop and there had been city sounds all about him. When they did stop it was in a garage, an integral one from which he was carried with the blindfold removed into the kitchen area of a house. Then into a room furnished with a bed and a bare mattress, a small room with a barred window like in his last habitat, and looking out onto a wall, this time brick not stone. Once again the effect of the injection was starting to wear off and he could make independent movements, small ones to begin with. The men looked down at him and the bearded man advised him to get some sleep because they might not be there long. Behind the two men Shard saw another man hovering, a small man with a yellowish skin, a look of the Far East. Nothing more was said and all three went away, locking the door behind them. Traffic sounds came to Shard, muffled but not too distant. They were not far from a busy road. A little later there was a smell of cooking, not very good cooking, greasy, and the smell was the horrible stench Shard associated with hamburger stalls.

Hamburgers it was. Two were brought to Shard on a cold plate, a mess, with chips and peas, already congealing. This was brought by a woman, guarded by the bearded man with a gun, and Shard's wrists were freed from the handcuffs while he ate. The woman stood watching; she was young, dressed in jeans and a sweatshirt advertising CND. The bearded man, even when on guard duty, couldn't keep his hands off her. Fondling, though keeping his eyes on Shard, he spoke into her ear.

"Tack's a lucky bastard."

"He's not here," she said, giggling a little.

"Ah, that's true enough." The bearded man's face suffused with anticipation but no more was said. Shard finished his meal and surprisingly felt better for it. The girl went out, came back with a glass of water. Neither of them spoke to Shard. When he'd drunk the water the glass was removed and they left. Soon after this the girl came back in and handed a newspaper to Shard. It was a national daily, no local clues, that morning's paper. For some reason or other, maybe neglect of duty but maybe because it didn't matter, the handcuffs had not

81

been replaced and Shard was able to read without difficulty. He was featured as expected. An intriguing mystery . . . total disappearance, but linked with the sick passenger off the train from Glasgow. It was not specifically suggested that Ho Suzy's unborn child was Shard's, but the juxtapositioning of the guesswork couldn't have left many people without that impression and Shard, although he had been warned, seethed afresh. There had been nothing further from Mrs Micklem but it was reported that she had been called, along with Shard's wife, to the Foreign Office. In his imagination, Shard relished the scene. But didn't relish what he knew would be happening around his home; siege by the press, reporters and cameramen snooping everywhere Beth went. He also read the guarded, more responsible editorial reactions. The Foreign Office was coming in for some stick. Like Hedge, Shard thought it was time some official statement was issued . . .

Beyond the door, from the hall, a telephone rang. It didn't ring for long. Shard heard heavy footsteps and then the Irish tones of the bearded man, answering.

"Hullo. Yes, it's Tim O'Carse." (Or it could have been Tim of course.) "Yes, we got here an hour or so. Yes. No, no, we've not questioned him at all yet . . . I've been waiting for more – yes." There was a lengthy silence from the bearded man, then a sound of annoyance, even anger. "What? You – " Another pause, then: "Ach, very well then, we'll come."

The receiver was crashed down, a show of temper – or disappointment. Tim spoke to the girl. "We have to go, it's your bloody . . . " A door banged and the voice was lost to Shard, who was left wondering. Inside the next minute his door was opened and the grey-suited man entered with the handcuffs, which he slipped onto Shard's wrists again while Tim stood in the doorway with his gun, looking angry enough to use it the moment he thought he needed to.

They left him, locking the door again. A few moments later he heard footsteps in the hall followed by the slamming of the garage door and the sound of the car starting up.

He listened for more sounds. None came. The house was silent, had a deserted feel, but he knew it wouldn't be deserted.

The girl and the yellow-skinned man would be there still, was his guess.

*   *   *

During the night Hedge was called from his bed: Detective Inspector Orwin, on duty in the security section, had had an urgent call from Defence Ministry –

"What is it?" Hedge demanded, sounding panicky.

"Faslane, sir – "

"Again?"

"Yes, sir, and – "

"What's happened, Orwin, just tell me!"

"Yes, sir." Orwin had been trying to do just that. "Faslane reports an explosion in the water, alongside one of the nuclear submarines – "

"Oh, my God. Damage?"

"Surprisingly little, sir. But whoever did it, got away. Could have been frogmen, the Commodore thinks. The whole of the Gareloch's being put under search. Defence Ministry expects positive news any time, sir."

"I suppose this is Detachment X?"

"Yes, sir," Orwin said. "There was another plastic notice."

"Oh, if only Shard was here!" Hedge said frenziedly.

"Yes, sir. Meanwhile that's not all – "

"Not all!"

"The U.S. base, sir. On the Holy Loch, the Poseidon – "

"The Americans!" Hedge was out of bed now, toes groping for his slippers.

"Yes, sir. Similar occurrence."

Similar occurrence, Hedge thought. The police never had any imagination. Nothing that affected the Americans could be called similar. This would be a diplomatic furore and the whole of NATO would fall upon his neck. Bees' knees . . . that, when Hedge had been a young man, was what the Americans had thought they were, hot as mustard and moved fast. This time they would move in his direction, unless he could off-load them onto Defence Ministry – which, having got involved, he probably couldn't entirely. Hedge began issuing orders: they tumbled rapidly into his closed line, into Orwin's ear. Orwin was to go north to Faslane at once; he was to go by air, the first available flight –

"Strike's still on, sir."

"Have you never heard of the RAF, Orwin?" Hedge had one arm into his dressing-gown. "Defence Ministry – tell them to provide air transport. Or a helicopter," he added, inferring that helicopters didn't rate as air transport like proper aeroplanes. "*And keep me informed* – I shall leave for the Foreign Office immediately."

8

There was, of course, no knowing how long Tim and his companion might be gone. But the fact they were currently off the premises was of some help, or might be if only Shard could take advantage of it. If he could, it would have to be done fast.

There was just one way: he had to get someone into the room. There was no prospect of himself getting out of it. He did the only thing he could do: he yelled and went on yelling. He shouted out that he was in great pain, feeling desperately ill too, a very sick man.

After a while the door was unlocked and a light switched on – it was dark outside now.

"What's the matter?" The girl's voice. Shard, who had shut his eyes since to do so might add colour to his deception, opened them and squinted as though the effort was torture.

"I don't know . . . the injection. I feel bad."

He heard whispers: he'd been right about the yellow-skinned man being left behind. He believed they were agitated. He'd banked on them not wanting him to die – there had never once been any threat to his life. Tim and the grey-suited man might react if they returned to a corpse. Shard gave a convincing groan, and made a retching sound. He said in a fading-away voice, "My stomach . . . I need to be on my back . . . it's cramp." He didn't add anything to that; he didn't want to mention the handcuffs specifically and it should be obvious to anyone who thought about it that he couldn't lie flat with his hands gripped behind his back.

He began to breathe rapidly, gasping for air.

He sensed consternation; the girl was asking the yellow man what was in the injected drug. He didn't know but seemed to think they shouldn't take chances. On the other hand, they obviously couldn't get a doctor. He suggested ringing Tim. The girl said, "He's gone to Tack's. Tack isn't on the phone. Uses a call box."

"Is he going to be long?"

"I reckon he is. He said – " The girl broke off; Shard opened an eye fractionally. She was biting her lip and looking almost desperate. Shard gave a cry, and jerked his body rigid two or three times, hoping the rigidity might bring rigor mortis to her mind. Perhaps it did. She came forward and squatted by his side, put a hand tentatively on his forehead. "Stomach, you said?"

"Yes. Griping . . . cramp. For God's sake . . . lay me out flat."

Breath hissed through her teeth and she straightened. Then she said, "Listen. I'm going to unlock the cuffs, all right? Just remember you're covered."

Shard had already seen the heavy revolver, with silencer, in the yellow man's hand. If it was used it wouldn't be used to kill, he was sure enough of that. Just to inhibit. He added a further touch: delirium. He talked nonsense, about Beth and babies and mothers-in-law.

"Oh, Jesus," the girl said, and bent again and pushed Shard over so she could get at the cuffs. The key went into the lock and she pulled the metal from his wrists and then he reacted with the speed of light. He got the girl round the neck, almost breaking it, then jerked both her and himself to his feet lifting her by the neck. She screamed loudly, mouth wide open,

86

eyes staring at the yellow-skinned man, who had brought up his revolver and was trying to find a point of aim clear of the girl. As the man teetered about, Shard flung the girl at him bodily, with every ounce of his strength. They crashed in the doorway and the gun came free and skidded away into the hall, and just as it did so the lie was given to the girl's belief that Tim wouldn't be back. Shard heard the car driving into the garage.

*   *   *

On the wings of the dawn Detective Inspector Orwin's helicopter put down inside the Clyde Submarine Base, to be met by Commodore Rushcroft in person.

Orwin identified himself, showed his FO pass. "Any luck, sir?"

"With the search?" Rushcroft swept an arm around the Gareloch. "Not a damn thing so far."

"Getting a little late now," Orwin remarked.

"Yes, you can say that, Inspector. I'd have expected some result." He pointed out to Orwin the visible points of the search: patrol boats, inshore craft, diving boats, naval motor-cutters and whalers with armed seamen embarked, helicopters, asdics in use, all that could be done, and, distantly on the farther shore of the loch, army and police in large numbers, from opposite Helensburgh to Garelochhead. "Either they got away to sea, or . . . "

"Or, sir?"

Rushcroft faced Orwin squarely. "Or they came from inside."

"Inside the base, sir?"

"Yes."

"But you don't believe they did."

"No, I don't. We're not that lax, we're not lax at all. But it has to be considered. There'll be an inquiry this morning, Inspector."

Orwin coughed. "Mind if I attend, sir?"

"It's your job, I suppose. No, I don't mind."

They walked together, towards the lochside and the nuclear

87

submarine berths. Rushcroft confirmed that the damage had been negligible, perhaps just a foretaste of what might be done in the future, something to hasten the nuclear missiles away from the Clyde, away from Britain altogether. Orwin asked about the Americans in the Holy Loch.

"They're not pleased," Rushcroft said. "I didn't think they would be. But there's no need for them to lift the bloody Pentagon and drop it on my head." They walked on. "Are you intending to visit them?"

"I've no orders to do that, sir."

Rushcroft grinned. "Then take your luck in both hands and thank your God, Inspector. You'd very likely have been lynched."

Detective Inspector Orwin spared a thought for Hedge. He was close enough to Grosvenor Square to have the US Embassy thundering at his door by this time.

*   *   *

Which, metaphorically, was what was happening. Hedge had hastened to the Foreign Office in his own car, speeding along an almost deserted Victoria Street past Scotland Yard and wondering if Hesseltine too had been alerted. Possibly not: it wasn't the Yard's pigeon. Defence Ministry, of course, that wretched fellow Hocking, he'd be busying himself and getting nowhere at much speed.

But within moments, literally, of Hedge dumping himself down in his swivel chair he was telephoned by his opposite number in the US Embassy, a man named Taft, no descendant of the one-time President of the United States but the mantle had been handed down as if with a pedigree and Taft wore it most of the time, by proxy.

"Now see here."

Hedge groaned: why couldn't they speak English? He said, "It's being investigated. At this moment I can't say more."

"Can't say more?" came the tones of sheer astonishment. "Why, see here, Hedge, you've said nothing yet, nothing at all, and my Ambass – "

"Yes, yes. I quite understand your position, of course. But

so far as I'm aware *very* little damage, actual structural damage, has been – "

"That's not the point – "

"And no casualties," Hedge said loudly, "either to your naval personnel or ours. It could prove a storm in a teacup."

"Of all the stupid things to say. A penetration's been made in water guarded by your own British Navy. That shouts aloud. And all you do is call it a storm in a teacup!"

Hedge said desperately, "Oh, really, I never meant to imply – "

"Listen, Hedge." It was better than see here, but Hedge gave a groan of dismay. He knew just what was coming. It did. Taft's ambassador had been dug out from bed and was awaiting firm reports and apologies and real assurances. But in fact he hadn't waited for long. Already he had been in touch with Downing Street – Number Ten direct and to hell with protocol. Hedge's heart went down into his boots: the PM was the hardest of nuts. Then Taft came out with it, flat. "All this business in the press, Mr Hedge."

"What?"

"Your man Shard. Need I say more? Well, maybe I should be plain. I – "

"I can't discuss that," Hedge said at once. "It's all rumour and I have positively no comment."

"Now see – "

"Positively no comment. Goodbye, Mr Taft." Hedge replaced his receiver, fuming and now very anxious indeed. If only Shard would materialise – Hedge couldn't fail to see something of the American viewpoint. Alleged bribery of a top security man, and the top security man vanished. That wretched girl Ho Suzy's pregnancy. The Americans were everlastingly on about the slackness of British security, and Hedge had to admit there had been too many lapses, not on his part of course or that of the Foreign Office, and now this, perhaps the last straw for the Americans who saw their Poseidon fleet at risk. This was possibly why Shard had been framed, a stupid attempt to break the Atlantic alliance, shatter trust, shatter NATO. Far fetched? Not really. The Americans were so touchy. Anything could happen.

Hedge waited in sick dread for the Permanent Under-Secretary to arrive.

*   *   *

Shard had gone after the revolver, butting the yellow-skinned man in the stomach as he too made a dive for it. Shard won out. The yellow man, small and skinny, skidded along the hall's cheap linoleum and lay winded at the foot of a flight of stairs. Shard got the girl before she had recovered from being thrown, wrapped an arm around her, lugged her to the front door and reached it before the men had come through into the back of the house from the garage. The back door opened just as Shard had slammed the front one and was heading with the girl down a short path for a gate. The area, he saw, was residential but there was still some traffic even though the hour was late. He was probably on a main through route somewhere. As he reached the gate there was a phutting sound and bullets came close enough to be noticed. Shard rushed the girl through the gate and then, from the cover of a low brick wall, he waited and watched.

The yellow-skinned man seemed to have recovered: now rearmed, it was he who came through, incautiously, taking a risk: he would be dead worried. He saw Shard in the same instant that Shard saw him and they both fired together. Slivers of brick burst into flight above Shard's head and the little weasly man clutched at his chest, spun twice, and collapsed. A passing couple on the other side of the road – out late, girl being taken home – stared for a moment through the traffic, then took to their heels, probably to find a policeman. Shard hoped they would find one, that he would use his loaf and not approach unarmed but instead report by radio, asking for police marksmen. The traffic rolled past unheeding, going fast at this hour along night-clear roads, concentrating on getting out of town – Shard didn't recognise his surroundings but there was the feel of London – and these days people didn't stop if they saw trouble, they didn't want to get involved.

He waited for the next attack. The grey-suited man and the bearded one, Tim, were still inside, presumably. The yellow

90

man lay still; there was a lot of blood welling from a hole in the chest and he looked to be as dead as mutton. Shard dragged the girl towards the spreadeagled body and felt for a heart-beat with his free hand: nothing.

Silence from the house: a getaway, via the back? The car hadn't come out, not surprisingly, perhaps, since it would have come out into Shard's gun range.

Time for a risk: Shard got to his feet. Another couple was coming into sight, beneath a street lamp, coming towards him on his side of the road. Useful cover, perhaps: probably the men in the house wouldn't risk more shots in full public view. He shoved the girl's body against the gate, pushing it open, told her to get down in the lee of the wall and keep quiet or else. Shaking like a leaf, she did as she was told. Shard grabbed for the yellow man's right leg and dragged him through. The legs spread and the left one tangled with the gate post. Shard freed it. Legs together, the body came past the gate. The couple outside, having seen something nasty, were beating it back the way they had come. Shard shut the gate, rolled the body into shadow against the wall, and retrieved the girl.

"Into the house," he said.

She was fully compliant. Maybe she knew he was walking into danger. Shard knew that risk too; knew also that he could leave now with the girl, report in, have the house cordoned and then, after a shoot-out, searched. But that wouldn't do. If the two men hadn't gone already, they would go the moment he left the scene but before they went they would remove anything that might be of interest to the police.

He went slow up the path, all senses alert, gun ready.

No movement anywhere, no sound. The front door stood open as the dead man had left it and the hall light was on still.

He went in cautiously, shut the door, went through to the kitchen. No-one. He was certain now that they'd gone and probably wouldn't have had time to destroy all evidence; that was when he began to smell burning outside – paper, unmistakably. He pushed the revolver hard into the girl's body. "Save me time," he said. "I take it there's a back way out?"

She nodded. "Other side of the garage leads to the back garden – "

91

"And a service alley?"

"Yes."

"And the burning?"

She shrugged. "I don't know."

Maybe she didn't, maybe she was playing for time, knowing what was burning. But the smell was coming through from outside, and she'd said there was a garden. Shard propelled her ahead of his gun, through the door, through the garage which had another door on its far side, out through this into the back garden, an overgrown area of brambles and long, unkempt grass that had once been a lawn. At the far end, a dull red glow and a low flicker of flames. Shard went fast for it, overturned a dustbin with holes in it, a makeshift incinerator. Very makeshift. Shard stamped on the flames. Burned paper swirled. However, something had been salvaged and it might be useful. No point whatever in going in search of the two men. They'd gone by now. Shard, however, could give an excellent description of them.

He had just about put the fire out when he heard cars pull up in front of the house and orders being given as doors slammed. That couple had done their duty nobly.

Still holding the girl, Shard went back into the house and was in the hall when the door came open and he saw uniformed men. A sergeant, armed, a police marksman, asked, "Who are you and what's going on?"

Shard grinned. "A certain amount of mayhem, Sergeant. And I'm Detective Chief Superintendent Shard of - "

"Pull the other one," the sergeant said.

The men hadn't removed his Foreign Office identification. He produced it. The sergeant looked at it in some astonishment and said, "I've heard about *you*, sir."

Shard felt himself react. He said, "I hope you don't believe all you hear, Sergeant, or all you read in the newspapers." He looked past the sergeant at police officers crowding the doorway. "I'm taking charge. I want a toothcomb run through the house, every inch. Even if it takes all night. And there's something to be collected from the back garden. Carefully."

*   *   *

92

Before the Permanent Under-Secretary had reached his office Hedge, still sitting nervously awaiting the summons but taking pains to appear nonchalant in the eyes of Miss Fleece, had the shock of his life when Miss Fleece, returned to her own office to fetch a document for study by Hedge, came back looking both flustered and overjoyed.

She said, "Oh, Mr Hedge, the internal phone."

"Yes?"

"The security section, Mr Hedge – "

"Yes, yes."

"It's Mr Shard, Mr Hedge!"

Hedge looked up sharply. "News? What is it?"

Miss Fleece's bosom trembled. "He's back! He's here in person. He asks shall he come up?"

Strange emotions shook Hedge. The news was good, of course. But how was he to react to Shard? All the fuss and scandal . . . it was going to be so embarrassing. *Could* Shard just step back into his official role, just like that? And if and when he did . . . a discreditable rat gnawed away at Hedge's mind. Shard always seemed to put him in the shade and he'd been doing well on his own . . . he recalled that on several occasions lately he'd said aloud that he wished to goodness Shard was back, but . . . oh well, anyway, he was. Hedge set his teeth a little and said, "Yes, of course, what's he waiting for?"

Miss Fleece went away and within the next minute Shard came in. He looked dead tired, Hedge thought, and not over-clean, as though he'd slept many nights in his rumpled clothing, and he was unshaven. Hedge said, "My dear fellow! I'm so relieved you've come back."

"Why, Hedge?" Shard's tone was rather harsh, Hedge thought.

"Well . . . why not? All this time – "

"All right, forget it. I just thought I detected a sort of nuance, that's all. A suggestion that the guilty man had seen sense."

"Oh, goodness gracious, Shard, *certainly* not! But do I gather – "

"I've read all about it. They showed me the newspapers.

93

And they confirmed it.''

"They?"

Shard said, "I've a lot to tell you, Hedge. But first I want to ring Beth.'' He reached out for Hedge's open line, but Hedge's hand got there first and clamped down on the instrument. Shard flushed. "What's that in aid of, Hedge? I said, I want to call my wife. I've not been home, I came straight here, after certain things had been done.''

Hedge asked, "Why did you not call her earlier?"

"Because I felt it my duty to report first – in all the circumstances.''

"Yes. Yes, quite.''

"And now I've done that – not fully. But I've reported back, and I want to set Beth's mind at rest, Hedge.''

"I'd prefer to have your full report first.''

"Why?" Shard was truculent, felt his fists clench, the nails dig into his palms. Hedge was a bastard.

Hedge said, not looking at Shard, "This dreadful business – you know what I mean. It has to be got out of the way between us before you contact your wife – surely you can see for yourself?''

"No. Or do I take it you believe I've accepted bribes?"

Hedge shifted uneasily. "No. Certainly not. But there have to be the – the formalities. I shall have to consult Sir Edmund, you know, and perhaps Hesseltine – it may be necessary to call in A10. Just a formality, of course – ''

"You've got your lines crossed, Hedge. A10 investigates complaints against police officers. In this case, A10's inappropriate. Isn't it?''

"Oh well – you know what I mean, Shard.''

"Yes, I think I do.'' Shard had not been bidden to sit down; he remained standing, staring down at Hedge, his eyes hard. "I think you're trying to nerve yourself to a suggestion that I might be suspended from duty. Isn't that it?''

"Well . . . er.''

"I see.''

"It might have to come to that, I don't know. If it does, it'll be the press to blame very largely. It's become a matter of public confidence.''

"You mean there has to be a scapegoat, and I'm the obvious one?"

"I didn't say that, Shard. You should know very well what the police procedures are. Any public scandal . . . oh, I apologise, Shard, indeed I do, but there's that pregnancy to be thought of as well as – as the rest. The baby, by the way, was not born. So – " Hedge broke off, coughed from a red face: he'd been about to say, so you won't be landed with fatherhood. He didn't know why; he genuinely didn't believe the dirt. He covered up, or tried to, with a mumble; but Shard had got the drift.

Shard said, "Some people can't help being four-letter men, can they? In the meantime, I'm still a detective chief superintendent on secondment to the Foreign Office. You'd better listen."

"Your report will be taped," Hedge said. This was in a sense routine, but the way Hedge said it showed he hadn't liked the reference to four-letter men.

*   *   *

Shard kept his report brief and factual, describing the series of events from the time he had left the Clyde Submarine Base to his eventual emergence into the streets of London – his guess had been spot on: the house had been on the North Circular Road, a clearway out of London. He gave full descriptions of Tim who might have been Tim O'Carse and of the grey-suited man. The yellow-skinned man, now dead, would be investigated also. The girl, who had so far refused to give her name, was in police custody, so far uncharged with anything. She would be brought to the Foreign Office if and when required, Shard said, but as in the case of Ho Suzy, Hedge preferred to keep interrogations away from the Foreign Office, which must still remain unsullied as far as possible. Shard mentioned the name Tack, the man whom Tim and the grey suit had been called away to visit. All these were now being sought with the help of the Yard's CRO and fingerprint computers. The house had been dusted for prints and some good ones taken; results should flow before long.

Hedge said, "You spoke of an incinerator."

"A dustbin, not very efficient."

"Tell me about it."

"I was about to. Inefficient for them, but there was something of help to us. There could be more from the half-burned bits and pieces – "

"Where are they now?"

Shard said briefly, "The Yard. Forensic. In the meantime . . . I found references to Faslane – "

"Ah! There's been another attempt. Orwin's up there now." Hedge told Shard of the report from Defence Ministry, the small explosions alongside the nuclear submarines. "The Americans now, so unfortunate, that man Taft at their Embassy." Hedge rung his hands. "He mentioned . . . well, never mind."

"He mentioned me."

"Yes, I'm afraid he did, Shard."

Shard could see it all without it being spelled out: the Americans wouldn't want any suspicions of disloyalty and none of it had yet been disproven. He forced it down to the bottom of his mind. He had a job to do, if he were to be allowed to go on doing it, and doing it successfully was the only way he could see of clearing himself. He said, "Faslane. That was indicated – in the dustbin. Both incidents, the plastic notice and the explosions. Also the Irishman outside RAMC HQ."

"The man McMahon . . . "

"Yes. All the orders – what's left of them, that is. It's sketchy unless forensic can read more. McMahon was a hiccup in a sense. For personal reasons he'd taken against the bosses, the bosses of Detachment X, and he was believed to be about to grass on – "

"Which he did, to the extent that he spoke of this – this bribery."

Shard stared. "He did?"

"You didn't know that?"

"The papers didn't have it, not the ones I was given. And those men didn't mention it. But isn't that proof of a frame, Hedge? The fact that McMahon revealed it?" Any straw . . . .

Hedge said, "I can't say and we must leave it for now – it

96

won't be forgotten I assure you. Now, do I take it McMahon was put on a hit list because he was about to grass?"

"Right."

"But why Millbank?"

Shard shrugged. "The coincidence of fate, that's all. He happened to be there when they got him."

"But a military establishment?"

"Not the army's teeth, Hedge. And I was coming to that – to military and naval establishments. More attacks are planned, or were planned – I'd say they'll be in abeyance now. The – "

"Where, Shard, where?" Hedge sat forward: this was where he stole a march or two on Defence Ministry and Hocking.

Shard said, "Devonport, the submarine and frigate pens. Portsmouth – "

"There was an explosion in the New Forest. Possibly premature." Hedge filled in for Shard. "I *said* it would be Portsmouth. Presumably the dockyard . . . anything else?"

"Yes. Salisbury Plain and Catterick."

"Ah. Aldershot?"

"No mention of Aldershot. But don't get too excited, Hedge. It's just a blind."

Hedge blinked. "What is? The non-reference to Aldershot, do you mean?"

"No. All the military and naval establishments or bases. There was a clear reference to hoodwinking . . . it's all intended as a drawing-off exercise, nothing more. We're supposed to concentrate all our thinking along the lines of those bases, Hedge. All our resources."

"You mean *something else* is under threat?"

"Yes."

"What?"

Shard said, "That's what I don't know. That dustbin – I found no pointers except in that general sense of something else. It's vague enough, I know. But the rest was burned. The only hope is forensic. It's not much of a hope."

*   *   *

Hedge had somewhat grudgingly allowed Shard to go home.

97

He'd checked with both the Permanent Under-Secretary and the ACC first and Hesseltine had been rudely caustic. When Shard had gone Hedge sat drumming his fingers and looking very worried. Something else, but what? He'd asked Shard if he thought Detachment X was big, but Shard had said size didn't matter. It was big enough to hit where it hurt most and in fact the fewer the operatives the better chance they might stand. You could never spot the one man with the bomb. London? Not necessarily, Shard said, and that coincided with the earlier expressed views of the Head of Security, still shingled and in much pain, that the provinces were equally at risk.

For God's sake, where and what? Hedge cudgelled his brains. Shard's dustbin information could be said to check with the opinion of the Garda men in Dublin that the military aspect was a blind. A renewed bombing campaign – but Detachment X wasn't the IRA. Or was it? Hedge was fogged. Detachment X had a nasty sound. If only Ho Suzy had been held and put under the grill – Hesseltine, not himself, had mucked *that* up. He, Hedge, had agreed to police bail but that was scarcely the point.

Put it all out of his mind for a while and something would come through. Hedge sent for Miss Fleece and got on with some routine work and in the middle of it Detective Inspector Orwin called on the closed line from Faslane. He had attended a preliminary inquiry and the result so far had been unhelpful. There had been no evidence of anything like outright treason or even of collusion by the base staff. Hedge thought it negative and rather naive: you didn't bowl out disaffected persons as a result of a naval inquiry. The navy was so stereotyped . . .

Shortly after this report was received, the Yard came through. Not Hesseltine but his deputy. Forensic hadn't been able to find anything more. The burned paper had simply been in a state of distintegration. Hedge slammed down the telephone and seethed. Sheer carelessness, either forensic themselves or Shard. Why hadn't Shard protected the charred paper in some way, perhaps glue and polythene bags, or something?

The rest of the day was quiet. Too quiet, a sense of

brooding. And the sun was scorching when Hedge left the Foreign Office for lunch at his club. It baked and burned and London was full of blasted tourists in stupid clothes. So many foreigners dropping litter, the American ones dropping chewing-gum or plastering it under park benches. London was reaching the bottom these days. It even smelled of sweat.

9

Shard rang Beth before leaving his section; he didn't want Mrs Micklem around when he got home, it might wreck the reunion. Beth was crying when he rang off, crying from sheer relief, but she was in control when he got there and Mrs Micklem had packed and gone. Beth said she was supposed to keep an eye on her but was convinced she would never in fact talk to the press again.

"What about that lot outside?" Shard asked, waving towards the roadway. The vultures had been out in force, but he'd pushed his way through and refused to answer any questions. His face had been forbidding and he hadn't had too much hassle.

Beth said, "I called a taxi. And there's been a DC watching. He helped."

"Where is he now?"

"He went with mother. I believe she was the main reason he was here."

Shard nodded, moved restlessly about the room, went out to look at the garage, for no real reason except that had been where the five thousand pounds had been put. The place felt unclean, been through by villains and by his own cloth, which hurt. The whole thing had made him feel unclean himself. When the law moved against you, being a detective chief superintendent, even an assistant commissioner, meant nothing at all. Even the Commissioner of Metropolitan Police himself, if ever he transgressed, would not be immune to having his collar felt by a p.c. The law itself stood above its officers. With uncleanness on his mind, Shard went upstairs to shave, bath and pull on a change of clothing. He knew he wouldn't have long at home; soon the questioning would start – Hedge had had no need to utter the warning. They would ring through during the afternoon.

They did: Harry Kenwood, to say he was required. He left immediately, watching out for trouble. Detachment X would be wanting him back, presumably. But he didn't spot anything. When he reached the Foreign Office he was faced with what looked like a board meeting or a court of inquiry – or a court martial. The Permanent Under-Secretary was there with the Head of Security brought from bed, plus Hedge and Hesseltine, and Hocking from Defence Ministry. But there was an obvious attempt to make the atmosphere pleasant and informal, and Shard's interrogators confined themselves to questions on his imprisonment and what he had gleaned as a result – largely a repeat of what he'd already reported to Hedge. He was told that preliminary questioning of the girl, identity still not known, had achieved a nil result and none of the men had been brought in. They had vanished. The prints had been of little help: nothing was known about the dead yellow man or the other two. Only Tack was known to the police: he had quite a record. Fraud, robbery with violence, sexual assault. No known connection with terrorism as such, but that could be something new for him.

Then the Defence Ministry man withdrew and there was an embarrassed silence and looks were exchanged, throats cleared. One or two coughs. Shard knew what was coming. It was left to the Head of Security to promulgate it.

"Shard . . . "

"Yes, sir?"

The Head of Security didn't shirk it. He said, "Those allegations."

"You've had my word, sir."

"Yes. I accept it unreservedly – I think I may say we all do." There were simultaneous nods and murmurs. A shaft of sunlight played on old mahogany furniture. Shard's eye followed it mesmerically. The Head went on, "But you're a policeman, Shard. Policemen look for proof. Mr Hedge has mentioned the man McMahon who released the information in the first place. Well – he's dead as you know. And what he said can't be taken as anything further than its face value, I'm afraid. Not at this stage. We need hard evidence that the money was paid without your knowledge or approval. I'm sure you can appreciate that." He added, almost in appeal, "As a policeman."

"As a policeman, sir, yes."

"None of us doubt for one moment that you'll be fully cleared as soon as this business is brought to a head – even before, if certain persons can be brought in and questioned. They will be."

Shard's heart was like lead. There was no need for anyone to underline it. In a voice he scarcely recognised as his own, he said, "But not by me, sir."

"I'm afraid not. You are suspended from duty pending further inquiries. I'm desperately sorry, Shard, but you see, there are other considerations . . . "

"I understand, sir." Hedge had already spoken of one of those considerations: the American interest. The alliance was of more importance than the fate or feelings of a detective chief superintendent. Much more important . . .

"Then that's all, Shard, thank you. You'll – er – you'll be required to give evidence when those men are brought in, of course."

Shard nodded without speaking and turned away for the door. He went down to his section to collect his bits and pieces and hand over to Detective Inspector Orwin.

*　　　*　　　*

Beth was shattered even though he'd warned her it might be going to happen. She was close to tears again, tears for a career

102

that might be wrecked unless the hard evidence was forth-coming. Shard did his best to cheer her, and cheer himself at the same time. He said, running a hand through his thick hair, "It's not desperate. It's largely expediency." He mentioned the American interest.

"But they can't - "

"Yes, they can, Beth. And I can understand it. British security's always been a touchy point with the Yanks."

"*They* can talk!"

"All right, so they're not much better. But they think they are and they have the upper hand. No use moaning about that. But I say again, it's not desperate. I don't doubt Hedge and the rest believe me, and Hesseltine's a good friend. In due course, I believe a statement will be issued, clearing me."

She said, "Yes, I'm sure it will," but she didn't believe it any more than he did himself. She wondered what the future might hold. Simon, sitting around the house, getting more and more despondent, losing his confidence, growing bitter and cynical, old before his time, a rejected copper who'd loved his job. And it was such a dirty charge, one for which she saw herself as partly to blame. If only she'd done what he always said and locked the garage, but it was too late for regrets now. In any case they'd have found another way. She said rather dismally, "I suppose they'll keep you informed, Simon."

"Yes, they'll do that. Bob Orwin's not only a good DI, but he's a good friend as well. Right?"

"Right," she said, looking a shade puzzled. His tone had been odd, she thought, unless it was imagination. And he seemed happier as he mentioned Bob Orwin. Then she clicked: Simon wasn't going to be sitting listlessly around the house. It wouldn't have been like him if he had. But that held dangers too.

*   *   *

Hedge took the call from the Yard and having taken it almost sent down for Shard before he remembered. He changed Shard to Orwin just in time. Hedge was in two minds about Shard: half was really quite glad not to be chivvied and treated with forebearing impatience by Shard, half knew Shard was going to be missed badly. Without him, they wouldn't bowl Detachment X out half so quickly, Hedge was convinced of that, and he, Hedge, was going to have to do a lot more work himself. Detachment X had been clever: the removal of a top man as something nasty drew towards its fulfilment had thrown a spanner into the works.

Orwin came up. "You wanted me, sir?"

"Yes. There's been some progress, a little, not much. The girl's broken." Hedge pushed things about on his desk, frowning. "Still won't give her name – at least, she admits to Joan Smith but they're not believing that at the Yard, quite rightly in my view. But some pressure was applied, the Yard wasn't specific, and she's shopped those men. Tim O'Carse, and a man she knew just as Blakey – the Yard's checking out any Blakes on their computer files – and the man Shard spoke of, Tack. She gave an address for Tack, with whom apparently she'd been living. Somewhere around Tottenham Court Road, between there and Portland Place. The Yard's putting on surveillance."

"Tack won't be lingering, sir."

"No, probably not, but it's something. Now here's the important thing, Orwin. This girl doesn't appear to know their forward planning but she believes they came south with intent – that it's in the south they go into action. That was to some degree corroborated in Mr Shard's report, of course – Devonport, Portsmouth, Salisbury Plain – oh, and Catterick." Hedge drummed his fingers. "Catterick's north."

"Yes, sir. But Mr Shard did say the military establishments were a blind."

"Yes, quite. I was about to say that – I do know what was in his report, Orwin."

"Sorry, sir."

"Now there's something else and it's much less helpful I'm sorry to say, very sorry indeed. It's this alleged bribery business, Orwin."

"Yes, sir."

"The girl confirms it. She says Mr Shard *was* taking bribes. She's quite positive. She says he was in the habit of visiting this

104

man Tack when she was there with him. Chapter and verse . . . ''

"But you don't believe it, sir," Orwin said firmly.

"Me?" Hedge looked up. "No, no, of course I don't. But it doesn't make things any easier."

"It doesn't, sir."

Hedge blew out his cheeks and sat back from his desk at full arms' stretch. "We have a good deal of *thinking* to do, Orwin. We have to get inside the minds of these men. Detachment X . . . Against The Holocaust. Well, we know that's rubbish now, a mere blind as Shard said." Orwin had the idea Hedge was going into repetition rather like the man who forgets what he was about to say next and goes back a stage or two to get his bearings. Hedge went on, "We have to try to get there before them as it were, Orwin."

"Yes, sir."

"Well, have you got any ideas to offer? I mean as to a target, don't you know."

Orwin shrugged. His mind was a blank and he said so. "It could be anywhere, literally."

"Neither us nor the police – nor Defence Ministry – can guard everywhere, Orwin. We must *narrow down*. Let me offer a few suggestions: Parliament, the Palace – the PM even. Westminster Abbey, St Paul's . . . " Hedge rambled on; he had many suggestions to make, some sensible, others less so. "Just to make you think, really, Orwin. Stir the imagination . . . "

Orwin got to his feet; it might be churlish, but he was a busy man. He had lines of his own to investigate, lines that at this stage he didn't want to talk about to Hedge. If you once put something to Hedge, however tentative it might be, he nagged away at it and wasted time and temper. Orwin went down to his section and put a call through to the Yard. Tack, he was told, had flown from the address given by the girl but the flat above the sex shop was under observation. There had been no further talking and so far no leads to Tim O'Carse or the man known as Blakey. The Yard hadn't yet got to the end of all the Blakes, but of course 'Blakey' could be just a nickname. Orwin then called Shard's home number, keeping him in the picture of events.

*   *   *

105

Tack had gone away soon after an expected telephone call had failed to come through from the house off the North Circular; that failure in communications had prompted Tack to drive past the house and he had seen police activity around it. That had caused him alarm and he hadn't returned home since. He had avoided all his contacts, just in case. After driving past the house he had gone on to pick up the A1 at Mill Hill and had then pulled into a lay-by to do some thinking. Having thought, he drove on until in South Mimms he found a telephone box from which he called a number in Grays, Essex. It should be safe enough; and there was just a possibility that the grapevine had picked up some news.

It had. It had picked up more than news. No names were mentioned but the instrument at the Grays end, answered by Blakey, was handed over to the bearded Irishman Tim. All Tim would say, and Tack didn't press for more, was, "Get here pronto."

Orders were obeyed. When Tack, an hour or so later after a mix of fast driving and traffic delays, was sitting in the Grays house he learned that his girl had been taken by the fuzz and Shard had got away. Tack reacted badly about the girl but was told to hold his horses by Tim O'Carse.

"You knew the risks."

"Right, I did. But I never thought – "

"Well, now, it's happened. It needn't be too bad for us. She'll be questioned, naturally, but she doesn't know a lot, remember." O'Carse paused, staring at Tack. "That is, not unless you told her anything you shouldn't. Did you now?"

"No," Tack said uneasily. "Course I didn't, not a thing, only what she needed to know, and like you just said, that wasn't much."

O'Carse nodded. "Right, then. I'm not worried. And I doubt if they'll find much to charge her with. They just may let her go . . . like they did Ho Suzy. Just may, if they don't get what they want by questioning."

"They'll put a tail on her," Tack said, still uneasy.

"That's to be expected. But she doesn't know this address. She'll lead them only to yours – which you'll not be visiting again. Is there anything there?"

Tack knew what he meant by 'anything there.' He said, "No. It's clean. You know I never – "

"Just checking. You remain here, Tack."

"What about Tracy?" Tack asked in reference to the girl. "Where'll *she* go?"

O'Carse grinned and scratched at his beard. "She'll be out on a limb, Tack. Homeless – no help to the fuzz at all. And we don't need her any more." He spread big, hairy-backed hands in a wide gesture. "Afterwards, we'll pick her up again. That's a promise. In the meantime you'll obey orders. From now on until we're ready, no-one leaves this house."

*　　　*　　　*

Later that morning there was a conference. Tim, Tack and the grey-suited Blakey attended it, together with the occupier of the Grays house, a man named Mussuq from one of the Gulf states, a man who, if ever he returned to his own country, would face death. Mussuq made no contribution to the conference, he was merely the provider of a safe house. Also present were four men who had come in singly at spaced intervals. Hard-faced men all of them, and all with Irish accents. Two of them were in working clothes and both were HGV drivers, expert handlers, by their own estimation, of artics and container lorries, very tough knights of the road; the other two were equally tough but were not lorry drivers. They had served in the British Army and they were the gun experts, trained marksmen as good as anything the police could provide. Blakey attended this conference with an outfit of road atlases and Ordnance Survey maps. There was a discussion that had the feel of a final going over, a last check that they'd got everything right, no snags, nothing left uncovered, every possible contingency thought of. This was going to be big – that was very much in the air. Something else, when the maps had been put away, also needed a last check.

One of the ex-army men got to his feet. "I'd like to see the stuff again," he said. "Just to be sure."

"That's okay," O'Carse said. He went out of the room with the other man and opened the door of a big cupboard beneath

107

the stairs. This was the armoury, totally unsuspected in its ordinary, day-to-day surroundings. Grays, Essex - dull but respectable and very handy for London. A workaday place where none of the men except Mussuq himself - and he had been accepted by now, after a residence of ten years or so - would ever be likely to be remarked upon. The armoury contained automatic rifles, Chief's Special revolvers, Colt .45 automatics and a number of detonators, currently safe, which could be activated by remote control.

The ex-soldier looked around, poked about, seemed satisfied, but asked, "Where's the police gear? I thought you were going to have it brought here."

"I am. Not yet, though. Time's not that short - and we still can't be sure what Shard found out."

10

The press had been a little restrained but not silenced; far from that. It was known by now that Detective Chief Superintendent Shard had been suspended from duty pending full investigation of the alleged bribes. The press was in fact being cautious about Shard, simply stating the facts. But there was speculation about what was going on in the Establishment and what the implication of the bribes might be. A house in northwest London had been raided by the police after a man had been shot, and it was after that that Shard had reported back. And a girl had been taken into custody but not so far charged with any offence, which was odd.

What was going on?

Faslane, the dying man at Millbank, the explosion in the New Forest near Southampton, Faslane again – it hadn't taken the Scottish newspapers long to get hold of *that*. Defence Ministry was saying nothing. They had put up a spokesman to say that. And Shard, of course, was a very special policeman attached to the Foreign Office . . .

There was dirt around, and a conspiracy on the part of the Establishment to keep quiet. It was the duty of the press to dig.

The public had to be held safe from danger, and there was a feeling of danger around London. The press skated round the point that the feeling was largely engendered by themselves; most Londoners were phlegmatic enough and went about their daily chores unheeding. If a high-ranking police officer took bribes, so what? That was his affair, and that of the police themselves. Explosions? Good grief, they were always happening these days! You took your chance, you took your life in your hands perhaps if you stopped to think about it, but then you didn't stop to think about it because if you did you would never go out at all. You'd starve in safety.

Then the thing started to become political.

There was always a politician around to stir things up his way or that of his party upon whom his career depended. The Opposition asked questions in the House. Could the Prime Minister give an assurance that there was no danger to security in the lapse of Detective Chief Superintendent Shard from the normally high standards of the Metropolitan Police? No, the Prime Minister could obviously not, pending the putting together of the results of an inquiry; but the honourable member who had asked the question should remember that Mr Shard had denied the allegations and there was no proof that he had lapsed in any degree. Ah – but he'd been suspended from duty, hadn't he?

"A routine measure," the PM said acidly. "May I make the point that if there had been no suspension in the circumstances, then the honourable member would be complaining on that account?"

There was a certain amount of uproar and cat-calling and a member was heard to shout out that the whole thing was a disgrace and reflected badly on all concerned and that there was a question now of public security being at immediate risk. Later the Prime Minister made it plain that extra security precautions were being taken in all military and naval establishments and there was no cause for alarm. When a minister passed a scrap of paper, and the PM read the message about Shard's report, there was something of a dither but the PM issued no correction to the statement on defence establishments or indeed any further comment. The matter was closed.

In any case, what Shard had reported about the attacks on the defence establishments being merely a blind was certainly not up for discussion in the House.

Despite the efforts of the Opposition to raise the temperature, the BBC news broadcasts were vaguely soporific: there was nothing to worry about after all and the government was doing all that was necessary. This blandness was not so apparent in the US Embassy and Hedge was once again put under verbal pressure by Mr Taft, who demanded audience.

"It's not good enough. Your man's under suspicion – okay, I accept that he's out of circulation. But what damage has been done already?"

Hedge said, "None, so far as I know."

Taft pounced on that. "So far as you know. But how much *do* you know, Mr Hedge?" When there was no answer, he went further. "Are you certain your man didn't reveal any secrets when he was being held by these people – that is, making the assumption he was in fact innocent of accepting bribes, are you certain he didn't succumb to pressure – "

Hedge interrupted frostily. "I have every confidence that Shard would have done no such thing."

The American's face said clearly that he didn't have the same confidence at all. The British were still too inclined to evaluate persons on an old-fashioned basis, a basis of trust and personal knowledge. Oh, sure they went in for screening, but once a man had been screened and passed okay he became one of the chaps and could get away with murder. There had been so many instances of that. And Taft didn't accept that Detachment X was now believed not to have any military target in mind: there were blinds and blinds. And sometimes a blind could, itself be a blind. Mr Taft talked on around this point until Hedge scarcely knew whether he was coming or going. The Americans, he had always thought, had curious minds. It was also very plain that Taft was thinking the same thing about the British. Anyway, after Taft had gone back to Grosvenor Square, Hedge began to believe he could be right: Shard could have been fed – or could have found in that house on the North Circular – some intentionally-laid false trail. Perhaps that was why he had been kidnapped and let go.

111

Perhaps it was just as well that all the defence establishments had been put on an alert and the security strengthened. There would be no diminution of that and never mind Shard's report.

*   *   *

Shard said, "I'm going out. I don't know when I'll be back. Don't worry about me."

Beth asked, "Where are you going?" She had her arms full of dirty washing, bound for the washing machine. There had been something in Simon's tone that said he wasn't just going for a walk. "Or don't you want to say?"

"The old patch," he said. That was all; he kissed her and left. He walked along to the tube station and caught a train going south, changed for Leicester Square where he got out and walked through to Soho. Once, back in his Yard days as a DI, Soho had been his patch. Not all that long ago; and he still had plenty of contacts, useful people who kept their ears to the ground and didn't mind earning a bit of tax-free cash now and again. What he proposed doing held its dangers for a suspended officer but the risk could be worth while. He pushed through the crowds, the mix of white and coloureds and Chinese, the prostitutes both male and female . . . even prostitution had changed these days, had largely lost its honesty. Return a girl's look and you were already half-way to losing a sizeable amount of cash. Fifty quid, she would say, and here's the key of my flat, see you there in fifteen minutes. That was the last you saw of her, the flat didn't exist and she had plenty more keys all cut for a few pence. Today they were well in evidence, all ages from sixteen to an unbelievable sixty. Some of the older ones recognised him and kept clear, turned up side streets or into shop doorways when they saw him coming along. Others tried it on and got a brush-off. He watched the respectable business men, umbrellas, city suits, brief cases, giving quick looks over their shoulders as they entered the massage parlours or the strip joints before catching their trains home. Soho appealed to a whole spectrum who found home life dull and matrimonial sex savourless. It would probably never

112

be eradicated and Shard hoped it wouldn't; massage parlours and prostitutes provided a safety valve, or the honest ones did. Get rid of them and the floodgates of sexual crime might open. Besides, Soho was always useful to the police, a handy concentration of vice, criminals of all sorts, and grasses.

Shard went into a strip show. Or rather, its 'front'. He knew the routine: a girl at a desk would relieve him of twenty quid and give him a piece of card, which he would take to another address as an introduction, and at this second address, if he wasn't sent to a third, he would pay over more cash – or use a credit card if he hadn't the cash, they were all on Barclaycard or Access or American Express and so on – before he was allowed to see so much as a bare leg. It was all reciprocal: other 'fronts' sent the punters here to this one. But Shard wasn't going through all that. He knew the girl and she knew him.

She smiled and said, "Hi, Mr Shard. Haven't seen you in ages."

"No. How's life, Mandy?"

"Life's okay – I s'pose. I take it you're not here as a punter, are you?"

Shard grimaced. "Hardly."

"Duty, then? What we done now?"

He waved an arm around. "This. But all right – it's legal the way you play it and suckers have only themselves to blame. But I'm not strictly on duty."

She nodded, looking sympathetic. "I did hear."

"I thought you just might." Soho was full of ears and it never took long for police news to penetrate. It paid for the shadier operators to know as many police facts as they could get hold of. "But don't believe all you hear."

"Mean you're not – "

"No further comment, Mandy. Except that my business is – well, call it personal. And I know you can keep your mouth shut, Mandy. When it suits you."

"That's right," she said, dimpling. She was a pretty girl, tall, slim, sexy, and she didn't spend all her time at the pay desk. Now and again she stood in for a stripper, pranced and pirouetted and bent down in front of the heavy-breathing punters drinking it all in and thinking their own thoughts or

113

fantasies as they stared wide-eyed from the gloom of the small auditorium.

Shard counted out five tens and they vanished as if by magic. Fifty accepted said positively you could trust Mandy: she wouldn't talk about Shard's visit. She asked, "Well?"

"Is the boss in?"

"Yep. Upstairs."

"I'd like a word. Tell him it's purely personal. He'll understand."

Mandy nodded and used a telephone. She passed the message then looked up at Shard and nodded. "You know the way," she said.

He went past the pay desk, held aside a dirty red curtain emblazoned with a yellow dragon couchant, and then went up a steep flight of stairs. The thump of music sounded from behind a shut door when he reached a landing and as he went past this door it opened and a naked girl came out, said, "Excuse me," and vanished through another doorway farther along. There was a smell of body sweat overlaid with cheap scent that lingered behind her. Shard tapped at a third door.

"Come."

Shard went in. The room was over-brightly lit by an un-shaded electric bulb dangling from the ceiling, an air of utility and economy pervaded the office but the man behind the desk, controlling his empire, looked well enough heeled. The suit was expensive if vulgar and the man was sleekly fat. He was smoking a cigar, a big one, with the band still in place, and a glass of whisky was at hand; the fingers showed gold and diamonds. Guts Flambardier, half French, liked people to know he was a rich man, everyone except the taxman that was. Or so it had been said. Years ago, Shard had done an investigation on Guts, when he'd been attached to CO(C6), the fraud squad. He hadn't found a thing; Guts Flambardier was clean vis-à-vis the Inland Revenue and the VAT and he'd been extremely grateful to Shard for clearing him.

He got briefly to his feet and waved a hand towards a chair. "It's good to see you, Mr Shard. And I'm sorry for what I hear. I tell you this: I don't believe a word of it. You're straight."

114

"Thanks, Guts, I appreciate your confidence - "

"The Yard, it must be out of its tiny mind. Suspend Mr Shard? My, my." Flambardier waved his cigar; Shard was surrounded by the expensive odour. "You'll have a drop of whisky, Mr Shard?"

"Thanks."

Flambardier heaved his stomach over the desk and went to a cupboard. He poured a stiff whisky and handed it to Shard along with his cigar-case. Shard took one and Flambardier flicked a gold lighter, then went back to his chair. "It is because of this trouble - your suspension from duty - that you've come to me?"

Shard nodded. "I'd appreciate a little help. The sort I believe you can give."

"Uh-huh?" Flambardier was cautiously non-committal until he knew more.

Shard said, "I have some names. You just might know them."

Flambardier relaxed. He was not being touched for a loan, something to tide over a misfortune - but of course Mr Shard would be on full pay, at any rate for the time being. He said, "Any help I can give . . . " He waved the cigar again, an expansive gesture of goodwill. "What are these names, Mr Shard?"

"Tim O'Carse. Blakey. Tack. A girl who calls herself Joan Smith. I'm trusting you, Guts. You don't mention those names to anyone else."

"That's understood, Mr Shard. You did me a good turn. I'll do you one - if I can."

"Are the names familiar?"

"No. To me they are not familiar." Flambardier leaned back in his chair and closed his eyes for a moment. "But there is someone . . . someone you'll remember from the past, who might be of some help, perhaps. No promises, of course."

"Who is it?"

Flambardier said, "Do you remember Charlie Dingo, Mr Shard?"

"Charlie Dingo . . . which wasn't his real name - "

"No."

"Charlie Dingo's dead, Guts."

"Oh, no." Flambardier smiled, enjoying Shard's total amazement. "He was assumed dead, yes, because of the circumstances – you remember?"

Shard remembered, all right. Charlie Dingo had been the objective of any number of villains from the Soho protection yobs right up almost to the Mafia and the Chinese tongs that had come to London over the years. Charlie Dingo, who had done more time inside than anyone else Shard could recall from his Yard days, had been highly prized by the police. In the days before the supergrasses as such had emerged, Charlie Dingo could have been called their first progenitor. He had a very wide range of contacts and the biggest ears in crime. And he had been hounded to his death – Shard had thought – by a gang from London's East End who had got word that he was in the Midlands. There had been a chase reminiscent of the Wild West without the horses, and Charlie Dingo had run for it, literally, into a moonlit canal. He'd been seen by some youths to lose his footing on an old and slippery tow-path and to hit his head on a rusted, derelict barge as he fell in and sank. The youths hadn't gone to his assistance: he'd appeared to have mates, who spread out along the bank. They didn't seem anxious to help and later the youths reported to the police and arrests were made. There was no further sign of Charlie Dingo thereafter and although the canal was dragged no body was ever found; but, as Guts Flambardier had just said, an assumption of death had been made. An erroneous one. Charlie Dingo had got away with it under cover of the dark when the moon had gone behind heavy cloud . . .

"You're sure of this?"

Flambardier said, "As sure as I'm sitting here. How do I know? Let us say, a little bird, Mr Shard. Charlie Dingo was a good friend of mine, but even I did not know until – until this information reached me. Oh yes, he's alive all right, under a different name now and a changed appearance, but still in some fear of the gangs – you will have to be discreet. We must trust each other now, Mr Shard. I shall not talk, you will not talk. Do you wish to speak to Charlie Dingo?"

"He'll be out of date by now, surely?"

"No, I think not. Gathering useful information has been Charlie's life for far too long, the habit can't be broken – "

"But he won't have any contacts, can't have!"

"Not the old ones, no. But new ones. I'm told that Charlie's doing very well in his new life," Flambardier added, grinning.

Shard asked what Charlie's line was. Illegal immigrants, Flambardier said, a network nationwide, providing faked passports, bringing in Pakistanis who disembarked from ships at sea, mostly in the Channel and the Irish Sea and landing them in boats of various sorts in the less frequented coastal areas. Plenty had been apprehended, apparently, but never Charlie Dingo. He was much too fly.

"Where is he now?" Shard asked.

Flambardier said, "That I don't know. I mightn't say if I did. This has to be left to Charlie himself. I shall send a word through and if he picks it up, then he will decide for himself. I can't commit him. And another thing: I don't even know what name he's using."

"How do I contact him, then?"

"You don't," Flambardier said. "I shall let it be known in certain quarters – that little bird of mine – that Mr Shard seeks his help and that Mr Shard was a good friend of mine in the past, and still is. From then on, you wait. If he wishes, Charlie will contact you. Leave me your telephone number before you go, Mr Shard." He raised his eyebrows. "Or – should I assume your line will be tapped?"

"I wouldn't be at all surprised," Shard said bitterly.

"Red tape – I understand. Then there must be an alternative. Can you suggest one, Mr Shard?"

Shard said, "I'll have time on my hands. Time to sit around in pubs, let's say. Ones where I'm not known."

"Such as?"

"The Golden Horn in Richmond. Classy, not for criminals – I'm unlikely to be spotted for what I am, a cop."

"Tomorrow evening, Mr Shard? Give me time, give Charlie Dingo time. Okay?"

Shard nodded. "When he rings, tell him to ask for John Dixon."

"Very well, I shall pass the word."

"I'm very grateful, Guts, I really am." Shard got to his feet. "One other thing: there's urgency around. I hope Charlie won't take too long."

"I'm sure he won't, if he's willing at all."

Flambardier got up to see him out of the office, clapped his shoulder in a friendly way. Shard went down the stairs, had another word with Mandy, and left the premises, walking back quickly to Leicester Square and a tube home.

*   *   *

When Shard reached home he found a watch on his house. This was not unexpected. The circumstances were such that the authorities couldn't really be blamed, but it did give the lie, in a particularly nasty kind of way, to all the expressions of confidence, of disbelief in his guilt. Henceforward he would be tailed. He had no difficulty in recognising the surveillance for what it was, though naturally he didn't recognise the DC on the job; that DC would have been sent in from some outlying division where Shard didn't know the faces. He wasn't worried except that if and when Charlie Dingo made contact, then the tail would have to be shaken off. Frankly Shard's hopes were low: Charlie would never take the risk, and couldn't be blamed for that. On the other hand, Flambardier carried weight. He had always been genuinely grateful to Shard for that clean report that had shifted a big load of worry from his mind and his business. He might even lean on Charlie Dingo; with his knowledge that Charlie was alive and working the illegal immigrant racket, he could lean with a considerable amount of effectiveness . . .

Shard found the house empty. There was a note: Beth had gone round to the library to change some books. Shard wandered into the kitchen and made himself a cup of tea, his mind playing around Tim O'Carse, Blakey and Tack, and the girl. If he rang through to the Foreign Office someone might tell him if the Yard had found out anything more, if the girl had been persuaded to dig further into her recollections, but there was that likelihood of a tap and it wouldn't be fair on whoever answered. Bob Orwin had taken a risk in telephoning through

118

earlier, to tell him of the Yard's lack of success. But perhaps Orwin had known the tap hadn't yet been arranged. Proper authority had to okay a tap and it was never a step lightly taken. It wasn't something Hedge could initiate, for instance. But from now on Shard had to accept that he was out of contact with his section and with the Yard, however many friends he might have in both places. Oddly perhaps, the thought of a tap hadn't occurred to him until Guts Flambardier had mentioned it.

Meanwhile time was passing. Shard had no idea whatsoever of the time scale the villains had in mind for whatever it was they intended to do. He might have weeks yet; but this he doubted. They wouldn't have come to London, left the anonymity of their remote hideout too early in the game . . . of course they'd been flushed out by that crashed Tornado, but Shard's guess was that they would have had other 'safe houses' in the north. London was always a risk; London was stiff with security and intelligence, with CID men working underground. All of which suggested to Shard that not only must the time be close but also that the target was somewhere in London itself. Something non-military, but what? Like Hedge, Shard racked his brains for ideas, but London had so many possible targets. Again like Hedge, it occurred to him that the papers could have been a plant, that he had been as it were set up to deliver false information, but that was a hard one to swallow – no-one could have timed that makeshift incinerator to burn away part but not all of the paper, and the yellow man had been intent enough on stopping his get-away.

Beth came back with her library books. She was being determinedly bright. Shard could almost feel the effort that went into it. She didn't ask him how he had got on; she was keeping off the subject, but he brought it up, said he would have to be out next evening and maybe more after that, but didn't say where he would be going. He knew she didn't like it; there was a reaction between them, a scared look in Beth's eyes, almost as though he was losing her trust. He tried to make up for it, but his efforts were clumsy and she remained withdrawn, giving him searching looks now and again when she thought he wasn't noticing. But he wasn't going to tell her where he was going, or why, because at the back of his mind was the fear that Hedge might decide to question her and he didn't want to put her in the position of having to lie to the Establishment as represented by Hedge.

*   *   *

That night, well after dark, certain movements from the house in Grays took place, supervised by O'Carse. Heavy packages were carried out to a car in the driveway and placed carefully in the boot. The car was a large one, a Volvo, black in colour. After it had driven away with the HGV drivers, making west and then south into Kent where it rendezvoused with two big articulated lorries, O'Carse used the telephone to call a number in Royston in Hertfordshire. O'Carse was terse. He said, "Bring the gear in first thing tomorrow, all right? Use the van . . . yes. All's well here, no worries." Then he rang off. Then he caught Tack's eye. Tack was sitting in an armchair and not looking so confident as O'Carse, who asked, "Nerves?"

"No. Not nerves."

"What, then?"

Tack, biting at his lip, said he'd been thinking of who the fuzz had got that might talk. His girl, Tracy – but they'd been into that, O'Carse said. Tracy didn't know anything useful except Tack's address, now closed down. So? Tack said the blokes in Dublin, being held by the Garda. They could be broken, he said. They had only to say who the explosives had been delivered to . . . maybe that was all *they* knew, but it would be more than enough.

O'Carse said, "Too late now. The fuzz still has to find us – and they won't."

"How about Shard?"

O'Carse laughed. "Shard's covered," he said. Tack's eyebrows went up but O'Carse didn't say anything further, and Tack didn't ask. It never did pay to question O'Carse. O'Carse came across with things when he was ready and not before.

11

Early next morning an Escort van drove up to the Grays house and made a delivery. The van, which was old, grey and dirty, bore legends proclaiming its owner's effectiveness at Car Repairs and MOTs While-u-Wait, Hot Water Systems, Plumbing, Fitted Kitchens, all work guaranteed. But it was none of these that were concerned with its presence in Grays. Four large brown-paper parcels were carried into the house and O'Carse opened them for a meticulous inspection before parcelling them up again and stowing them in the cupboard from which the guns and detonators had been removed. The contents were police uniforms, complete and entire, all genuine, all correct for wear by two police sergeants and one chief inspector. They had been made to measure to fit, in the case of the sergeants' rig, the two ex-army men and in the case of the chief inspector, O'Carse. Other police uniforms had gone to an address in Tilbury.

As O'Carse put the parcels in the cupboard, the van was heading into London carrying Tack. O'Carse was feeling a surge of preliminary excitement. Just three days to go. And everyone on the ball. Just one more thing to do, and that was up to Tack – and Blakey, already in London and waiting for Tack.

* * *

The van was driven into a builder's yard in Chiswick and high wooden doors were closed behind it. Tack and the driver got out, went into a hut serving as an office and were greeted by Blakey. Blakey was out of his grey suit and wearing floppy jeans and a T-shirt and the gun in the ankle-holster was unnoticeable unless he sat down and pulled his jeans up. He said, "Now for a wait. Check – any change in the time?"

Tack shook his head. "No change. We get moving at ten p.m."

Blakey nodded and handed cigarettes round then produced a pack of cards. "Fill the time in," he said. "We don't leave here all day. Lunch'll be brought. And supper. No booze. How's Tim?"

"Confident," Tack said. He said it sourly; he still had doubts on his mind. He played cards desultorily, not concentrating. Around nine o'clock another man came in, the builder in person, with newspapers. They all read them. The scare was dying down except for the Americans, still bellyaching about lax security. There was no further mention, directly, of Detective Chief Superintendent Shard. The papers read, the cards were resumed. At twelve-fifty-five Blakey got to his feet and went over to a paper-littered shelf on which stood a small radio, which he switched on. All the faces were expectant now, awaiting the news broadcast: Radio Four, The World at One.

When it came its content was no surprise to the men in the builders's yard or to Hedge, who had had the report an hour earlier from Defence Ministry: there had been an explosion, a big one, in the Rosyth Naval base on the Firth of Forth. A device, remote-controlled, had gone off close to a frigate armed with guided missiles. By some freak there had been no structural damage, or virtually none, to the frigate, but there had been a number of casualties to the ship's company working on the upper deck, dead and wounded both, and there had also been damage to a warehouse. There had been civilian casualties as well; that was bad, Hedge knew. What would the public's reaction be now for heaven's sake? The armed services were one thing, civilians quite another. Civilians didn't expect to get hurt and now they would shout aloud. The casualties apart, there were similarities with what had happened at Faslane and the Holy Loch: nothing really serious. But in all three instances, Hedge said, that could be no more than luck. He asked, "I suppose no-one was apprehended?"

He had Hocking on the line, and Hocking said, "No. Clean getaway. A car was found parked outside the main gate of the dockyard – stolen, as has been established. It's being checked for prints as a matter of routine but nobody expects very much."

The car, Hocking went on to say, was believed to have contained the remote-control outfit, but they could be wrong. Hedge fancied they very well could; surely, after an explosion in the dockyard, *somebody* would have noted a rapid retreat by a man or men outside the gates, and in any case why hadn't they *driven* away? Hocking said there could have been another car. There had been a degree of panic, he said, and no-one so far questioned remembered seeing anything at all at the time.

Hedge said savagely, "There's one thing certain now in my opinion."

"Well?"

"Shard had it wrong. It's perfectly clear these people, Detachment X, are after defence targets."

"It does seem so," Hocking said. "You may be sure we'll be taking due note of it – "

"And doing what, may I ask?"

"All possible precautions – "

"I thought you were doing that already, my dear fellow."

Hocking said rather nastily, "Oh, we are, don't worry. Now there'll be *extra* security."

Defence Ministry rang off; Hedge sat fuming and tapping fat fingers on his desk. Defence Ministry, Scotland Yard . . . it was all running away from him now, rapidly passing out of the orbit of the Foreign Office, yet he'd been the first one to be sent in at Faslane – how many days ago now? One lost count of time. The FO had become initially involved because of that dead Arab and the thought that he might represent one of the international terrorist organisations with silly initials. Who could that Arab have been? Perhaps he wasn't an Arab at all? That had stemmed from Commodore Rushcroft, who had stated dogmatically that he knew an Arab when he saw one. Well, the navy wasn't always right even though it always thought it was.

What was really behind Detachment X? If only something positive would come through. Hedge believed it was still a Foreign Office matter, that the influences came from beyond Britain, beyond the Irish Republic too. He mustn't lose his grip, his control of events. Yet even about that he was in two minds: honour and glory were good, of course, and success meànt much to him, but on the other hand if you shed the responsibility then you couldn't be blamed for other people's mistakes and, as he had reflected to himself earlier, he was beginning to feel his age.

He stiffened his back, sitting up straight with something of a glitter in his eye. He was Hedge – Hedge of the Foreign Office. He must never forget that. Responsibility, danger – they were what he had been trained throughout his life to accept. He took up his internal line. "Ah, Miss Fleece – "

"Yes, Mr Hedge?"

"Memos, Miss Fleece. Kindly come in."

*   *   *

The six o'clock news that evening carried the story in full of the attack on the frigate in the Forth. There was concern in Whitehall and Defence Ministry was reacting. Security in all military establishments was being tightened, the Portsmouth and Devonport naval bases were now closed to the public for an indefinite period, no more visits to the *Victory* and never mind that it was the holiday season and a number of organisations had been booked to arrive in coaches – Cub Scouts, Brownies, church groups and so on. The guard was being reinforced to keep all persons without authority away from Catterick, Tidworth, Aldershot camps. Extra MOD police were being drafted to these places as well as to Greenham Common and all

124

other RAF airfields, even the ordinary ones. The civil police were assisting as well, the MOD force not being a particularly big one. Henceforward there would be fewer bobbies visible on the streets.

The men in the builder's hut, growing bored and impatient with inactivity, greeted this news with wide grins. Blakey gave the thumbs up sign. "Stupid bastards," he said.

"It's what we were aiming for, Blakey."

"That's right. But they're still stupid bastards. Like sheep really, eh?"

They went on waiting for zero hour, ten p.m. At a little after six, not so far away in Richmond, Shard entered the saloon bar of the Golden Horn, followed at a distance by a – to him – very obvious tail who looked around for somewhere from which he could watch two doors. Shard heard some of the BBC's broadcast. Scotland again, and a naval target. And now service and civilian casualties . . . the barmaid and the few people who'd drifted in early were full of it. There was a lot of head-shaking and sour comment about terrorists and how the authorities never seemed able to cope with them. But a defence target again: *had* he been wrong, Shard wondered wretchedly? If only he'd been still on the case, got the first reports for himself and knew the real score. It was hard to be in limbo, no wiser than the general public. He acknowledged to himself that he could have been wrong, that he might have picked up a blind after all. But, obstinately, he still didn't believe he had. In the meantime it was clear from the news broadcast that the Establishment was back to the military and naval targets, concentrating heavily in that direction. Natural enough, if their minds were one-track; terrorism was desperately hard to bowl out before it struck.

Shard sat on a stool at the bar, propped up on one elbow, looking as dispirited as he felt, and chatted now and again with the girl behind the bar. He drank shandy; he had to keep his wits about him while he awaited the call from Charlie Dingo. If it came at all . . . he didn't say to the girl he was expecting a phone call, that would do when she answered the ring and then asked if there was a Mr Dixon in the bar.

Seven o'clock, no call. Seven-thirty ditto. Shard hoped

125

Charlie Dingo had got the message. But Guts Flambardier knew the urgency, and the grapevine from Soho was always first-class. Shard bought another pint of shandy, not enjoying it, wishing for a large Scotch. The girl was aware of his gloom. Plenty of sad people came and sat on stools, seeking company so long as they could afford it. The bar wasn't all that busy and she was sympathetic, leaning close to Shard, her long fair hair hanging almost over the shandy. He was one of the sad ones and was good-looking with it, which was sad in itself, a man like that . . .

"Cheer up," she said. "It may never happen."

Clichés. But she meant well. Shard responded with a grin that lit his face while it lasted. He said, "No, that's right, perhaps it won't."

"Terrible, that business in Scotland."

"Yes."

She was studying him closely, frowning a little and giving her hair a toss out of the way from time to time. She knew just what the trouble was: a row with the wife. Make it up and she wouldn't be seeing him tomorrow. But she didn't speak the thought aloud, it might be tactless, though some liked the chance to talk. This one didn't look as though he would, which was a pity, because she would be willing . . . she gave a slight giggle at the thought of what she'd be willing to do for him, then blushed, because he had a sudden look in his eyes as though he thought he was being laughed at. She moved away, a little embarrassed and sorry, and as she did so the telephone rang in a passage leading from behind the bar and she went and answered it.

Shard's grip tightened on his glass as he awaited the summons. It didn't come. The girl said, "Oh, it's you, Marty. Yes, it's okay, we're quiet tonight . . . " A long conversation, with intermittent giggles and oohs, followed. Shard gritted his teeth. Lovey-dovey, and it could block Charlie Dingo. It went on and on until a man sitting in a corner with a woman Shard fancied was not his wife got up and came to the bar and banged a glass on the counter and the girl looked round into the bar and rang off. Time passed, dragging. Beth would be wondering and probably worrying, but she should be used to

126

the lot of a copper's wife – but just now was different, of course. He wished he could have taken her into his confidence but there was still that thought of Hedge and what he might do. Hedge was like a fat, overfed pigeon, watching with beady eyes.

Eight o'clock, eight-thirty. Nothing. The telephone didn't ring again, not even Marty for another conversation. People came and went. After two more shandies, Shard had to go and relieve himself but still didn't draw attention to himself by saying there might be a call for him. He was as quick as possible but was thereafter haunted by the thought that Charlie Dingo might have rung in his absence.

Nine o'clock and the BBC broadcast more news, a repeat of the six o'clock really, all about the frigate. By now the bar was crowded and when the news was over Shard caught the comment, also a repeat: it was a wicked state of affairs and it was time the authorities did something about it. All service personnel were at risk and it was a crying shame; and civilians had got it too. At the same time there was a sense of detachment, of remoteness: Scotland was a long way off and thank God they were not near any service establishments in Richmond. They soon got down to the full enjoyment of their drinks again, plus pop music.

Ten o'clock. Charlie Dingo wasn't interested, didn't want to break his anonymity. He could scarcely be blamed for that, but Shard nevertheless thought hard thoughts about him. In the meantime Shard hung grimly on, getting funny looks now from the barmaid as he sat hunched on his stool. She was whispering about him to one or two regulars at the other end of the bar, he could tell that from the way they tried not to show they were looking at him, but they weren't really interested. Just another bloke drowning his sorrows, it was always happening. Could be hilarious if the bloke fell arse over tit off his stool, that was all . . .

The girl was calling time and giving him somewhat cautious looks now as if he might give trouble when ejected when the telephone rang again.

She answered, said, "Just a minute," and came back into the bar. "Is there a Mr Dixon here?" she called.

127

Shard said, "Yes."

"Well! There's a call for you. Don't take too long, will you, I'm – "

"Not as long as Marty," Shard said. She clicked her tongue crossly and brought the telephone through on a trailing lead.

* * *

Prompt at ten p.m. the dirty grey van left the builder's yard in Chiswick and headed north-west. They had quite a way to go, in and out, across main traffic arteries and along small streets until London's solidity of buildings began to thin out a little. Out here the air was fresher and you could begin to breathe. The builder, who knew his way around London, drove. By his side was Blakey, and Tack was in the back, very uncomfortably, bracing himself against the van's sides and having his bottom jolted. Apart from Tack, there was little in the van's body, just some clutter to be expected of a repair and plumbing outfit, but what there was of it shifted around and a washbasin hit Tack. He was greatly relieved when at last the driver said, "This is it, Blakey," and slowed.

"Doesn't seem to be any fuzz," Blakey said.

"I told you. Stand out like a sore thumb."

"Still . . . " Blakey picked at his nose, obviously uneasy. "Could be round the back, I s'pose." He knew Shard would be under surveillance. Then he saw the bus shelter, opposite the end of the road as the van cruised past. From it there was a clear view down the road, which wasn't a long one, and in it a figure was huddled, tramp-like, as though sleeping it off. "That's it," Blakey said. "Or I reckon so."

"So what d'you want now?"

"Keep going ahead, turn, and come back past the bus shelter." Blakey looked round. "All right?" he said to Tack, and Tack nodded. Blakey said, "Right, let's go."

The van pulled ahead, reversed into a side road, and came cruising back towards the bus shelter, where it stopped. Blakey put his head out of the window. "Hey, mate."

The figure came to life. It was a girl, a young one. She had

128

spiky hair, multi-coloured, and was dressed in what Blakey would have called an Indian outfit, a sort of sari, but she was white. She could have been anything, a prostitute, a down-and-out, a junkie; but there was something that to Blakey said very positively, and he should know, that this was what he had expected, at any rate apart from the sex – a dick doing obbo on Mr Shard's house. A female dick; it wasn't nice but it couldn't be helped and it was all the fault of the rights for women brigade who had pressured the fuzz into giving women DCs men's jobs.

"What is it?" the girl asked.

"Got ourselves lost, haven't we?" Blakey produced a street map and thrust it through the window. As he did so, Tack began easing the rear doors open; they'd been left unsecured on the outside. "We're looking for Bastow Gardens. Don't happen to know it, do you?"

"I'm a stranger around here," the girl said. She hadn't moved from the shelter. Blakey cursed to himself. When you asked the way in a street, the bloke – or woman – you asked usually came up close, within handy range. Blakey thought fast, leaned back in his seat and spoke in a hiss to Tack.

"Get out when I get out and move fast."

Blakey leaned forward again and spoke through the window as he began to shove the door open. "Look. You may still be able to help. The map – "

He flourished the map. By this time he was out and on his feet and Tack was moving in as ordered. The girl hadn't a chance. Blakey reached her first and grabbed for her arms as she came upright fast. He held her tightly and she hadn't time to yell out before Tack had gone into action. He had a garotte in his hand and this he slipped over the girl's head, down over the hair spikes until it was around her neck and then he pulled the thin cord taut, like a snare. It was done in a flash and there was no more than a gurgle. Blakey and Tack carried the girl fast into the back of the van and Tack got in with her while Blakey got back in front. The van started up, did a sharp right turn into Shard's road. Tack kept up the strain on the garotte and the girl's face bloated. As the van stopped outside Shard's house Tack felt in the clothing. They'd been spot on and he said so to Blakey. The girl had a two-way radio, very small, very neat. She'd never had a chance to use it.

"Fine," Blakey said. "All ready?"

They all got out, leaving the body. They went together up Shard's path, solid and official-looking. Blakey rang the bell. After a minute, Beth answered, keeping the door on the chain. She asked, "Who is it?"

Blakey said, "CID, Mrs Shard." He pushed a card round, an authentic one. "Mind if we come in, please?"

Feeling shock, wondering what was in the wind now, Beth pushed the door a little way to and released the chain. The three men crowded in. "Mr Shard, please. He's wanted."

"He's not in," Beth said. She was in a dressing-gown, having gone to bed, feeling she just couldn't wait up for what might be an indefinite period. Then she saw the gun in Blakey's hand and she felt like collapsing.

Blakey said, "Not a peep out of you or you're for it." He glanced at Tack. "You two, check everywhere."

Tack went up the stairs, fast. The builder did the downstairs and then the back garden and integral garage. They reported no sign of Shard. Blakey swore viciously. Tack asked, "What do we do, eh?"

Blakey's face was hard, angry. He said, "We take what's available now, don't we? We take the woman."

12

Charlie Dingo hadn't, of course, spoken himself. The man who called said the name didn't matter but Mr John Dixon could make a fair guess what this was about and might learn something to his advantage if at ten-thirty next morning he was hanging about outside the entrance to Green Park tube station reading a copy of the *Daily Mail*. Shard would be recognised easily by his contact; there had been photographs in the press recently.

That was all. No opportunity for Shard to ask questions. He left the Golden Horn, was aware of being picked up again by a tail, a different man this time but obvious enough to anyone who'd ever been in CID. The tail was quite unnecessary; Shard was going home, where he would be handed over to the officer on obbo near his house. It was all a ridiculous performance, Shard thought. They knew he knew he was under surveillance but they had to go through the charade of dressing up in all sorts of different disguises. Getting out at his home station he walked through to Bastow Gardens, the tail some distance behind and not bothering much since Shard's

131

destination was now perfectly obvious. As he approached his road an Escort van turned out of it, going in the opposite direction and going fast once it had turned into the main road. From the corner of his eye as he turned into Bastow Gardens Shard was aware of the tail crossing the road towards the bus shelter.

He went up his path, brought out his key and went in. The house was silent; Beth would have gone to bed. He flicked on the hall light. He felt the increased beat of his heart as he found signs of a disturbance: doors standing open, a shattered bowl of flowers and water spilled on the hall floor, the stand on which the bowl had rested lying on its side, a tear in the hall wallpaper.

He shouted for Beth and there was no answer. Fear for her ripped through him. He searched the house, ran outside, went into the garage. The car was there still. What had happened to the officer on obbo – half asleep, not doing his job?

Shard went out into the road, looked around, saw the tail from the Golden Horn coming along towards the house. Shard went for him at the double. He said, "All right, there's no time for the play-acting now." He took a deep breath. "My wife's gone and there's signs of a struggle."

"Gone, sir? That's funny, because – "

"It's not funny to me."

"No, sir – sorry." The DC seemed puzzled rather than anything else. "The woman DC – she's missing too, sir."

Breath hissed out through Shard's teeth and he said crisply, "Come back to my house and we'll contact the Yard at once, by phone."

*   *   *

A commander crime took the call at Scotland Yard, took it from Shard personally. He said, "But you're under suspension, Shard, I – "

"I'm reporting a crime, sir. A kidnap – "

"Put the DC on."

Some people . . . Shard ground his teeth but handed the phone to the tail, who made a full report. Before he'd rung off

132

Shard said, "Tell the Commander, Mr Hedge is to be informed right away."

The DC did so. Shard said, "I don't know, of course, what your orders are in connexion with myself, but I'm going to the Foreign Office immediately. In my car. You can come if you want – if those are your orders, not to lose sight of me – but I'm going to suggest you remain here. Still on obbo. All right?"

"Yes, sir."

"I doubt if anyone'll approach, but you'll know what to do in that event."

Shard reversed his car out of the garage, locked the doors behind him, and drove fast through quiet streets to the Foreign Office. He didn't know whether or not to expect Hedge, but he could call him on the closed line from the security section. When he got there Harry Kenwood was on duty and told him that Hedge had been rung, had sounded sleepy, and had said it could wait till morning. Strictly, it was a Yard job. He would await a report from the Assistant Commissioner Crime before committing the Foreign Office.

"Balls to that," Shard said. "Get Hedge again, please, Harry."

Hedge was furious at the second interruption in his sleep. "Really, Shard, I don't know what things are coming to. You're under suspension – "

"You're the second person to say that tonight, Hedge. It's my wife that's involved, don't you realise that?"

"Yes, yes." Hedge was impatient. "I'm sorry, very sorry – "

"Then just listen. I'd say it's obvious who's got her, Hedge – wouldn't you? Detachment X – "

"But *why*?"

Shard said, "I don't know. Hostage, perhaps. I aim to find out."

"You're under – "

"Not again, Hedge. I'm asking to be put back on duty."

"Don't be ridiculous. It's simply not possible, you *must* know that. The routines . . . and it's even more impossible now you're personally involved through your wife – "

"I want you to speak to the Permanent Under-Secretary, Hedge, and to the ACC – "

133

"It's not the ACC's affair, it's mine. I'm sorry, Shard, but I'm saying no." There was a suspicious pause. "Just where are you ringing from?"

Shard told him. Hedge said in an accusing voice, "I thought so – closed line, it had to be . . . you've no business to be there, Shard . . . I'm astonished. I advise you to leave immediately – oh." Hedge hissed angrily into the telephone: Shard had had the impertinence to hang up on him. Police! They were quite impossible. All sleep had gone from Hedge by this time; he bounced crossly out of bed, bare white toes feeling for his slippers. He left his bedroom and went into his study, where he kept whisky handy in a cupboard. He poured himself a strong one. He blew out a long breath. It never rained but it poured. After Kenwood had rung the first time, he'd had the whole story from the Yard . . . a woman DC disappeared while keeping surveillance on Shard, attached Foreign Office. There had been something in the Yard's tone that suggested Hedge was in some way to blame via Shard, but he would soon get Hesseltine to sort *that* out, he wasn't going to be high-and-mightied by a mere commander CID. He tried to concentrate: the woman DC had obviously been taken before whoever it was had gone to Shard's house, just to stop her reporting. A natural thing to do, of course. But why the interest in Shard's wife? That was a puzzle to be sure. A way of getting Shard back in their hands? But there wouldn't be much point in that, surely? Of course, Shard was the sort of man who would try to pick up the trail even though he was under suspension from duty, but Hedge still couldn't see why 'they' should want him back.

Hostage? Shard had used the word himself. But again, why?

It was all too much; Hedge poured himself another whisky and sat in a comfortable chair staring, without seeing, at a painting of the Forth Road Bridge. After a while the painting came into focus. Down by the northern end Rosyth dockyard nestled, not very clearly, but it was there. Symbolic? Hedge drank up his whisky. That was putting it too strongly; but Hedge believed that this thing, having begun in Scotland, at Faslane, was going to end there.

Would they blow up the Forth Road Bridge?

It could certainly be done by determined men and the results

134

could be catastrophic. And it would link with defence, since the wreckage would block Rosyth. The ships currently in there wouldn't leave for months, and nothing would enter. Rosyth would be written off. But was Rosyth all that important? It wasn't Portsmouth or Devonport and it wasn't the Gareloch. Could they block the Gareloch, and at the same time seal the Americans into the Holy Loch? Hardly both at once . . . but even that wasn't impossible, Hedge supposed, two simultaneous explosions.

Hedge got little sleep the rest of that night, his mind was too active. He'd been much upset by Shard's banging down the telephone on him. As for Shard, he got virtually no sleep: he prowled his house, a prey to a terrible frustration. The tail stayed with him, was relieved at two a.m. by another man, and Shard was glad of the company even though the DC was acutely embarrassed by his duty, a young man overawed by a detective chief superintendent at the best of times. He tried to make the point that he was only there as a sort of protection, a crime having been committed, and Shard let him think he believed the point was valid.

In the end he fell asleep in an armchair in the sitting room, and woke stiff, chilled and headachey. Around eight a.m. a woman DC turned up on relief. She looked like the backside of a bus but she was motherly and insisted on going into the kitchen to prepare breakfast. Shard, not hungry, knew he must eat and did so. Cornflakes, fried bacon and eggs, toast and marmalade, plenty of coffee. He felt better afterwards though his mouth was like the bottom of a parrot's cage after too many cigarettes throughout the night.

At nine-fifteen he left for Green Park. He wasn't, as he remarked wryly to the woman DC, under house arrest. Walking along Bastow Gardens for the station in the main road, he was well aware of another tail, who looked something like a gas meter reader without an official cap and no meters to read. Shard had to get rid of him before he made his contact at Green Park and it wasn't going to be easy.

In the station he took the first southbound train to enter. He might be able to shake the tail at the interchange.

*   *   *

135

For Beth, the night had been traumatic. In the back of the van, gagged very firmly so that breathing was difficult and with Tack's gun handy, she had been jammed against the body with its blotched, bloated face. Whenever the van came under a street light, she could see it plain. The very stillness . . . she had never been close to death until now, in fact had never even seen it. Not even her father; she hadn't been able to face it, to see the familiar features that would never move again, the lips that would never utter. The van seemed to drive for hours, time passing slowly. None of the men spoke: it was as though they too were dead, even the driver, who sat erect, staring ahead, full of concentration. This would be no time to risk an accident, any brush at all with the law. After they had been driving for around half an hour there was an exclamation from the man sitting in front beside the driver and the first words were uttered. The man twisted round and spoke briefly to Tack.

"Blindfold."

"Christ, yes!" That should have been thought of earlier. Tack put his gun down and brought out a handkerchief which he placed over Beth's eyes and knotted it round the back of her head. That made matters worse: Beth swayed and bumped into things, hard things, soft things, Tack's gun being one of the hard objects, a nasty reminder. Beth worried herself sick about Simon: had he, too, been got at? It had been late and no sign of him. Except when he was on a job, he wasn't a late bird, not unless they were both out together, dinner in the West End, or a show, that sort of thing. But then she remembered what one of the men had said back in the house: they'd wanted Shard – that was why they'd come, of course – and she was second best. All that added up to the fact that they hadn't got their hands on Simon. But what would he do now, when he found her gone? He wasn't the sort to sit back tamely, under suspension when she was in danger, and he would stick his neck out, risking the chop.

At last the van slowed, took a sharp turn, jolted her as a wheel over-ran something like a kerb, then stopped. The back doors were opened up. Tack's hands fumbled, removing the handkerchief. Beth was pulled out, drawn along the body of the woman DC, and set on her feet. She was in a garage, the doors of which had been closed behind the van. There was a door leading into the adjoining house, and she was pushed through this. It was still dark, and lights were on in the kitchen.

*   *   *

Shard changed at Acton Town and again at Earl's Court, trying to shake off his tail but without success. He left the Piccadilly Line at Earl's Court, changing back again onto the District Line. He got off at Victoria and hurried into the main line station, which was pretty packed although the first pandemonium of the rush hour was over. He went into the ticket hall, came out again and went down the steps to the gents. Leaving the gents he went in through the back entrance of the Grosvenor Hotel and out through the front. So far, so good - he couldn't see the tail, but he found a taxi coming empty down Victoria Street for the station and he flagged it. He got in, told the driver to take him to Green Park subway, and then he saw the tail again. He knew the tail had seen him, too. And as luck would have it there was another taxi, which the tail nabbed. Shard could imagine the order: follow that cab, real Sherlock Holmes stuff. He had half a mind to re-direct his taxi and hope to throw off the pursuit but this tail was obviously a good one and time was passing. If he didn't keep his rendezvous, Charlie Dingo's man wouldn't wait, might smell a non-existent rat.

He had to take a chance now. The tail, of course, wouldn't interfere with the contact, but would do his duty and report. Shard would have to take that as it came; sitting in the back of the taxi, he swore savagely. Hedge and the Yard . . . in their eyes he could be showing all the signs of guilt. Even Shard himself didn't really believe they would lift his suspension. That had just been his first desperate reaction to Beth's disappearance and was unrealistic.

He was set down near Green Park subway and as he paid the driver he saw the tailing taxi drift past and stop farther along.

Well - so be it.

137

He had bought his *Daily Mail* at Earl's Court. He moved slowly, casually, towards the entrance to the subway, then rested rump and shoulders against the wall, lit a cigarette and shook out the pages of the newspaper. The time was ten-twenty-five. He kept a sharp watch as he made a pretence of reading. The tail was loafing eastwards, looking into the big windows of a car showroom, still looking like a bereft meter-reader. For a moment he vanished into the doorway and Shard wondered if he was reporting in, using his pocket transceiver. He reappeared and began drifting around the windows again, an unlikely-looking sort to buy a Rolls Royce, but these days you never could tell. Shard disregarded him, watched exclusively for his contact to show. Piccadilly was crowded; the tourist season in full swing seemed to have brought the world to London, all shapes and sizes, all colours, every possible accent and language from Texas to Singapore, Amsterdam to Africa. The clothing was incredible but you couldn't call it drab: this wasn't the anorak season. And it was a very hot day; Shard sweltered. Used-up air blasted from the subway like some monstrous blower at full pitch. A police car, lights flashing blue and syren in action, tried to thrust its way along Piccadilly towards the Circus. Not looking for him – not yet. Perhaps some junkies, or transvestites in the public lavatories beneath Piccadilly Circus.

Shard glanced at his watch: ten-thirty-five. He would wait till eleven, not longer. Charlie Dingo could have had second thoughts. The tail would be getting more and more interested, no doubt.

People brushed past him, some of them roughly and looking irritated: he was being a nuisance, standing there in the way. It was just after ten-forty-five when a man spoke to him.

"Got a light, mate?"

"Sure." Shard brought out his lighter and flicked it. The man drew on his cigarette, face close to Shard's. He was a thickset man and middle-aged, around forty-five, dressed in a worn blue lightweight jacket and green trousers, a sartorial mess; black hair turning grey, solid, respectable, alert, could have been an army NCO once. Not, Shard would have thought, Charlie Dingo's sort, and perhaps he wasn't. But he

138

was. Drawing on his cigarette he remarked casually on the *Daily Mail*.

"Usual stuff, eh?"

"Yes. Strikes in the shipyards. Unemployment up again. Threat of an autumn budget. Four murders, same number of sexual assaults. Baby carved up in Brixton."

"We live in a lovely world. Brink of war too, I s'pose."

"Naturally."

"We'll take a walk, Mr Dixon. All right?"

Shard said, "I have a tail – "

"Oh, Godalmighty!"

"I couldn't shake him. So long as we stay here, he won't come close, but if we move – "

"Yes, I understand." The man scratched his cheek, looking baffled and angry. He'd have expected better of a top copper, his expression said, "Where's this tail?"

Shard told him; he swivelled aimlessly, but took a good look without appearing to do so, then nodded. "All right, we'll talk here. Won't take long . . . when we part, that tail won't know which to follow."

"He'll radio in for assistance – "

"Won't take that long, Mr Dixon. Now. You wanted to know about Tack, Blakey and O'Carse. You're well vouched for by . . . let's say, a mutual friend. You know who I mean. We know about Detachment X. There's a house in Grays, Essex." Quickly he passed the address. "Man named Mussuq owns it, brother of a bloke killed up at Faslane on the Gareloch. You suss out that house, Mr Dixon."

"Do you know anything else? Do you know what these men's objective is?"

The man shook his head. "That, we don't know, but – " Very suddenly he broke off. A silenced gun had been used; Shard had seen nothing, heard nothing in the traffic's sound and the crowd noises, but the man had crumpled and now fell flat on his face and Shard saw the bullet holes in the back. Any single person in the close crowd could have been responsible. There were screams from those near at hand, a surge of people away. As he saw the tail pushing through the crowd, Shard beat it down into the subway.

139

In the last analysis he obviously couldn't avoid being picked up: but not yet, not if he didn't go home. He believed Beth would be in that Grays House. He wasn't going to have Beth caught up in the cross-fire if the security forces moved in. And apart from Beth he had that other personal business to settle once and for all.

13

Hedge was feeling a looseness in his stomach: sent for by the Permanent Under-Secretary, he was informed of unpleasant duty.

"I think it'd be desirable to have a senior presence in Scotland just now, Hedge. It's my view that things seem likely to lead that way."

"Ah." Hedge, with a flutter in his heart, did his best. "Of course, the Head of Security . . . being still on the sick list, Under-Secretary, would it be wise for me to be in – "

"That's all right. I've been in touch. He'll be in his office, you needn't worry. That gives you clearance."

"He's – er – not fit to go to Scotland?"

Pippin frowned. "No. And couldn't be spared anyway, as you should know." Hedge spared a bitter thought for the Head of Security: damn the man, up and down like a yo-yo, in one minute, back in bed the next, what a carry-on. Hedge hoped he wouldn't meet Hocking in Scotland, which was bad enough on its own, always rumbling in its belly about Sassenachs . . . Hedge felt himself to be a kind of human lode star beaconing the combined effort in the right direction to bowl out a national catastrophe. Wherever he went, he would find Detachment X following, a personal vendetta.

Dispiritedly he returned to his office and set Miss Fleece busy on arranging a flight to Glasgow – the strike had been settled now – and soon after he had done so another blow fell. Hesseltine was on the telephone from the Yard. There had been a shooting in Piccadilly, Shard had been close to the scene, and Shard had disappeared. He had not gone home so far. That was all that was known. Hedge at once informed the Permanent Under-Secretary, who did not countermand the trip to Scotland. But by this time Hedge was feeling quite relieved at being on his way out of the London crisis.

*   *   *

Shard left the underground system at Leicester Square and walked through to Soho minus tail. He went again to the strip joint. Mandy was on duty again at the reception desk, and rang through to Guts Flambardier, who said send him up.

"So what is it this time, Mr Shard?"

Shard said, "Shelter, Guts. Just shelter till after dark, that's all." He paused, then said, "Charlie's man bought it," and explained what had happened outside Green Park station. Guts was rattled, thinking like Charlie Dingo of possible moles in his own organisation.

He said, "You got an address, you said, Mr Shard."

"Right."

"Reported it?"

Shard shook his head. "Not yet."

"Risky for you."

"I have personal reasons, Guts. Pressing ones. I know the risks but even coppers are human. I've got something to do . . . I may find I need police assistance, probably will. In which case I'll report. If I can't do what I want, then I'll report anyway. Does that sound confusing?"

Flambardier grinned. "Yes, Mr Shard. You said, personal reasons. The bribery – of course."

"That, yes. More important, I think Beth could be at that address."

142

Flambardier lifted his eyebrows and looked concerned. "They got your wife, Mr Shard?"

"Yes. I'm going in. On my own in the first instance - "

"When?"

"Tonight."

"And you want to hide up here till then, is that it, Mr Shard?"

Shard nodded. "They won't think of coming here, Guts."

"No, no. If you're sure you weren't tailed here, Mr Shard?"

"I'm sure. So - can I stay?"

Flambardier said at once, "Of course. There's a room available and you can have it as long as you like - me, I shall be busy, so - "

"You won't want me to hang about in here. I understand. Thanks a lot, Guts. I'm very grateful."

The fat man waved a dismissive hand; it was, he said, his pleasure. He flicked a switch in his intercom, spoke briefly, and almost at once a girl came in, dark and slinky, to take Shard over and show him where he could spend what would be a very long day. He found that the window of the room gave him a view down into the street and though he couldn't see the entrance to Flambardier's joint, not without opening the window and craning, which might be a risk, he could keep a fair watch on the approaches. He watched for some while but saw nothing of any interest, and this he reckoned was the final proof that he hadn't been tailed.

* * *

Hedge reached Glasgow airport in a semi-dismal state of mind. Scotland again but this time in better comfort, by which he meant an MOD car, a chauffeur-driven, plain dark green Rover three-and-a-half litre that met his flight and smoothed his highland path. The urgency had precluded, praise God, a self-drive up the motorway system and never mind government economies this time. Accommodation had been arranged at the Clyde Submarine Base; but first Hedge told the driver to take him to Rosyth, where there had been loss of life and they

143

would expect a VIP. Of course, they'd already had one from Defence Ministry but they'd appreciate another. So it was the M8 for the Forth Road Bridge with the driver wondering why the dickens the old bugger hadn't made up his mind from the start and flown for Edinburgh rather than Glasgow . . .

At the Rosyth naval base Hedge was taken to the scene. All had been cleared up now but the warehouse was in a bad way and the frigate's starboard side plating showed dents and gashes. Hedge was asked to go aboard and gingerly he climbed to the deck, to be met by the ship's captain. He expressed his commiseration and as a courtesy was taken round the frigate. It was quite an experience and he found it claustrophobic below decks, so many narrow passages and not much head-room, mostly taken up with huge pipes and projecting hand-wheels and any number of electric cables and nasty things underfoot to trap the unwary. Hedge gave his skull a very unwelcome crack against something hard when he negotiated a high coaming in the deck plating of an alleyway – part, he was told, of the vessel's watertight system.

He rubbed at his head, felt a lump. It had been a nasty jolt and he had staggered groggily until given a steadying arm. "I call it dangerous," he said huffily. No-one answered this; Hedge thought them rather off-hand but wondered why anybody went to sea and a few minutes later dropped thankfully into a vinyl-covered settee in the wardroom where he was offered gin. He appreciated the gin, though he would rather have had whisky, but was even more thankful when he was safe ashore again and in his car. He had been terrified throughout in case these demoniac people should strike again while he was aboard and the relief that they had not done so was enormous. He found he was shaking like a leaf as he sat back for the long drive to the Gareloch. They were brave fellows in the Navy; he would make a point of mentioning that when he got back to the Foreign Office. The gin had been quite a strong one and Hedge found a mellowness descending. England still had stout hearts . . .

When at last he reached Faslane, once again having run the gauntlet of the peace women who seemed to have grown dirtier in the interval since his last visit, he was met – he was glad to note – by Commodore Rushcroft in person. And Hocking, unfortunately. And a message. He was to ring the Permanent Under-Secretary at once.

Rushcroft said, "My regards to Pippin, Mr Hedge."

"Yes, of course." Hedge was taken to a security line and put through to London. There was some delay before the Permanent Under-Secretary came on the line. "Hedge speaking, Under-Secretary. From Faslane," Hedge announced.

"Ah. There's been a development. It could be the break-through."

"Good heavens!"

"What was that?" It was a very poor line; Hedge hoped it was not being tapped – in theory at any rate security lines couldn't be tapped, but theory was one thing and Hedge was never inclined to trust gadgetry too far. He said hoarsely, "I merely said good heavens, Under-Secretary – "

"Oh. Well now, listen carefully." The voice exploded again in fizzes and crackles but Pippin didn't seem much bothered about taps, more fool he Hedge thought. "Dublin's been on the line, the Garda. Those men."

"Phelan and – "

"Yes. They've broken, or rather one of them has, the man Garrity. He's admitted being concerned in the supply of a large quantity of arms and explosives to one of Shard's villains, the man O'Carse – "

"Good heavens!" Hedge said again, involuntarily.

"What?"

"Oh, nothing important, Under-Secretary. Was there more?"

"Yes. The supply was made from one fishing-boat to another . . . transferred in the Irish Sea and landed at a lonely part of the coast – or rather a lonely island just off the Welsh coast, in the Bristol Channel. Sully Island. It's connected to the mainland by a narrow strip of land that's under water at full tide apparently. No-one lives on the island, and a boat approaching from seaward wouldn't be remarked upon . . . and the off-loaded cargo was driven to the mainland at low water, in a Land Rover."

"Really," Hedge said, a trifle blank. "Why Wales, Under-Secretary?"

"Why *not* Wales?" The Under-Secretary sounded irritable. "What we don't know, and what Garrity doesn't know either, is where it went from there."

"Scotland," Hedge said, quaking a little. Through a window he could see the bows of a nuclear submarine.

"That still seems the most likely in the light of recent events, though of course we still can't be sure. However – I'm grateful to you, Hedge, for placing yourself in what may well be the most likely place of danger. That's appreciated."

Just as though he'd volunteered . . . Hedge said, "Thank you, Under-Secretary. I shall not be found wanting I assure you."

"What?"

Damn the line. Hedge shouted a repeat at the instrument and the loud repetition made him feel foolish. A moment later the line went dead. Hedge remembered he hadn't had any lunch, but no offer was made to provide him with it. It was well into the afternoon by this time and since it was expected of him that he would want to tour the base again, he was trudged around until his feet, in town shoes, began to feel dreadfully sore. It was quite beyond him to take in the technical detail and he found it very annoying that Hocking knew this and kept on uttering supplementary explanations in an over-loud and supercilious tone. But Hedge was pleased enough to see that Faslane's security had been tremendously increased even beyond his last visit, which just went to show that his warnings had been properly heeded. It was he, Hedge, who had stressed Scotland and the navy should be grateful; it was more than Hocking had done. This afternoon, every other man seemed to be a security guard and there was a good deal of activity at the southern end of the Gareloch, where it met the Clyde. Extra anti-frogmen precautions were being taken. And Hedge thought about the approach to the main gate: policemen everywhere, somewhat impeded by the peace women as usual, but if and when the crunch came to Faslane the police had more than sufficient numbers to deal with turbulent women.

It had been the same at Rosyth. No peace women, of course,

146

since Rosyth wasn't a nuclear base even though they serviced ships carrying, for all Hedge knew, nuclear weapons. No women but plenty of police, on the watch for nobody knew what. Scotland was ready. Hedge stared out across the waters of the Gareloch, now an astonishing and very beautiful shade of purple, just like the heather.

"So peaceful," he said. "One can quite imagine the Scotch liking it."

A look passed between Rushcroft and Hocking but Hedge was unaware of it. From the distance he heard the sound of the pipes, wild, haunting, nostalgic across the Gareloch. Hedge believed the tune was 'Scotland the Brave'. Well, they were going to need to be, perhaps.

All of a sudden he felt an odd weakness in his knees; and was overcome by an intense desire to be back in London. Curious sounds were coming from the berthed nuclear submarine: someone was banging, as if with a sledgehammer. Surely that was stupid? But Rushcroft didn't seem bothered and neither did the wretched Hocking.

Hedge fought down incipient panic nobly. The Foreign Office didn't panic.

*   *   *

The Head of Security, racked with shingles still and wincing at every sudden movement of his head and neck – even brushing his hair was agony – was in conference with Hesseltine and Hocking's boss in Defence Ministry, Sir James Ruff, and another man from the Home Office. The Home Office was worried about the dilution of police strength. So many officers had been moved hither and yon, said the Home Office, that ordinary crime was being given a fine chance if it cared to take advantage. It hadn't yet, but it would, it was bound to.

"National emergency," Sir James Ruff said, in prompt support of his ministry. "Must take precedence."

"Oh yes, I quite agree. But not for ever, you know. How long is this thing going to go on?"

"If any of us knew that," Sir James said heavily but didn't add anything further. The Home Office had taken the point.

147

What, in particular, appeared to be bothering its present representative, a Mr Futlock, was, of all things, traffic control. In the view of all the others traffic control, though obviously important, had to be relegated to a very secondary position for the time being. Not so, Futlock insisted: he was a pugnacious little man with thick glasses, balding and with a pot belly. And he stuck to his point. There was, he said, the question of the holiday traffic. Miles and miles of snarl-ups and tail-backs, even on the motorways, and there were going to be accidents. They all knew, for instance, what the M25 was like now, so many delays at the Dartford Tunnel bottleneck.

"That's precisely why I'm here," Mr Futlock said, glaring through his lenses. "There's those coaches, remember."

Sir James stared back. "Good heavens, Futlock, *what* coaches?"

"The European Parliament party – "

"Does it matter?"

" – the children, with some mothers and schoolteachers. Long delays wouldn't be welcome . . . we were not able to arrange coaches with lavatory facilities and you know what children are."

Sir James blew out a long breath. "What *is* all this about?"

Futlock said, "The arranged party. A kind of treat, a tour of Britain. All the Common Market countries, but confined to children of MEPs. And, as I said, some mothers. Do you mean to tell me you've not been *informed*?" He was aghast.

The Head of Security came in on that. "We've all had other things on our minds, Mr Futlock. It's the first I've heard of it. Sir James – Hesseltine?"

Result negative. But Hesseltine said, "It's not my concern, of course, traffic's B Division, but Mr Futlock does have a point, though I think he's exaggerating the problem. The constabularies involved can't be that short of mobiles. They'll be got through."

"But not without delays," Futlock said firmly.

"Well – no."

Futlock compressed his lips. Sir James asked, "What's the route? Do we know?"

"Of course we do," Futlock said. "They're coming in by

sea, four coaches from the Hook to Harwich, an early arrival. The day after tomorrow. They're not taking in London at that stage, that'll come on the return journey. They go first to Chartwell and then along the south coast to Portsmouth and Southampton . . . '' He outlined the remainder of the tour, then went back closer to its start. They would leave Harwich by the A604, taking the A12 at Colchester to join the M25 motorway at Junction 28. "The big delay, you see . . . the Dartford Tunnel. And being the holiday season the roads'll be packed all the way through to there as well. What we in the Home Office would like to see is a police escort and traffic held back where possible to let them through. All those children, you can just imagine – and no service areas unless they deviate. You understand?'' Futlock gave a cough. "If any of them haven't *been* – you know – before disembarking, and if they've drunk bottles of pop and so on, Coca Cola, and coffee in the case of the mothers . . . well, you can imagine, surely?''

There were nods, impatient ones. Futlock said earnestly, "It's not just the natural functions, it's really not. It's the fact that Britain's organising this and it's got to be a success. Our Common Market partners. It's very important, or I think it is anyway – *very important* – that we do our best and impress them, give them an insight into this country and its achievements and so on, make them want to see more, improve relations within the European Community . . . ''

Futlock was known to have always been a keen and convinced Marketeer, right from the start, one of Heath's pioneers. And, all things considered, it was a small enough point. As Hesseltine had remarked already, the police were not that stretched. There was agreement that Futlock should have his way. But when the conference broke up, Hesseltine stayed behind for a word with the Head of Security. He had something on his mind, was looking thoughtful and came out with it straight.

"Dartford Tunnel,'' he said. "What does that suggest?''

"As Futlock said – delays, tail-backs.''

"Yes. And – a confined space. Automatic tamping.''

There was an indrawn breath: the Head of Security had got there. "Of an explosion, d'you mean?''

149

Hesseltine nodded. "I'm only using my imagination, of course."

"Detachment X? They're not out for that sort of thing!"

"Probably not. Just a thought. On the other hand . . . the Common Market. NATO. There are links. Destruction on our soil of our partners in the EEC. It wouldn't help, would it? And there's another point that looks like a possible link. Something came through just before I left the Yard. I didn't mention it at the conference because . . . well, our Mr Futlock for one. He's a gasbag – never disloyal, of course, but can be indiscreet in a normally harmless way."

"Well?"

Hesseltine said, "You'll remember that Arab, dead at Faslane. We've never identified the body, but Garrity in Dublin apparently came out with some further bits of information, extra to the Garda's latest report about the landing of explosives. They put on pressure, real pressure because they knew he was holding back. Well, that Arab, who'd always got away with it until he tried Faslane, was a fringe member of the Baader-Meinhof gang and responsible for the assassinations of Jacques van der Bergh, Egon Knudsen, Roger Poujade and Gerhard Schmidt. Belgium, Denmark, France, Germany. All those men – "

"Keen marketeers and the assassinations never nailed on anyone . . . yes, I remember. But I don't see – "

"That Arab was in cahoots with Detachment X – right? We never did believe the bit about the holocaust. That was cover." Hesseltine added, "It's worth bearing in mind."

"Well, perhaps. It's a long shot, Hesseltine."

"Yes, it is. But in my opinion it's vital those coaches do have a police escort, at any rate from Harwich until they're through the Dartford Tunnel. Just in case."

"And we should check the tunnel itself?"

Hesseltine said, "Yes. Minutely – as soon as possible, and from then on it'll be watched. Discreetly. We'll try to nab our villains rather than scare them off. Scare them off, and they'll still be around to try something else."

"Yes." The Head of Security wagged a finger. "But don't put too many eggs into the Dartford basket, my dear chap. I

150

say again, it's a long shot and I'm certainly not convinced."

After Hesseltine had left for the Yard, the Head of Security reviewed the state of their knowledge, which was not a lot even now. He had a shrewd idea that the Permanent Under-Secretary didn't wholly believe Faslane was at further risk but thought poor Hedge was better out of the way. There was something in that, of course. Faslane had had its warning and was now one hundred per cent awake, no easy target. Hedge *was* something of an incubus . . . and there was another point as well: Detachment X would probably know by now that Hedge was back in the Gareloch and from this might well deduce that Whitehall was concentrating on points north.

Well – leave Hedge in Scotland, then. It might be worth the Head's own while – he thought – to go to Dublin, though he didn't relish the idea, not with shingles. It might in fact be better to leave Garrity to the Garda: Hedge had only been allowed to listen in and not actually interview. That chap Futlock – he'd started something in Hesseltine's mind and that had overflowed. Children, the innocents to be used as unsuspecting pawns, to be blown to little pieces as an explosion rocked and ripped and split the confined carriageways, in red-lit darkness and smoke and screaming panic?

What would be the point?

There was a fast answer to that one: there would be a demand, as yet unspecified, the children and the mothers would be hostages. Plus Shard's wife for good measure? And perhaps this was why they had wanted Shard originally. Even the bribery, those payments . . . a defected Shard joined up with the villains . . . the mind boggled. One thing would be certain: those coaches wouldn't be blown straight away. There would be a breathing space before the end came, the holocaust in the Dartford tunnel.

But it was all conjecture.

14

Shard left the strip joint a little after nine p.m. He left alone, although Flambardier had offered the services of a strong-arm mob, a small mob of two men. Shard had declined with thanks. Flambardier had given him the men's names, and Shard knew them by reputation. They'd both been on the Moor and in Parkhurst and Pentonville: GBH, years ago, and then murder. Shard was in bad odour as it was and he didn't want to make matters worse. This had to be his show. He believed Flambardier had simply made a gesture and was relieved it hadn't been taken up.

Shard made his way to Fenchurch Street main line station and took a stopping train to Tilbury, where the liners of P. & O. and the Orient Line used to berth. Since then the Orient Line had been swallowed whole by P. & O. and the whole caboosh had shifted to Southampton, leaving Tilbury derelict from a seaman's point of view, a useless leviathan of docks and warehouses and customs sheds and platforms where the boat trains used to come and go. The rail journey was a deadly one. City backs, slums, open spaces and patchy re-development, not worth looking at even in daylight. In Shard's carriage was a couple who appeared high, probably on glue. They intertwined and squirmed and felt. If they had a car it might well bear in the back window the legend, COMMUTERS DO IT IN RAILWAY CARRIAGES.

The train halted at Grays, last station before Tilbury. Shard got out; the glue-sniffing couple fell rather than got out, picked themselves up and staggered to a bench on the platform and carried on where they had left off.

Shard walked out of the station. He had never been in Grays before, nothing to take him there, but Guts Flambardier had provided a street map and he knew where to go.

It was a warm, clear night. There was a moon. That didn't help anyone's anonymity but it had to be put up with. It was quite a walk from the station and Shard took it fast, thinking, as he had thought all day, of Beth. He was convinced he would find her in the house he was aiming for, though Charlie Dingo's man hadn't said anything about that – he might have got around to it if he hadn't been killed first. Or he might not have known: there hadn't been much time, certainly, since Beth had been hooked away from home. It would have had to have been a very fast grapevine, even for Charlie Dingo.

There were quite a few people about but they thinned out as Shard approached the road where the house was. The safe house of Detachment X, but it wouldn't be for much longer. A police mobile cruised past, seemed to slow a little as it came up by Shard and he had a feeling he was being scrutinised, but the mobile didn't stop. He had happened to be in some shadow, between two street lights and the moon temporarily cut off by a high rise building. Lucky: the local coppers would be, like all coppers everywhere, on the lookout for Detective Chief Superintendent Simon Shard, suspended from duty and now vanished. How dirt could stick! Probably half the force believed he'd taken bribes. He felt more and more unclean: to be shrinking away from a mobile, it was the end. And he had to admit that the fact he'd vanished after a killing wasn't doing him any good at all. During the long day in the strip joint, Guts Flambardier had come along to tell him he was being a fool. Flambardier had been genuinely concerned.

"You should report, Mr Shard," he'd said. "Tell the Yard, leave it up to them."

He wouldn't. Maybe he was just obstinate, maybe his powers of judgment had gone for a burton, the result of the stigma of suspension, of the sheer nastiness of the faked-up charge against him, which still stood in fact because it had to. Police routines were rigid. Shard had begun to feel for the criminal, or anyway the innocents who got themselves landed with a charge they knew to be false. It had always got him in the guts, like a twisting knife, when a man eventually proved his innocence after some years in gaol. All the wasted, frustrated years, the grating injustice. It would, in his case, drive him to madness he felt sure. However, the principal, indeed really the only, reason he wouldn't report was what he'd already told Flambardier: his first thought now was for Beth. The men of Detachment X had to be fanatics; they wouldn't hesitate to kill a hostage if they saw the fuzz closing in, a hostage who might already have learned too much and whose evidence had to be silenced for the benefit of the rest of the iceberg of which O'Carse and Tack and the others were almost certainly just the tip.

Something like that . . .

Flambardier had seen the determination and had given up. Now, in Grays, on his own, Shard was facing the practical difficulties. He had to remain unseen, he had to penetrate the house quietly after he'd sussed out it and its surroundings. Not an easy thing to do. For one thing Grays wasn't quite asleep yet. He looked down the road, the one he had to penetrate: there was light showing from most of the houses, which were all detached and standing in their own grounds – not large, but one of the good roads in Grays. Not all that good; they'd seen better days, gone down in the world, perhaps a result of the withdrawal of the liner companies from Tilbury. There were bangers parked in the driveways of the nearer houses, and motor-bicycles. There was, Shard found as he drifted along the road, almost an air of a council estate. The house he sought was at the far end.

He turned and walked back again, going instead into the next road now that he'd had a preliminary recce of the target road itself. He moved on, normal walking pace: a lingerer could be an object of suspicion. From beside him there was a scuffle, a sound of anger and fright, and a spitting cat sped across the roadway pursued by a dog that now started a frenzied barking. The cat vanished into a garden, darting through a hedge, and the dog was brought up short by an iron gate, and yelped. From a house a little ahead of Shard a front door opened and the dog's owner came down the short drive.

"*Endersby*! Bad dog, Endersby. Come here."

Endersby, some name for a dog. Anyway, Endersby came back surlily, the cat having gone beyond his capabilities. Beneath a street light, Endersby's owner caught Shard's eye and grinned.

"Bane of my life, that dog."

"Dogs will be dogs, when there's a cat."

"That's right. Good night to you."

"Good night," Shard answered. Endersby had just missed fame: dog of the man who might have recognised Shard and reported to the police. That was the way things happened sometimes: dog chases cat and bowls out villain. But the man had been totally unaware.

Shard moved on. When he reached the end of the road he would need to shift round to the target road to identify the house. After that, ingress to the back garden. He'd noted a service alley of a kind, more of a beaten track really, between the roads. It shouldn't be too difficult; he wasn't necessarily looking for a fight. What he wanted was to suss the place, learn all he could, and then contact the local police and insist on going in with them to ensure Beth's safety.

*   *   *

That same afternoon, allowing no grass to grow, Hesseltine with Home Office backing had got things moving vis-à-vis the Dartford Tunnel and the route of the four coaches from Harwich. There would be a police escort which would break away a little south of the tunnel exit. The tunnel itself had had a preliminary check and so far all was well. From now on until the Common Market party had passed through there would be a police watch, mounted by plain clothes men at both ends of the tunnel. And the carriageways would be under continual monitoring by the military, also in plain clothes, the bomb squad from the Ordnance Corps keeping guard with their detector apparatus. Once all this was in train, Hesseltine relaxed on that score. If Detachment X had designs on those children, they wouldn't succeed in the Dartford Tunnel. Of course, there were other places – almost anywhere in fact – but none so tailored for nastiness as the enclosed stretch of the tunnel. A check on the route of the coaches showed nothing similar. No more tunnels. Going north ultimately, they were to head through Newcastle itself which meant they wouldn't go through the Tyne Tunnel. After that Scotland – no tunnels, but some bridges. That wasn't the same thing at all. But the bridges would be watched. It was possible – not easy, but possible – for armed men to seal both ends of a bridge and hold coaches in the middle. No chances would be taken. But they could be barking up the wrong tree. Hesseltine wondered if he was guilty of a bee in his bonnet about those children, over-doing it. Too much concentration on a mere idea that wasn't even a hunch.

The Head of Security had put a call through to Hedge in Faslane, keeping him in the picture. Hedge had pooh-poohed the notion. Typical of Hesseltine, he said.

"How d'you mean, Hedge?"

"Tangential thinking. He allows his mind to . . . to dart about – "

"Better than mental constipation, I'd say. But I'm not committed to his ideas. We're by no means neglecting the defence side. How are things on the Gareloch?"

"Quiet," Hedge said.

"Keep in touch." The Head of Security rang off, and Hedge shook his head in wonderment. Children! Really not at all likely, though if anything did happen to them it would bring the whole show very much within the scope of the Foreign Office, the name of which would be mud and very unfairly so, since it would be a purely police matter to protect coach parties. But the Foreign Office would incur the opprobrium

156

since the children were *foreign*. Although Hedge, having racked his brains in the few moments after taking the telephone call, could remember nothing about the visit being brought to his notice, he knew that it must have been submitted to the Foreign Office, and that the Foreign Office must have given the whole tour its blessing. Hedge brought out his handkerchief and dabbed at his forehead and cheeks, which were shiny with sweat. It was so hot. So hot that he could almost fancy the heat was drawing extra smell from the peace camp and its inhabitants. On the phone, his boss had spoken of demands possibly being made, the hostage element . . . had Hedge any ideas on that? Hedge had not; he thought about it as he emerged into the open, risking the stench, making for the room that had been allocated to him – he felt in need of a rest on his bed. What demands? Nothing very substantial occurred to Hedge. Oh, of course, in a general way, defence. Detachment X Against The Holocaust? Well, yes . . . they might demand the dismantling of the nuclear bases, all of them, but that was scarcely a practicable possibility. It would take months to dismantle everything even if there was surrender on the part of government, and no terrorist could keep four coaches sealed up that long. A promise? But promises could be broken, and would be the moment the coaches were driven out.

No. It wasn't on at all. As he'd said – typical Hesseltine and Yard thinking. The EEC party was safe enough and he, Hedge, was at the sharp end as usual. He was convinced that something dreadful was going to happen at Faslane. And he believed the Head thought so too. And Pippin. He was really quite flattered at the trust being reposed in him. His ego was assaulted only by the presence of Hocking.

Then all of a sudden he recalled something, and recalled it with a flutter of his heart: there *had* been a submission of some sort about a party from the EEC, though he couldn't recall anything about children, and he'd dictated a memo about it to Miss Fleece, scarcely giving it a thought at the time. It hadn't seemed at all important; it had been a long time before the advent of Detachment X in any case. Hedge screwed up his eyes and thought frantically back. He hadn't even passed it to the Head, he seemed to remember. If only he had Miss Fleece

157

with him. There had been something about a guarantee of safety, a sheer formality of course, but . . .

Oh, dear. It *couldn't* be the children, surely? But if it was, then that submission and that memo would come to light and it all bore his initials. He would be stuck with it, and it would hurt.

*　　　*　　　*

The recce round the front of the house had established for Shard which back gate from the service alley would connect. He moved back into the service alley. Three rear gates from the bottom he stopped and eased the gate open. No sound. And now no moon. Cloud had drifted up: heavy cloud. The weather could be breaking. Cautiously Shard moved through an over-grown garden. Shrubs, brambles, long grass, unkempt hedges round the perimeter and another cat. The cat hissed and moved astern, then took off at speed. Thank God there was no Endersby. Shard moved towards a light, glowing red behind a thin curtain. There had been no light in the front of the house. If he was going to pick anything up, then the lit window was the place for eavesdropping. The night was hot, sultry – thunderstorms around? The window might be open.

There was no guard. Shard hadn't expected one. They wouldn't see the need. There was a lot of anonymity; you didn't expect international terrorism to shack up in Grays, Essex. Grays was a very unlikely core of earth-shaking events. And you didn't destroy your anonymity by a parade of guard dogs and gun-toting toughs.

It was a longish garden – long and the width of the house and garage. Shard's approach was very quiet. No more than an occasional crackle from the undergrowth. He got right up to the window, stepping onto a neglected flower bed and flattening his body against a brick wall. The window was, as he had hoped, open a little way at the top but he was unable to hear any conversation. The light was on still and Shard found a small field of vision where the curtain had been pulled away a fraction from the side. He couldn't see anything and he fancied the room might be empty. Then a man moved into his sight. A bearded man whom he recognised as the Irishman O'Carse. And O'Carse – there was no doubt it was him – was wearing police uniform, that of a chief inspector. He was visible for some thirty seconds and then he moved away. The house remained quiet. *Was* Beth there? Currently Shard could see no way of finding out short of an entry. Anger mounted in him; for a moment of madness he thought of crashing through the window, throwing O'Carse into confusion, and then blundering about in a frantic search for Beth. And it *would* be blundering about, and not for long either. He couldn't assume O'Carse was on his own.

There was only one thing: wait a little longer and hope to overhear some talk, then beat it fast for the police and rely on them listening to a suspended officer, and heeding that officer's demand that he should lead the squad that went in, because his wife was, or might be, in there with the villains.

The light remained on: Shard waited. After what seemed like half the night there was movement again in the room. Two men now, two men talking. There was a reference to a woman, no name mentioned. Beth? That apart, the conversation, so far as Shard could pick it up, was uninteresting, irrelevant, no more than chit-chat. It could be he was wasting time, but he was kept there by the possibility of Beth, so near and yet so far, a cliché that really meant something now.

There was a drop of rain and quite suddenly the temperature had dropped too. A light wind came up, eddying round the house. Within little more than half a minute the rain was coming down fast, lashing at Shard against the wall. From the middle distance a rumble of thunder followed some brief summer lightning. Then the light in the room went out, the curtains were pulled back, and the window was thrown up from the bottom. Shard moved a little farther away.

A man leaned out. Shard couldn't see him very well, close as he was, but the build was that of the man from Glasgow Central, the man in the grey suit.

The man said, "It's a soaker, Tim. A real soaker."

Shard scarcely breathed. He hadn't been seen, but the man was still looking out of the window, leaning out, not minding the rain evidently. It had been a long, hot summer and rain was pleasant. That was when the next lightning came, accompanied by its heavy roll of thunder, now very close. The lightning, summer lightning again, lit the garden like day and held it for some seconds. Shard was clearly outlined against the wall, like a pinned butterfly.

15

Blakey had seen him, and reacted fast, calling out to the Irishman in the police uniform. Both men were through the window in a flash. In the instant he knew he'd been seen, Shard had made for the party wall dividing the gardens to his right. A hedge, as unkempt as the rest of the garden, grew against the wall. That didn't help. Shard was heaving himself over the wall when a hard grip went around his legs and he was yanked backwards, dragged through the hedge as his handhold was pulled from the wall. He fell on his face, hitting gravel. Before he could utter he was dragged up again and O'Carse sent a fist crashing against his jaw. Another blow; then he sagged dizzily until he was put right out by the barrel of a heavy revolver coming down on his temple.

He came to with a dry mouth, a bloodied face, a pounding head and feeling sick. He was on the floor in a barely furnished room; and men were looking down at him. O'Carse, Blakey, a Middle Eastern person unknown to him, and an equally unknown fourth man – Tack.

"Welcome back," O'Carse said, grinning. But the grin wasn't meant to show humour and it quickly vanished. O'Carse squatted on his haunches and stared into Shard's face. In his hand was a cosh, pliant and heavy. He said, "You're going to answer some questions. If you don't, you get this. First question: how did you get on to this address?"

Shard gave no answer. O'Carse repeated the question and then struck with the cosh. Lightly: it didn't have to be hard and it hurt wickedly, taking Shard's temple where the gun-barrel had hit and left a discolouring lump. The room seemed to lift and move around him.

"Now," O'Carse said. "Spill it, right? Or else."

"It'll have to be else," Shard said. Again the cosh came down. The sick feeling mounted. Shard said, "Contacts."

"Sure. Which?"

"Anonymous. A grass. Phone call. That's all I know."

"A suspended copper?"

"That's not necessarily known widely."

"All right, so you had a tip-off. What else were you told?"

"Nothing else. What about my wife?"

O'Carse made a coarse remark, looking savage, but wasn't giving anything away about Beth. He asked, "How far did this tip-off go? Who else got it?"

Shard said, "I don't know. It could have been only me. On the other hand it might not."

"But you didn't pass it on yourself."

"No," Shard said, it being the only thing he could say. If he'd passed it on, he wouldn't have come in on his own. O'Carse obviously knew that. But O'Carse could be left in the air all the same, not knowing if the word about his safe house had spread or would be spreading. And it was clear enough to Shard that O'Carse was worried: a decision had to be made, get out quick or stay. Not an easy decision for anyone to make; villains never liked being forced out of HQ before they were ready. It tended to throw off the details of the organisation, upset the fine balance of the plans. Whatever they might be: for what it was now worth, Shard might be able to find out.

He sensed irresolution in the air as O'Carse tried to reach his decision. For now, there was no further use of the cosh, though O'Carse was swiping it against his free hand as though it might be brought into play again at any moment. Shard made an attempt at probing on his own account.

162

He asked, "What did you want me for in the first place?" He added, "Back on the Inter-City from Glasgow. Why?"

"You'll find out soon enough."

Shard persisted. "When you lost me, you went for my wife instead . . . to use her as bait to get me back, perhaps. From which I assume you have a use for me. I find that reassuring."

"Why?"

"Because it seems to tell me you want me alive."

O'Carse said, "I wouldn't bank on it, Mr Shard." He paced the room, pulling at his beard. He was distinctly uneasy but there were no more questions. He would see no point: the fact of Shard having come to the house was enough to be going on with. Meanwhile Shard thought about that police uniform, which was now off. A trying-on session was what it had been, probably. So somewhere along the line there was to be impersonation, possibly some police officers marked down for killing, with O'Carse and his mob taking their places. Where? That was the big question. In many ways Detachment X had it made already. Or would have had if he hadn't turned up in Grays to throw a spanner in the works.

And that spanner seemed to have lodged in a vital spot.

O'Carse reached his decision. "We're getting out," he said to the Middle East person. "I'll call Tilbury and the depot."

Depot? That sounded interesting to Shard, who after being handcuffed by Tack was left on the floor of the room while O'Carse did his telephoning. The thunder was rolling still and there was more lightning but the storm was moving away now. Shard caught scraps of conversation: something about marked cars and more uniformed men, and something about explosives too, but nothing that was remotely useful if he should manage to get away, nothing to put the finger on anything, any locality, any target. Explosives were nothing new: that was what he had been facing all along, something to be blown up.

O'Carse finished his telephoning and came back into the room. He nodded at Tack and said, "That's it. No real problem. But we won't waste time. You and Mussuq, get the stuff loaded fast as you can."

Mussuq: that was the name Charlie Dingo's man had

163

mentioned just before he'd been shot down at Green Park. And Charlie's man had said Mussuq was a brother of the Arab shot at Faslane. Well, that was interesting, like the mention of the depot, but currently it wasn't a lot of use. Lying on the floor, Shard heard a good deal of work going on, shifting sounds and heavy breathing as feet moved in and out of the house, probably between it and the integral garage. By guesswork, it took them around half an hour. Then O'Carse, who'd gone out to give a hand, came back into the room and told Shard to get on his feet. Shard did so, staggering until O'Carse got a grip on him and steadied him. He was taken through into the garage, where an Escort van stood with its rear doors open. Inside were arms and boxes of ammunition and hessian-wrapped packages of strange shape and what looked like radio loops, or aerials. There was no room on the floor of the van: Shard was to ride on top of the cargo. He was gagged and blindfolded and then, still with the cuffs on his wrists and Tack holding a gun on him, he was lifted bodily and thrown like a sack of potatoes to lie on the load. Another of the men got in with him. He heard the other three get in, something of a squash in the front, and then the van was backed out. It stopped.

"Garage," O'Carse said. Someone got out and secured the up-and-over door, got back in with a slam. They reversed again, swung and went ahead.

There was no sign of Beth.

*   *   *

Shortly after the van had driven away from Grays two apparent police cars, mobiles with uniformed crews, had left a warehouse in Tilbury, a relic of the liner days now used by an outfit that repaired crash damage, and had driven fast along the A126 to Purfleet where they picked up the A137 through Dagenham for West Ham and the southbound Blackwall Tunnel beneath the Thames. From here they had driven into Woolwich and had gone to ground in a disused dairy where behind a high brick wall they joined another marked police vehicle, currently empty of a crew. There was a light on in a

164

derelict office. The four men from Tilbury crossed the yard to this office, where two men were playing cards and drinking tea. One of them looked up.

"All right, Squib?"

One of the newcomers nodded. "All correct. You got the word from Grays, did you?"

"Yep. No bother. Best get out of them uniforms."

"Can't wait," the newcomer said. He and the others went across the office, through a door at the back. Here, in a larger room, mattresses were laid on the floor, a dozen or so of which seven were already occupied by sleeping forms. The men from Tilbury began stripping off the police uniforms in the light of a bare electric bulb that one of them had flicked on as he went through from the office. The two ex-army men were among those already bedded down. One of them woke, cursing the light.

"Keep your hair on. Won't be a tick."

The light was out again within a couple of minutes. Soon after this O'Carse came in from Grays, in the Escort van. The slower vehicle had been passed by the mobiles the other side of the river. The van was unloaded and the contents transferred into the boots of the mobiles while Shard, still cuffed but with the gag and blindfold removed, was sat in the office. There was no talking until O'Carse had finished the transfer and come into the office. Then, speaking to one of the card players, he said, "Know who this is, do you?"

"No."

O'Carse told him. The man said, "Didn't need the wife after all, then."

"She'll help too. Where is she?"

Shard felt the heavy thud of his heart, felt the blood mount to his face. The card player said, "Safe. In the caboosh."

There was no knowing what or where the caboosh was but Shard didn't like the sound of it. But Beth was said to be safe, and that was a lot. Meanwhile the other man was asking O'Carse if Shard had come across with anything useful. O'Carse said no, he hadn't, but his main part was of course yet to come, and at this there was a laugh. The atmosphere was easy, relaxed. There was confidence around. Shard really

165

hadn't made much difference by barging in. And still there were no clues. There was some inconsequential talk and then O'Carse yawned and said it was time they all got their heads down. They felt very secure inside what was evidently the depot. Shard was led through a doorway and then told there was a mattress for him to lie on.

"No tricks," O'Carse told him. "You'll be guarded all the way through."

So someone wasn't going to get a full night's sleep.

It was, he believed, some hours later when he woke to hear the ringing of the telephone the other side of the door.

*   *   *

In Faslane Hedge had turned in early after a good dinner and rather too much brandy but had not been able to get to sleep: there was so much on his mind, which went whirling round in circles, getting him nowhere. At any moment something might happen, a bang in the night that would obliterate half the Clyde and himself with it. He wondered why he had been sent: no-one seemed to want him. Oh, they had been very polite, of course, but there was a hint that the navy could look after itself. He was beginning to feel superfluous, which was an uneasy feeling. He could be in Scotland for months for all he knew, facing the most appalling danger minute by minute. He almost found himself wishing Detachment X would hurry up and end the terrible suspense. His nerves were playing him up very badly. In the middle of the night he got up, took an aspirin and ate two tablets of Ginseng, which he always found steadying – he was currently on a month's course of Ginseng and had forgotten to take his ration after dinner, thanks to the brandy. Automatically he checked his bedside table: wrist-watch which he always removed at night, wallet, cheque-book, small change, torch in case the electricity failed, cigar case, lighter, Rennies. Then, on a sudden impulse, he picked up all these items and put them in the coat pockets of his suit, on a hanger in the wardrobe, so that he could save time if Detachment X should strike during the night.

166

Then he laid down again on the bed. He was snoring as dawn broke over the Gareloch. The peaceful, un-blown-up Gareloch, with that great black nuclear-powered submarine still at its berth.

*　　*　　*

In the Woolwich depot the telephone had been answered and O'Carse had been woken with urgency. When the Irishman had taken the call he was in a bitter mood. The call had been from a contact, a plant who'd grown in a propitious field. O'Carse called out some of the men from the mattresses and held a conference in the office. Shard strained his ears but couldn't pick up anything. Not until the conference was over and the door from the office came half open. He heard the Irishman's voice.

"Could come to a shoot-out, and then a bloody fast move. Bloody load of kids!"

That was all. It meant nothing to Shard. He fancied he might be in for another question-and-answer session but that didn't happen and he was left in peace. A suspended copper would hardly be in any position to give up-to-date information in any case, if something fresh had come up.

He drifted off into an uneasy sleep, having nightmares about Beth. The day came up, the men woke. There was a tension in the air now, very noticeable to Shard, but nothing happened except that some food was brought by one of the men, pre-packed sandwiches, tea from a flask. Unhungry, Shard ate just to keep his strength up. Time drifted slowly by. There was no sign of O'Carse for most of the day, but he re-appeared after dark and called another conference. The last one, Shard heard him say.

*　　*　　*

Behind the closed door O'Carse repeated his remark, the previous night. "Bloody load of kids . . . just because they might want to pee." He'd had a bad day, trying without success to glean more information. His contact had told him

167

the Home Office was worried about seasonal traffic problems and delays north of the Dartford Tunnel, the big bottleneck in the holiday months. It was believed the police escort would break off at the exit from the tunnel and would head back north once the coaches were clear. But what if they remained in company ahead and astern along the M25? Any police presence at that stage could be disaster. In any case, it could mean the fuzz was on to something even though they'd have got their wires crossed. If they didn't believe they had something, why else provide an escort for a bunch of EEC kids right through from Harwich just until they were clear of the tunnel?

Didn't make sense.

O'Carse didn't like it at all, but knew he was in a cleft stick. To delay was not on, definitely. There was a rendezvous and it had to be made. The chance would not recur.

Tack tried to be reassuring. "Could be just what the bloke said: traffic problems. No more in it than that."

"Sure. But that doesn't help, does it? The point is, the fuzz are going to be around. And we have to pick up the artics at the A2 roundabout . . . at the very bloody time the coaches are coming through!"

"Last night you mentioned a shoot-out."

"Right! If we have to, we do. I don't want it, it could sod up the whole show. But the orders stand, we stay in business, move out 5.30 a.m. and make the rendezvous at 6.15."

That night the tension was very much increased, the atmosphere in the dormitory almost electric, and Shard believed that most of the men were as sleepless as himself. In his case his insomniac state was largely due to the sheer frustration brought about by his helplessness.

16

"Right," O'Carse said, standing by the leading police mobile early next morning. He was wearing his police chief inspector's uniform; two men, the ex-army men, were in sergeant's uniform, the rest being dressed as constables.

Shard asked, "Where's my wife, O'Carse?" There still hadn't been a sign of Beth.

O'Carse laughed. "Safe! She stays here. But her safety depends on *you*, right? I can be in instant touch with the depot all through. Any trouble, she gets it. Bear it in mind, Mr Shard."

Shard was ordered into the lead car with O'Carse. The Irishman got in and the convoy moved off, sharp on 0530 hours. Leaving the gates Shard picked up the landmarks: high brick walls surrounding the dereliction of what had been the arsenal, farther on barracks with a wide parade ground, then the old Royal Military Academy, no longer used as such. They were in Woolwich. As they swept up a hill O'Carse told Shard that if for some reason they were stopped by genuine fuzz, then yes, he was Shard and he was under arrest. If he said a word further, Beth would suffer. O'Carse repeated what he'd

169

already said: there would be communication with the depot throughout. They had him all ends up; and they had that use for him, so far unspecified. Shard knew that O'Carse in his chief inspector's rig would carry the authority to retain him if there was any argument as to whose property he was. The cuffs and blindfold were no longer being used on him: if difficulties arose with the genuine police, the presence of handcuffs and a blindfold on a senior officer just might arouse a few suspicions, or so O'Carse believed. The convoy of cars moved fast; at this hour the traffic was not heavy and the only delays were at lights along the Sidcup Road and elsewhere. O'Carse kept on checking the time; they had to be as spot on as possible but it would be better were they too early than even a shade late, and you could never forecast what the traffic might do.

O'Carse was on edge now: they all were. The man in p.c.'s uniform alongside Shard in the back of the mobile was thin-lipped, taut as a drum. Shard was well covered; the man was ready for any move he might try.

A little before 0600 the cars slowed short of the roundabout where the A2 trunk road fed into the M25. No heavy vehicles approaching the roundabout from the A2 . . . O'Carse wasn't worried, though the traffic was light yet. Moving slow, the phoney police cars halted on a hand signal from O'Carse. O'Carse and his mob watched out ahead and to the left, towards the exit from the Dartford Tunnel. Traffic went past, traffic came from the tunnel, still not heavy. O'Carse watched the time constantly. At any moment a police escort might come through and he wasn't going to jump the gun. Meantime he was early so it didn't matter; but he would move out on time and chance it. If the coaches and their escort didn't show . . . well, it would obviously take a long while for four coachloads of kids, mothers, teachers and drivers to relieve themselves in the conveniences outside the tunnel. Non-appearance would be no more significant than that.

Then they came, rolling up from the distant exit. O'Carse said, "Coaches. And I reckon they've dropped the escort. We're okay to go – right on time." As the four coaches came up from the tunnel towards the roundabout free of their police escort, O'Carse waved his cars on and into the roundabout.

170

They were all in as the coaches slowed to enter, giving way to the supposed police mobiles coming in on their right. Shard saw the loads of children, waving from the windows, all looking excited and happy.

*　　　*　　　*

The first report went to Hesseltine in Scotland Yard and he rang through at once to the security section in the Foreign Office.

"Through the tunnel," he said. "All safe."

It was Detective Inspector Orwin who had answered. "Nothing happened, sir?"

"Not a thing, thank God. We were on a bum steer after all."

"Back to square one, sir." Orwin paused. "Shall I inform Mr Hedge at Faslane?"

Hesseltine said, "No, leave him to me." When he'd cut the call he sat back for a moment, frowning. Back to square one was right, everything just as it was before he'd gone overboard for the Dartford Tunnel theory. The defence establishments were still at risk and there was no knowing when or where Detachment X would strike. Or it could still be a civilian target . . . he took up his security line again and called Faslane. It was early, but Hedge could be dragged from bed. The dragging took some time and Hedge sounded peeved: he'd just managed to get to sleep, he said. And what did Hesseltine want?

"Dartford Tunnel – "

"Yes?"

"Coaches through and clear. No blow-up."

There was a snort. "I never did think there would be, my dear fellow. Never! A stupid theory all along."

"But one that had to be covered, Hedge, once it had been considered. I'm sorry."

"Well, so I should think! I trust you'll be getting those mobiles back where they belong – watching over the military targets. So much time wasted, so many policemen diverted – "

"Just two cars, Hedge, that's all."

"That's as maybe. Have you any word of Shard?"

171

"No."

"It's all very suspicious," Hedge said. Hesseltine rang off without comment and Hedge put the handset down with a bang, bad-temperedly. He gave a sudden shiver, as though he'd suffered a premonition: it was all back to Faslane again, he thought. No evidence, just a feeling, but a nasty one. Faslane was such a prime target, along with Greenham Common the very nub of the nuclear defence system. But perhaps they would hit at Greenham Common after all. And Hesseltine was a fool, a fool who had talked everyone into co-operating with his stupid ideas about children from the EEC. Of course, as Hesseltine had said, it was a case of only two mobiles . . . but it had got everyone into a fruitless way of thought.

*   *   *

Once O'Carse had entered the roundabout he saw the two articulated lorries coming up as expected to the junction from the direction of the Medway towns. They were coming up fast and came into the roundabout ahead of three of the coaches, following out along the M25 behind O'Carse and the leading coach, which had nipped in. The other fake mobiles, recog-nising the vehicles, which were being driven by the HGV drivers who had attended a session in the Grays house, slowed and let them through, holding the three rear coaches back. It was some nasty driving but police cars could get away with it. O'Carse, once out of the roundabout again, increased speed. Behind him the driver of the leading coach did likewise, following the apparent police car. All the drivers were Belgians: they had not been told to expect another escort after the Dartford Tunnel; but here was one and it was to be presumed there was some good reason for it. The leading driver had Britain's problems with terrorists in mind: he had believed, although it had never been said, that the first escort had had to do with possible threats to his EEC passengers. Falling in as it were behind the mobile, he shrugged: he must of course obey the British police. Immediately behind him was one of the lorries. Behind that, the second coach put on speed

172

to pass the second HGV and keep behind his leader. Then came the third coach, and behind it the second lorry. Behind that, the driver's mirror told him, were two more police mobiles, one of them coming out to overtake. Lastly came the fourth coach.

* * *

Sitting next to O'Carse Blakey said, "They're coming with us. The coaches."

"Too right they are," O'Carse said, quite calm.

"Extricate 'em?"

O'Carse grinned. "We bloody don't! Too late to muck about now, traffic's building up." It was; the lanes were busy in both directions as they all swept down fast for Junction 3, closely bunched. "Played right into our hands, Blakey, just where we want 'em. Something fortuitous we didn't expect . . . concentrate the mind of the brass even more."

"You mean take the kids with us?"

"Right! They're coming anyway, aren't they? They'll follow like sheep – you'll see. Kids . . . they're a sight better than a load of cars and vans and such, solo driver jobs, no passengers." O'Carse added, "It's their own bloody fault for being there."

Blakey gave a whistle and a nod. Too true, what O'Carse had said. Kids . . . kids from the EEC, what a bleeding headache for the brass! Blakey hugged himself with glee; neither he nor O'Carse were exactly philanthropists and young lives didn't particularly register. He obeyed orders when O'Carse told him to make hand signals through the rear window, to the mobiles and the HGVs, indicating that they were to keep the four coaches closed in and closed up tight with no chance for a break-out. The mobiles would get the message all right: they were to drop the original idea of bringing any other hostage vehicles into the convoy. O'Carse drove on. The police car that had been overtaking now slowed to tuck in behind the rear coach after its driver had given a thumbs-up in response to Blakey's mouthings and flapping hands.

Tight together, they all peeled off into the exit for the A20,

173

signposted for London and Orpington. The leading coach driver was surprised to say the least at the change in his route but accepted it as necessary for reasons unknown. The other three drivers simply followed him. Like sheep, as O'Carse had said. They came onto dual carriageway: a good, fast road at this time of day. O'Carse again increased speed: before long, someone was going to tick over, his immunity couldn't last for ever. The convoy sped past a lay-by, past a snack bar in another lay-by. London was now signposted at seventeen miles; and just after this the dual carriageway widened to three lanes. They went over a railway line . . . rugby pitches, both sides of the road after the railway . . . housing estates . . . on into the outskirts of Bexley and down again to two lanes. More traffic and O'Carse was obliged to drop his speed. Here the official limit was fifty and there were law-abiding drivers in front of him. London fifteen miles; and now down to a single lane, more buildings, bus stops, a big roundabout at Ruxley Corner. Here there was something of a hiatus: the second of the two articulated lorries, its driver having failed to comprehend and being anxious about the coaches ahead of him, between him and O'Carse, managed by some dangerous driving to pass the rear coach and tuck in behind the third one. Now the area was considerably more built up, an industrial complex. But back again to a wider road, with a suicide lane down the centre. O'Carse used this, disregarding speed limits, forced the oncoming traffic from the overtaking lane ahead. Another roundabout at Crittall's Corner, Central London A20 straight ahead. Shard was trying to work things out: why in heaven's name Central London? Back now to dual carriageway with O'Carse in the fast lane all the way. London twelve miles, speed limit fifty. O'Carse pushed it up. They crossed the A222, lights at green. Central London eleven miles. Up a short hill on the Sidcup by-pass, back to single lane and the speed forced down again: the next speed limit was forty past the National Dock Labour Board's sports ground. Dual carriageway again, and urban clearway. They came into the London Borough of Greenwich. The sign said Nuclear Free Zone and O'Carse gave a sudden laugh.

"One explosion's as good as another, they all kill," he said.

174

That was all. No-one else spoke. They were grim-faced, tensed up now. Sidcup Road, still forty mph . . . dual carriage-way again, traffic lights at Five Ways Corner and the speed dropping as O'Carse came up to a tail-back. The lights changed before he had to stop. Now on the A2, more traffic lights, green, a pub called the Dutch House with a big red neon sign reading TAKE COURAGE.

O'Carse laughed again.

Beneath a railway bridge, and then another roundabout. O'Carse took the exit signposted for the Blackwall Tunnel and the A102M, crossing the South Circular Road. Still dual carriageway . . . lights and a right turn, again signposted for the Blackwall Tunnel. Playing fields both sides of the road behind iron fences, a wide road with a suicide lane which once again O'Carse used, his rear mobile keeping the convoy closed up like sheep dogs . . . tower blocks, council flats. The road narrowed again past Kidbrooke Station, over a railway bridge, single lane, past the Thomas Tallis Youth Centre and under a footbridge, right turn – Blackwall Tunnel again, into a narrow, twisty sector which O'Carse took as fast as the traffic allowed . . . past a public house, a left-hand turn. Traffic really pressing now although it was still early, no chance to overtake anything, council estates, onto the A102M. Down a cleavage with high walls to either side, a number of road bridges crossing overhead, walls becoming higher and then fading away as the road widened into three lanes and the red lights flashed their speed-limit warnings, twenty mph and the Blackwall Tunnel, busiest of all the Thames crossing points, now five hundred yards ahead. Gantries with lane instructions and general warnings: one said no explosives or inflammables in the tunnel, and O'Carse laughed for the third time. Instruct-ions about weight, length and width limits also amused him. Past the Victoria Deep Water Terminal on the left.

And into the Blackwall Tunnel.

*   *   *

The time elapsed had not been long: forty-five minutes from Junction 3 on the M25 to the entry to the Blackwall Tunnel.

175

The convoy's progress had been noted and reports had been going in minute by minute: London had never seen anything quite like this before and it was a miracle there hadn't been a massive accident. The reports reached the Yard and Hesseltine: the four coaches with the children embarked had entered the Blackwall Tunnel northbound, accompanied by police mobiles, two articulated lorries mixed in with the coaches and behind the convoy an assortment of the usual day-to-day traffic. B Division was on the ball and mobiles were moving as fast as possible to be in position at the exit roads north of the tunnel.

Hesseltine didn't expect anything to emerge after the innocent traffic ahead of the coaches had cleared away. He was right: nothing did. North of the Blackwall Tunnel, from there to the various exits to the A11 and other routes, the roads stood empty.

Once again Hesseltine was on the line to the Foreign Office. "This is it," he said. "Detachment X for my money, holed up in the Blackwall Tunnel."

The Head of Security, early in his office, was rocked. But he said they could only wait. There was bound to be a contact. Detachment X must be wanting something; if they intended to blow the tunnel – and that would of course be the big stick – they wouldn't blow it yet. He said, "I'll inform the Permanent Under-Secretary. Keep in touch, Hesseltine."

"I'll do that." Hesseltine rang off, wondering what the results would be of a blow-up in the confines of the Blackwall Tunnel. The results above ground – they could all visualise what the scene would be like inside, the shatter, the blood, the wreckage, the mangled bodies. No doubt similar to what would have happened had the explosion come in the Dartford Tunnel, but this was closer to London's heart, the East End heart at all events. What effect would the downpouring of the Thames have, if the explosion didn't all travel out of the exits and the roof burst through? Millions of tons weight of water, swilling through to spill out at either end, one of the capital's main traffic arteries gone for a long, long time to come. Hesseltine knew the statistics: the Blackwall Tunnel was 6200 feet in length, and of this 1222 feet were below the river itself.

176

External diameter twenty-seven feet, sixteen feet width of carriageway, sidewalk of three feet one-and-a-half inches, headroom at the centre seventeen feet seven-and-a-half inches . . . for what it was now worth, it had taken five years to build.

Hesseltine sweated, drummed his fingers on his desk. His telephone rang, the security line. It was the Permanent Under-Secretary himself offering the usual Civil Service panacea.

"There's to be a conference, Hesseltine, immediately. Get over, will you? I want everyone together . . . ready for when these people make contact."

*   *   *

O'Carse in the leading car, behind the early-morning build-up of normal traffic, had touched his footbrake three or four times, bringing on his brake lights as a warning to the coach behind. Gradually the speed came down. O'Carse stopped at a couple of hundred yards past the midway point. Behind the police car at the tail of the coach-and-lorry convoy, other traffic was still coming in. Nothing from ahead: the southbound traffic used the separate tunnel to the east. O'Carse's men got out from the car and stood by it with automatic rifles in their hands. They answered no questions. There was already a degree of panic; the traffic was already forming a tail-back, streaming away south of the tunnel. Now there was no way out other than on foot along the narrow walkway.

There was a movement out of the cars. Still the armed men in police uniforms would answer no questions: it was very sinister. Drivers and passengers hoisted themselves to the sidewalk, and streamed back south. The armed police didn't interfere. Not until a helmeted London bobby was seen moving in alongside the halted traffic. When that happened one of the armed men lifted his rifle and opened fire, and the constable fell in a pool of blood and lay still. There were screams and shouts, and more people left their cars and ran for safety. As the racket died away, there was a total silence until it was broken by a police syren and then more gunfire from the northern end, echoing along the tunnel.

177

17

The northern gunfire was more sustained: a police mobile, a genuine one, had entered the empty mouth of the tunnel and come on with its blue lights flashing and its syren blaring out a warning. The three men who had been with Shard in the lead car had already got out, and now they crouched, waiting, automatic rifles aimed ahead.

O'Carse gave the order the moment the mobile came in sight round a bend in the tunnel. All three opened fire and the mobile slewed a little as its driver died, and came crabwise across the carriageway to hit the side wall and stop. The firing was kept up, then O'Carse went forward at a crouching run behind his gun. He took a look then walked back.

"All dead," he said. "And they've made a nice road block if their mates come in. Now – Mr Shard. Pin your ears back and listen. There's all the time in the world, but there's no point in delay. First thing, get out."

Shard came out from the back of the car. As he emerged and came upright he looked back along the line of lorries and coaches. The children were dead scared, staring white-faced from the windows, the coach lights on. Armed men from the police vehicles were moving up and down, making their weapons obvious to the coach drivers, who were remaining in their seats and looking as scared as the children. O'Carse, his face streaming sweat now in the tunnel's closeness, held his rifle with one hand and with the other took a grip on the front of Shard's jacket. His face was thrust close and the look was hard, determined, fanatical.

"This is where your part starts, Detective Chief Superintendent Shard of the Foreign Office. Starts right now. Ready?"

Shard stared back. "I doubt if you really expect me to cooperate."

O'Carse laughed. "I *know* you will, Mr Shard. I *know* you will. Now listen. You're going to walk ahead with an escort until you're in the tunnel exit north. You're going to find fuzz – your own mates, right? You're going to talk to them. But you're not going to do anything else and you're going to say nothing beyond what I tell you to say, and when you've talked you come back. You'll be covered all the way by the guns . . . and then there's the other thing, isn't there? Your wife. First thing that looks like going wrong, she gets it. Now: ready for your speech, Mr Shard?"

*   *   *

The Foreign Office conference was well attended. Besides the Permanent Under-Secretary and the ACC there was the head of B Division – traffic – and high-ranking men both military and civilian from Defence Ministry. In addition, this being now very much an EEC matter, the Common Market ambassadors were in attendance in person. There was a man from the Cabinet Office, plus the Home Secretary, also in person. Indeed the only VIP not present was Hedge, distant on the Gareloch.

The Permanent Under-Secretary started the ball rolling: like the Head of Security earlier, he said there was nothing to be done in any direct sense until the men in the Blackwall Tunnel made some sort of contact; but in the meantime, since they all had explosions in mind, certain dispositions had to be made. Many had; Hesseltine reported that all traffic for the southbound tunnel had been halted some way back from the entry and the immediate area was now clear. He had been in touch with the Port of London Authority and all river traffic over the tunnel had stopped as well. Efforts were being made to clear the contiguous areas north and south.

"An evacuation?"

"Yes, so far as possible. We don't want unnecessary casualties . . . we don't know how much time we've got and it's a big operation to – "

"Quite. I understand that. Troops?" Sir Edmund looked across at a major-general from Defence Ministry.

"London District's available when required, Under-Secretary."

Sir Edmund nodded, seemed undecided. "What can they do, I wonder?"

"Depends how the situation develops, of course." The Major-General was abrupt, largely because he didn't know the answer to that either. "GOC London District's awaiting orders, and in the meantime is moving troops closer to the vicinity of the tunnel, north and south."

"They can't get away with it," Sir Edmund said. "Can't possibly. Must be a suicide squad." He paused. "I suppose we could . . . er . . . mount an assault, General?"

"On what?"

"On the tunnel mouth. From the north, where I gather the entry's clear of traffic."

"I don't think so, Under-Secretary. That would only precipitate their actions. As you said yourself, we must wait. It's nasty – doing nothing. But it's inevitable. We've done, or are doing, all we can for now. I – "

"If I might put in a word?" This was the man from the US Embassy, Hedge's bugbear, Taft; but he was interrupted by the sudden burr of the telephone that stood in front of the Permanent Under-Secretary. Everyone tensed up as Sir Edmund answered. He nodded and said, "Thank you. Yes, I'll hold the line." He looked up, looked around the intent faces, tucked the mouthpiece below his chin for a moment.

"Tunnel, north exit," he said. "Shard has been seen in the tunnel mouth."

*   *   *

The men were behind Shard, their automatic rifles aimed, but they were keeping out of sight from beyond the exit. Shard could see police officers, all of them armed, keeping handy for cover. He knew what he had to say. He knew too that if he spoke out of turn the threat to Beth would be carried out. He knew his own risk as well: a gunning down on the instant. He was no thin red line of heroes but his own risk he could accept: it was part of his life as a copper. It was not part of Beth's. Nor was it part of those children's lives, or the mothers and teachers, or the coach drivers; and he didn't see what he could achieve in any case since he could only tell the truth, give the story as it was.

He called out to the police beyond the tunnel.

"My name is Shard . . . "

A chief inspector answered: "We've recognised you, Mr Shard."

"Is there anyone from my section there?"

"No, sir."

Of course, they wouldn't have known until now . . . Shard spoke steadily, in a carrying voice. "I'm under duress, as is everyone in the tunnel. One hundred and sixty-eight children and some women . . . I have a message from Detachment X." He swallowed.

"Listening, Mr Shard. Go on, please."

"In the tunnel is a massive amount of high explosive in two articulated lorries." His voice was almost emotionless. "If it goes up . . . but it can be prevented."

"How?"

Shard looked around for a moment at the deserted roadway. There was a heavy silence where there should be the increasing roar and thunder of London's morning traffic, the start of the rush hour. It was an eerie silence; he answered the chief inspector's question: "A safe conduct is asked for, that's the first thing. Detachment X will leave the tunnel when the safe conduct is granted. They're to be driven in two police mini-buses to a private airfield the whereabouts of which will be given once they're on their way. Aircraft will be waiting for them. If the safe conduct is broken, the tunnel will be blown by remote control. That's one thing. Here's the other – they have

181

demands." Shard paused, took a deep breath, and went on. "They concern Northern Ireland – and the Republic. All political prisoners other than Ulster loyalists are to be released unconditionally from the Maze and Crumlin Road and all other prisons north and south of the border. They know this can't be done quickly. But the tunnel's at risk until it *is* done. All the people inside remain there however long it takes. They'll be released twenty-four hours after the demands have been met."

There was a silence. It was broken by the chief inspector. "Do you believe they mean all this, Mr Shard?"

"Yes."

"You've been told to say that?"

"Yes. But I believe it. They'll do it – have no doubt about that."

"And the tunnel – once those men have gone under a safe conduct – "

"No-one will be able to move in or out. The lorries carry equipment . . . a beam will cover the exits, both ends. Any movement in or out will trigger the explosion. And overall, the remote control facility remains."

Another silence, broken this time by the voice of O'Carse in rear of Shard. "Okay, that's it. Back now."

*   *   *

The conversation had been reported as it was taking place to the Foreign Office and the intent ear of Sir Edmund. When the call was finally cut he said, "Well, now we know." He added, "Shard's gone back inside." Item by item, he had repeated the report to his audience. They all knew the score. It had been something no-one had suspected.

Taft said, "Well now, see here . . . that Shard. Is he in cahoots? That bribery. Doesn't sound too good to me and that's a fact."

Sir Edmund said, "I have every confidence in Shard, Mr Taft."

"Sounds funny to me. Insisting they'll do it – you know? They put him up to say just that – "

"*I* believe they'll do it," Sir Edmund broke in sharply. There were nods all round: they all knew the dedication of communist terrorists. Neither the IRA nor INLA, who could be behind Detachment X, would call themselves that, of course; but no-one doubted that the background had to be international communism since wanton terrorism had never been imputed against the ordinary Catholic population living in the Six Counties except insofar as they had themselves been terrorised into co-operation. Even the representatives of the EEC countries seemed quite convinced that the threat was for real. They, too, had had their problems with terrorists of various sorts. Now they were concerned with another threat to their nationals, this time on British soil, and were not overly concerned with the British position in Ulster.

Children, one of the ambassadors said. You couldn't condemn children to death, which was what it would amount to.

"I agree, of course," the Permanent Under-Secretary said. "But we're in a cleft stick, aren't we? They can't be got at, can't be extricated. This is the very devil . . . but it's gone beyond me, obviously. Beyond all of us here."

His face white and showing the strain of a long series of events, he took up his telephone and called Downing Street. He made a full report, speaking first to the Foreign Secretary then to the Prime Minister in person. He was told that an emergency meeting of the cabinet would be held at once and then a statement would be made in the House that afternoon. In the meantime there would be procrastination in regard to the safe conduct. The PM felt safe in doing that: Detachment X wouldn't blow its trump card while the men were still inside. Which in itself was the government's trump card as well. Or was it? Sir Edmund was not convinced. Suppose the gun mob simply came out into the open, taking a chance if they were kept waiting too long? What could in fact be done about them? Arrest them and let someone else operate the remote control procedure – for there had to be someone, somewhere, apart from themselves, standing by to do just that? You couldn't tooth-comb the whole of London and the controllers would be mobile anyway, keeping one jump ahead of the military and the police.

He said as he put down the handset, "Once again, we wait. Masterly inactivity." He took up another telephone and called Detective Inspector Orwin in the security section. "Orwin? Pass to the police at the tunnel, they're to contact verbally and tell Detachment X their request is being considered." Then he turned again to the assembled brass. "Dublin and the Northern Ireland Office are being informed of the development. The PM wants an FO presence in Belfast and I'm sending the nearest ranking diplomat, geographically speaking."

The Head of Security asked, "Hedge?"

"Yes – Hedge. Tell him, please. Fill him in. Then he's to be helicoptered at once to Stormont."

* * *

In something of a dither Hedge was on his way in obedience to changed orders. His brain whirled: such sudden and startling developments, not that he was sorry to leave Faslane but Belfast would be little better. There was physical danger there as well, although he could of course count on being well guarded in view of his importance. His actual orders were imprecise: he was simply to liaise and that might mean anything. It might even mean nothing more than that he was to be a sort of exalted messenger. There had been something in the Head of Security's tone that had conveyed something like that. The PM wanted someone in Belfast and it didn't much matter who. Hedge hadn't liked that and his underlip had jutted out at the telephone, but he wasn't able to argue the point because the call had been abruptly cut.

Soon after that another call had come, this time from Defence Ministry: Hocking was to go as well. So Hocking had made a pier-head jump, as Commodore Rushcroft had put it in his navalese, and was now in the helicopter with Hedge. He kept on talking but there was so much din that Hedge could scarcely hear him even though he was shouting in his ear. Hedge caught something about the likely reaction from the Ulster loyalists who might take matters into their own hands.

184

He shouted back, "It's being treated as top secret. You know that, my dear fellow. Only the Secretary of State and the military and – "

"It'll spread."

"What?"

"*Spread*. Spread like lightning."

"The facts about the tunnel may. But not their demands. In any case . . . really, I can't see what the loyalists can *do* about it. Not from Belfast."

"You don't know the Irish," Hocking shouted grimly.

"Nor do you." Hedge didn't hear the next shout and in any case preferred to disregard it. A shouting match in a naval helicopter was undignified. But Hocking's words had sunk home: the Irish were a very unruly lot, especially so, like the Scots, when drunk, and drink was a part of Irish life, the more so when they had something to drink about. And Hedge understood that most of them were armed. The moment the nature of the demand was known, there would very likely be bloodshed, mobs tearing through the streets with their guns, firing indiscriminately, looting, burning. The whole province could quickly become a shambles and it might be necessary to declare a state of emergency and impose Martial Law. There was no end to the possibilities; Hedge worked himself up to a high degree of fear during the short flight and felt like a jelly when he disembarked on a summer-green lawn at Stormont and was taken inside – he was much relieved to see a two-man bodyguard close in on him with bulges under their armpits – to attend a conference with the Secretary of State and the leaders of the main political parties. Here he found them in agreement with Hocking's views: trouble indeed there would be the moment the truth leaked.

It must not leak. It *would* not leak, the Secretary of State said firmly. Of course, the drama being enacted in the Blackwall Tunnel was known by now; a terse and edited statement had already been made on the BBC news – that had had to be done, obviously. But there had been nothing about the demand and no mention at all of Northern Ireland or the involvement of Southern Irishmen such as O'Carse.

It had to stay that way, the Secretary of State said, and there was full agreement on this too. It was Hedge who struck the note of unease on the secrecy aspect, having just thought of something.

He said, "With respect, Secretary of State. I would suggest that it's really no longer fully secret even now. There was Shard's contact with the police outside the tunnel, remember. There was nothing secret about that . . . admitted, there wouldn't have been many people around apart from the police, but we can't assume there were none at all, can we? The moment anyone who heard speaks to the press – well, no threats from Government are going to hold *that*."

This was only too true. The fear was acted upon at once. The army, already on a full alert, was ordered to increase the strength of all its armed patrols and with the RUC to take up strategic positions throughout the province.

*   *   *

The tension, the whole atmosphere in the tunnel beneath the London River, was coming up to boiling point. Everyone was in a state of fear: the children, comforted so far as possible by mothers and teachers, young women themselves distraught and not understanding what was going on, looked out at the armed men of Detachment X wide-eyed, many of them crying. The air itself was frightening to them: close and still filled with the exhaust fumes that had puffed out until the engines had been switched off. The great hulking articulated lorries, so sinister, the police uniforms that were now being worn slackly, shirts half out of trousers, ties removed, caps gone – this surely wasn't the way of the British police? And why were they not moving? The way seemed clear ahead, except for the crabwise police car in which the dead bodies still lay and were visible to those in the leading coach. That car could have been moved. And in Britain police didn't shoot at and kill other police.

The four drivers did what they could but they had no more knowledge than their passengers. All they could do was to try to keep their spirits up, keep them occupied. In the leading coach the Belgian driver, a fat and jolly man himself a father of seven children, got them singing, or tried to: they were not all

Belgian and the driver knew only Belgian songs. But a thin sound came from the coach and was heard by Shard, who had been put back in one of the cars, but still had his hands free. The frail sound of the singing struck at his heart. He believed them all to be doomed, no hope left. He didn't believe for one moment that either the British or the Irish Government would concede. They couldn't concede, it was not possible. In Shard's view the inevitable remained even after a police loud-hailer had started up and a voice had shouted that the demands were being considered. O'Carse had seemed happy enough but Shard had known the message for what it was, a mere ploy, a time gainer.

He racked his brains, trying to find a way out of an impasse. Both sides were in fact stymied; and before long O'Carse would be faced with having to make a decision. He wouldn't wait indefinitely, it would all smell a little high. What would he do then? Get himself and his mob out, taking the chance without a safe conduct, relying on the big threat he would leave behind? If he did that, would he be allowed to get away with it?

The answer was probably yes, since the remote control could be used if he were impeded in any way . . . Shard believed that the remote control would be found in Woolwich, the 'depot' with which O'Carse could be in touch when needed. Found with Beth, perhaps left behind with more intent than just to be used against himself. She could be a kind of hostage for the whole remote-control set-up, but it was pointless thinking about that now. More useful to concentrate on that beam, the sealer beam. But Shard was not well up on the propensities and capabilities of beams, though this one, he supposed, could be similar to those that controlled the opening and shutting of doors as people approached. One thing: he decided it couldn't have been switched on yet if O'Carse was to get out. Anything moving could presumably activate it. Even the outward scurry of a rat, if rats lived in the Blackwall Tunnel . . .

One of the men – one of those who had seen service in the British Army – jumped from the tail of the leading HGV. He had been busy inside, setting up the operation. He approached O'Carse; Shard overheard the conversation.

"All ready. Better get the vehicles shifted into place and the carriageway cleared south." The two men began to move away but Shard had got the drift. The vehicles bunched behind the lethal convoy, now empty of their drivers and passengers, had to be got rid of. Any vehicle half across the entrance, half across where the beam would operate, would break the seal. Probably that could lead to an automatic and premature explosion as soon as the beam was switched on. In the next half-hour there was a good deal of activity. The engines were started up and the first articulated vehicle pulled ahead of the leading coach while the second manoeuvered in reverse until it was behind the convoy. The coaches were now sealed right between the two explosion centres and Shard judged that the whole lot would be smack in the centre of the tunnel, right beneath the river. Once this had been done a big operation took place, obviously with co-operation from outside, from the Met, co-operation under the guns of the phoney outfit: the vehicles just inside the entry were shifted out in reverse once room had been made for them by dispersing the tail-back over a wide area outside the entry. Thereafter the whole approach to the tunnel, all the lanes, became one big parking lot.

The men came back and the army experts re-entered the leading artic. They jumped down again and with assistance from the others brought out two square metal boxes like television sets without screens. One of these was carried back towards the entry, the other to the northern exit, each trailing a long lead.

In the back of the police car, which was now with the coaches between the two artics, Shard was in a bath of running sweat, breathing petrol and diesel fumes left behind by the manoeuvrings of the heavy vehicles. What it must be like in the coaches, stuffy and sick-making . . . outside the car, even one of the armed men was looking sick, his face pale in the light from the overhead electric lamps running down the centre. Shard wondered if someone outside would get those lights switched off to help confuse Detachment X, but the fact that they hadn't yet done so could mean they didn't want to frighten the children even more. If those lights went out . . . but of course the coaches had their own lights.

188

It sometimes happens that people in widely separated situations think alike.

The lights went out.

*   *   *

From Stormont the Secretary of State for Northern Ireland had been in frequent telephone touch with Downing Street; Hedge for his part was in communication with the Foreign Office. He was, he told the Permanent Under-Secretary, keeping his fingers on the pulse of events.

"Ah, good," Sir Edmund said. "And the situation now?"

"Under control, but there are elements who might disturb the peace at any moment, Under-Secretary – "

"I can guess who," Sir Edmund said. "What's being done?"

Hedge told him about the further orders to the army and the Royal Ulster Constabulary, following upon his expressed fears of a leak via persons who might have overheard the conversation at the tunnel exit. "The press, Under-Secretary," he said.

"The press will remain silent." Hedge's fears, Sir Edmund said, had been thought of in London. The press had been told, no words minced, that any editor who transgressed secrecy requirements would be in big trouble, even charges of treason being mentioned. Hedge said he still wouldn't be one hundred per cent confident in a situation like this. There were so many ill disposed persons . . . not, of course, the press, he hastened to add. In the Foreign Office the press was always accorded a degree of sanctity in conversation until they actually did transgress, for the press was undeniably powerful. But this time it was not to be the press anyway. Hedge, his report passed, went into a bar that had been set up in a room leading off the conference chamber and was about to get himself a large whisky when the news broke via Hocking, who came into the bar to round up the relaxing constituent parts of the conference.

"Trouble," Hocking said.

"What?"

"There's been a broadcast – "

189

"Good God! D'you mean about – "

"Yes. Not the BBC, of course, and not any of the pirate stations either. Someone's spilled the beans – people speaking for Detachment X . . . they weren't on the air long enough to be traced, but they've announced the threat. It'll have been picked up all over."

Hedge shook like a leaf. Here he was, in Belfast, at the very dead centre of it all, representing Her Majesty's Secretary of State for Foreign Affairs and at any moment there could be rebellion! Things *always* escalated in Ireland. Sinn Fein, the IRA, INLA – they couldn't fail to take full advantage of a most dreadful developing situation. The IRA would be bringing up all its strength, reinforcing its wretched Belfast Brigade and blowing things up willy-nilly . . . the words, rather haunting ones with an extraordinarily catchy refrain, of a terrible revolutionary song came to Hedge as he made his way back to the conference, feeling a loosening in his bowels: *Come all you gallant Irishmen, Come join the IRA, And strike a blow for freedom, When there comes a certain day* . . .

Hedge now believed that day had come.

*   *   *

In the tunnel, just for a matter of perhaps half a minute until the men ticked over, ran for the vehicles and flicked on the headlamps, the only light came from inside the coaches. Patchily the dun-coloured, dirty walls came up; elsewhere was deep shadow. Shard reacted fast, taking what might be his only opportunity. He was out of the car before the man on guard duty had accustomed his eyes to the sudden gloom and he had jumped him, bringing him flat. He wrenched the automatic rifle from the man's hands and as he struggled up he slammed the butt into the head and the man went down again, out cold.

Shard ran for where he had last seen O'Carse.

That was when the headlamps came on.

A man moved fast, back from near the northern exit. Shard saw the rifle come up, heard a shout from a shadowy O'Carse, an angry shout of warning. Another man ran up from behind. There was no firing but Shard found his body gripped from

190

behind by powerful arms that came close to crushing his ribs, and the automatic rifle was wrenched away.

O'Carse came up, eyes hard. "Don't try that again, Mr Shard. You've just risked that wife of yours. You won't get another chance. Nor will she. Don't be a fool." He nodded at the man holding Shard. "All right. Let him go. But watch him."

Shard realised that it had been the shout from O'Carse that had saved his life, stopped the guns before they'd opened. So he wasn't to be killed – yet. Why?

18

The answer to Shard's wonderment came in the next moment when O'Carse said he and his mob were leaving: everything was ready now, he said, looking at his watch. He was confident they wouldn't be impeded, not with all those kids likely to go up. Shard was being left behind to talk again to the police, through the beam barrier, to keep up the convincement that this was all for real, that the moment O'Carse gave the word the explosion would be triggered off and the Blackwall Tunnel and its prisoners would vanish into history by way of a cataclysm that would bring devastation to a good deal of London at the same time.

Looking at his watch again, O'Carse began moving with his fake police for the northern exit. Shard asked, "How do you get through the beam, O'Carse?"

O'Carse laughed, still moving, still clock-watching. "It's on a time switch. It'll come on just ten seconds after we're clear."

Then they moved fast, backing away and keeping the guns aimed at Shard and, beyond him, the coaches. The last man had just passed through when Shard heard a loud click from the nearer HGV. O'Carse had made it in the nick of time.

*　　　*　　　*

Hesseltine got the message from the police officer in charge at the exit. A number of men had emerged. What were the orders now?

Briefly Hesseltine reported to the brass, still in session, remaining a cohesive group until the situation jelled one way or the other. He said, "I advise letting them have their way for now. Or else."

Sir Edmund, grey-faced, gave a nod. "No option. Provide transport for wherever they want to go. I want a report immediately the destination's known."

Hesseltine passed it on. The Permanent Under-Secretary called Hedge at Stormont. "What's the situation?" he asked.

"Tricky, Under-Secretary. There's an extraordinarily fraught atmosphere . . . it's on a knife-edge. I understand there's tremendous tension in the Catholic enclaves – Falls Road, Bogside in Londonderry, you know the – "

"Yes. That damn broadcast! Now there's something else." Sir Edmund passed the word that the men had left the tunnel. "It can go up at any moment, Hedge. Any moment, that is, after those men have got to safety. We don't know where safety is . . . but we assume it's outside the UK itself. I doubt if they'll blow while they're airborne and that may give us time, we don't know how long. Possibly not very long. They may head for the Republic and it's my bet they will."

Anywhere in the Irish Republic wasn't more than about an hour or so from anywhere in the UK – one hour maximum was the safest assumption. Sir Edmund said Dublin was being informed of the British Government's assessment.

Hedge asked, "The Irish as well as ourselves will track any aircraft, presumably, Sir Edmund? When they pick it up, what happens?"

"To O'Carse and his thugs? That's still in their own hands. The threat from remote control will remain. My mind is

193

running along the lines of a possible parley, probably somewhere on the border.''

"Yes, very likely, I agree, Under-Secretary - ''

"And that'll be up to you in the first instance - the man on the spot. Highly suitable. The right level, you see. It would be inappropriate at this stage to play this thing at too high a level - you'll understand that, of course. You'll be kept informed and so will Dublin. They'll be told you're immediately available in Belfast.''

Hedge didn't like any of it. He felt an onset of near panic, the walls of Stormont closing in on him and swaying away again, a nasty feeling. His mind seemed to shoot out from the top of his head and dwindle into the sky and then come back with a thump. The future was going to be extremely dangerous in a physical sense and also appallingly difficult to handle, even though he was being entrusted only with the initial stages - being used, he tended to suspect, knowing the Permanent Under-Secretary, merely as an agent for delay until Whitehall had gathered its wits and its response. But in the meantime he had to put up a good show. And there were compensations: he would be out of Belfast. But the border would be no picnic, of course. It was soon after this that reports began coming in of full-scale mobs on the move, the start of riot. Some RUC men had been shot up and missiles used against the troops, and a number of explosive devices had gone up without warning in shops and banks. There were bloody clashes between Catholics and Protestants.

*   *   *

There was hysteria in the coaches. When the armed men had gone the drivers got out and gathered round Shard, arms waving, faces tense. Why had he been left behind, who was he? They asked their questions in good English. He told them who he was but couldn't be sure they believed him. He told them not to approach the tunnel entrance and to make sure the children didn't either - he told them the full facts about that; the knowledge could worsen the incipient panic but they had to know.

194

"The children," Shard said. He had half a mind to get them out of the coaches: they *might* be safer near the exit, they just *could* make it or could be blown clear without the wholesale slaughter that would come if they were caught in the coaches, dead centre and confined. But children were children, there were four coach-loads of them and they couldn't all be watched all the time, and if just one of them should make a break for what looked like a clear exit, then the end would come. It just wasn't on. He said, "Keep the kids in the coaches and make damn sure they stay there." Lying in his teeth he went on to say the situation was in hand from outside. The Metropolitan Police were there in strength and would cope. They were going to get out. They didn't believe that. They were done for. Panic was going to be fatal and Shard did all he could to nip it in the bud and stiffen the drivers. The children, he said, depended on them, the men in authority, the familiar faces that had been with them all the way from home and would see to it that their passengers came to no harm. He said, "I'm going to get up into one of the HGVs and have a look around. I'm leaving you to your jobs. All right?"

He turned away, found himself thinking of Beth. He'd already put her in danger once by reacting automatically to a chance. But he couldn't have done less and he mustn't dwell on private matters. He swung himself up to the big rear doors of the northernmost HGV, double doors that stood open with the wires running down to the TV-like box that had been placed on the sidewalk platform just inside the exit. If he wrenched out those wires . . . no, that would activate the explosion, probably, just as surely as if the beam itself were broken. Too great a chance to take. He got inside. The HGV's interior was filled with packed high explosive with the primers and amatol detonators ready and the beam leads from the northern end of the tunnel running into another large, square metal box of similar size to the others. A fast examination told him that the box was completely sealed against any interference. And if, say, he should interfere with the detonators, that also could be lethal. Any pulling at wires and leads and connections, even any heat applied by hand to the amatol, might tip the balance of a delicate and intricately organised spider's-web.

195

Sweat ran into his eyes. He dashed it away. A feeling of total hopelessness almost overwhelmed him. He looked at his watch: 1030. They had been in the tunnel – what – more than three hours now. He was shaking, he could be a danger in himself if sheer vibration close to the detonators set anything going – amatol was a very, very volatile explosive and one that would have needed very careful packing for the journey in.

He got down from the vehicle, heaved himself up into the second HGV in rear. A similar set-up: and the other beam box would be positioned at the southern end.

Nothing to be done. Nothing – except try to keep the children happy as time passed, so slowly, towards what seemed an inevitable end. He spoke again to the drivers and suggested ways of keeping the children occupied. Word games, singing. They'd sung before; they sang again, each lot in its own coach with its driver acting as choirmaster. It could go on for days . . . Shard thought about starvation, thirst. Rationing . . . the EEC party had brought things in cellophane packets and bottles.

Beth kept intruding.

Beth and the remote control . . . just a faint, faint chance? He couldn't be entirely certain where it might be situated. For one thing it could be mobile. But he still believed it could be in what the villains had spoken of as the depot. In Woolwich. It wouldn't be at the Grays house, that had been shut down once his own intrusion had put it at risk. But Woolwich: he'd not been blindfolded on the way out and he could pick up the route in reverse as it were.

He might be able to get it across to the police outside; if he could, it was worth a long shot, but they would have to be pretty bloody careful or the remote control might be activated and the whole tunnel would go up – but *would* it, without orders from O'Carse?

Shard moved fast for the northern exit. Shouted instructions to the police . . . but he had approached the tunnel's end, standing well clear of the intruding beam, when there was a racket from behind him, shouts and crying.

He turned, fear piercing like a knife.

A number of children were racing down for the exit, pursued

196

by two of the coach drivers, coming past the abandoned police car.

Shard yelled out, "*Get back! Get back for your lives!*" He stood like a goalkeeper, arms wide, body ready to jump this way or that to field the running children from the exit. But he couldn't be everywhere at once. Three or four of them evaded him and as the first passed through the beam there was whirring sound from the metal box on the sidewalk. From deep inside the tunnel, in the sector below the river where the lorries and coaches stood, there came a series of loud clicks, clicks like revolver shots.

*　　*　　*

A telephone rang; Hesseltine answered. "Airborne," a voice said. "Two light aircraft, SD360 commuter planes – "

"Where from?"

"Just a field, sir. Near Biggin Hill. Heading north-west and being tracked."

"Keep me informed," Hesseltine said. He reported to the Permanent Under-Secretary, who nodded and took up another telephone.

This was answered immediately by Hedge in Stormont. Sir Edmund was ordering the stand by. Dublin would be contacted immediately, he said, and would be asked to call Hedge direct when more was known. Sir Edmund was now making the firm assumption that the aircraft were heading for the Irish Republic. This, he said, would be confirmed as soon as more reports came in.

Hedge dabbed at his cheeks as he waited, got up, prowled about, sat again with his hands shaking and face wobbling. Within an hour the confirmation came: the aircraft had crossed the coast over Anglesey and were heading north of Dublin.

The Dublin government would take over now.

*　　*　　*

The children who had run through the beam were met by uniformed police. They were picked up and run to the police line as fast as they could make it. Reports went at once to Whitehall, Downing Street, Scotland Yard. In the tunnel's vicinity the mobiles were being pulled back, with the foot men now aboard with the escaped children. Inside the tunnel, Shard, expecting the big blow at any moment, had run back towards the coaches between the HGVs, shouting to the drivers to get their passengers out pronto. He fancied there was a smell of burning from the lorries but if so it didn't last. Something small could have burned out; this was no time to stop for a look.

Now the children and the handful of hysterical mothers were streaming out through the exit, disregarding the beam, showing every sign – naturally enough – of panic. No explosion came. It passed through Shard's mind that there had been a monumental coincidence: O'Carse's remote control could perhaps have been activated in the precise moment that those children had run through and one set of controls had reacted against the other . . . something like that. But no: it was much too soon for O'Carse to blow the tunnel, it must be. With that remote control on his mind Shard ran from the tunnel to contact the police line. Ahead of him a small girl fell flat, screaming; Shard picked her up and raced on. Police were coming now, picking up the slower runners and then beating it fast to the rear.

Shard reached the mobiles.

A chief superintendent, a man he knew, had arrived to take over. Shard looked at him warily: there was a constriction, even in this situation, as though the chief super was in half a mind to arrest him, wondering if he should do his duty or not. As the children were piled into a convoy of police vans Shard said, "You'd better report pronto. Situation changed! Then I want a mobile . . . destination Woolwich. I want to find my wife."

Some of the vans and mobiles were already on the move out as the report went through. There was no explosion. Bluff? Shard didn't believe it had been – the high explosive was real enough, so were all the trappings. Before Shard was in the mobile, armed now with a police revolver, the Foreign Office had come through: for the time being all word of the tunnel's evacuation was being held under wraps as far as possible. In case of accidents not even Hedge or Dublin would be informed yet. Detachment X had to believe they were still in command.

*   *   *

The call came through from Dublin, for Hedge: the light aircraft had touched down near the village of Ballymullion, in County Cavan, around four miles from the border with Ulster. O'Carse had been in touch by radio, demanding a meeting with representatives of both governments.

"That's what we expected," Hedge said.

"Yes. We know. The meeting's to be at Clones, that's just our side of the border. O'Carse reminds us of the children. We have to play along so far as we can . . . and our understanding is that your people feel the same way."

"Yes, quite so."

"You'll also understand that we in Dublin, no more than you, want to see terrorists set free from our gaols – "

"Yes, yes."

"Then if you'll arrange to be in Clones as soon as you can, Mr Hedge."

"Yes, very well," Hedge said. "Mind, I shall make no decisions and I shall agree to nothing. I shall dismiss nothing. I shall in fact say as little as possible. I shall commit neither myself nor my government. Good-day to you."

The man in Dublin rang off sourly, wondering why anybody was bothering to send a speechless mouthpiece. Hedge busied himself, making quite sure that no aspect of safety had been overlooked in regard to his forthcoming trip across an uneasy border to Clones: he was to be helicoptered as far as the border itself, continuing into the Republic by road, in a mobile to be provided by the Garda. There were niceties to be observed, the Republic's sovereignty respected.

*   *   *

Shard had the route well in mind. When he was within one street of the disused dairy he told the mobile's driver to stop: he

199

would go the rest of the way, circumspectly, with just one plain clothes man. The mobile – and others were following up – would remain on station to give assistance if and when called upon. Shard had been given a two-way radio, which was now clipped to an inside pocket. He and the plain clothes man, a detective sergeant from the Yard named Farrow, went at a run towards the target premises. En route from the Blackwall Tunnel's vicinity Shard had given Farrow a detailed description of the lay-out and their objective was to be the one-time office into which Shard had first been taken on his arrival from Grays. He wouldn't, he said, expect to find many of the villains loafing about the yard, but there would almost certainly be someone on watch, just in case. Someone who would be keeping hidden himself.

Farrow said, "It's likely this O'Carse will have passed back information, sir. That he's away and clear."

"So?"

"May have dropped their guard a little, sir."

"I wouldn't bank on it," Shard said.

They went on; when the premises were in view at the end of the street Shard called a halt. "Time's of the essence," he said, "but no bulls at gates. There's an alley ahead there, see it – "

"On the right, sir, just this side of the – "

"Right. I'm going in there. I want you to go ahead, drift past and take a dekko, then come back and report. All right?"

Farrow nodded and went on as Shard broke off into the alley. Shard had already seen that the gates into the dairy were shut; but beyond the premises there was rising ground, a short, steep hill and from its top Farrow should be able to look down into the yard. Shard had remarked on the time factor: that counted still, even though the children and the rest were out. No-one wanted an explosion beneath the Thames, no-one wanted the casualties that could result in the immediate area of the Blackwall Tunnel. And a baulked O'Carse, if baulked he knew himself to be by this time, could radio through at any moment to the dairy set-up.

*   *   *

200

The helicopter from Belfast had taken off, Hedge shivering though the day was warm. He was about to come face to face with murderers and anything could happen to him and probably would. From the windows as the machine swung away from the city Hedge could see the red glow of fires and shooting flames and more explosions, and army vehicles, armoured troop carriers and such, on the move.

The border was reached quickly. Hedge was put down and transferred; the Garda mobile, driven by a grim-faced, taciturn man, lost no time in heading south for the Clones rendezvous.

At Clones there was a strong presence of the Irish Army and the Garda to meet and accompany Hedge: the British troops and the RUC were conspicuously absent, another reminder to Hedge that he was no longer on British soil. In the circumstances he found that a naked feeling. At a roadside, a lonely spot a little way south of the town itself, the hard core of Detachment X waited, headed by O'Carse. It was O'Carse who started the parley. He shouted across the gap between the two sides.

"That's far enough. Who're you?"

Hedge called back, "My name doesn't matter. I am from the British Foreign Office and as such I represent the British Government. I have to say this: Your demands can never be considered – "

"Can they not indeed? Just listen: kids. EEC countries. You know what'll happen." The voice was without any feeling, and was entirely confident. Hedge felt his stomach loosen. He really had no bargaining counters at all. "Well?"

Sweat poured from Hedge. Hoarsely, desperately, he called out, "I'm not negotiating. My function is to liaise, that's all. I shall transmit anything you say to Whitehall . . . and Dublin will also, of course, be informed." He paused. "That is all I can say, all I can promise."

They waited for O'Carse to speak. The tension was at a very high point now, the whole thing on a knife-edge. O'Carse was fingering a sub-machine-gun. It would have a very wide spread of fire and unless someone acted very fast there would be nothing between it and Hedge.

* * *

Farrow wasn't back yet. Cautiously Shard peered round the corner of the alley. Then he saw the DS coming into view from the top of the rise. Just as he saw him, there was a bleep from his pocket transceiver. He pulled it out, flicked a switch and a voice came through. "Chief Superintendent Rice, from the tunnel exit." There was a pause. "Not all those kids came out – the teachers have just reported after calling a roll. Panic . . . some were injured, I suspect. Some of my lads have gone in to get them out. Over."

Shard blasphemed.

Rice said, "Just be careful, Shard. Just be careful. *And bloody fast!*"

Shard pushed the transceiver back into his pocket. Farrow, not hurrying, sauntered round the corner, looking unobtrusive. "Well?"

"Not a bod in sight, sir." Farrow saw Shard's expression. He asked, "Anything up, sir?"

Shard told him. "I don't know how many. But up to a point we're back to square one. I'm going in, Farrow. Frontal assault, blast our way through. It's the only way now."

He remembered Rice's words: be careful. But Rice wasn't here; he was. In his view, sheer speed had to take precedence. The sudden rush that might catch Detachment X on the hop, the speed that might get him to the remote control transmitter in time.

And to Beth.

A lot would depend on Hedge. Before leaving the tunnel area Shard had been told that Hedge was standing by in Belfast and that the Detachment X aircraft was believed headed into Ireland. If Hedge could use delaying tactics convincingly, then O'Carse wouldn't be forcing any issues yet. And usually Hedge was pretty good at evading issues, fogging points and so on . . .

He and Farrow moved down the road, towards the gateway at the foot of the rising ground. Farrow said, "Chances are it won't go off anyway, sir. You said there was a fault."

"Yes. A fault in the operation of the beam. We can't assume for sure the remote control won't send it up."

Farrow nodded but said nothing further. Shard's police

revolver was out now; he felt the increased beat of his heart as they came down on the gate. He was about to get Farrow to give him a leg up to the top of the gate when he heard a car's engine start up in the yard behind and a moment later the gates came open. A car nosed out, a car Shard hadn't seen before, a Ford Granada, fitted with two big arced aerials, one on either side, sweeping back from the bonnet. In the car were four men, and in the back, between two of the men, was Beth.

Shard saw that he had been recognised: the Granada accelerated fast, away left down the road. Shots came back; Shard felt the glancing sting of a bullet across his left shoulder and then he and Farrow had opened fire, both of them aiming for the tyres.

They missed. Shard swore luridly and brought out his pocket transceiver, calling up the mobile that was waiting a couple of streets ahead. From then on, things moved fast, very fast. With Farrow, Shard ran on in the Granada's wake and almost within seconds he saw the police mobile coming out of the side street, right across the bows of the speeding car. The Granada's brake lights went on, there was a scream of tortured tyres, the vehicle rocked and slewed and by some amazing driving executed a U-turn away from the mobile, heading down again towards Shard and Farrow under fast acceleration. Shard and Farrow went flat to the ground as the men in the car opened fire; once again the police revolvers were in action and the mobile was coming fast down behind the escaping Granada. Then one of the revolver bullets took a tyre, and the big car swung, the brake lights glowing red again, turned across the roadway and crumpled into the brick wall of the dairy. The bonnet buckled and steam came from the shattered radiator as Shard raced up. He saw Beth, white-faced, her mouth opened in a scream. The Granada's driver, no seat belt, had gone head first through a shatter of glass from the windscreen and hung there pouring blood. The man in the front passenger seat was firing across the driver's back, while one of the men in rear, a man with headphones clamped to his ears, was bending down in what seemed to be an attitude of concentration.

Alongside Shard, Farrow said, ''The transmitter!''

Likely enough, Shard thought; but O'Carse would surely

hold his horses, ordering the transmit only when the sands had run right out, using it purely and simply as an act of revenge. He moved towards the Granada, keeping low, dodging bullets. The Met officers were out of the mobile now but grouped behind it and using it as cover. Then Shard heard another desperate cry from Beth; the blood pumped through his body and risking the gunfire he got to his feet and raced towards the Granada, flat out and direct, firing almost frenziedly as he ran. At least one of his bullets hit the target: just as something seemed to explode in his shoulder and against his head - just before he fell to the roadway - he was aware of the man with the headphones crumpling to the floor of the car. Then, as though Shard's collapse had acted as a signal, the men from the mobile were running down the road to close in for the kill.

*   *   *

At the Clones rendezvous another car drove up behind Hedge, a car with an Ulster registration, moving fast along the country road. It came to a halt with a scream of rubber and a man got out and approached Hedge, a small, dapper man wearing an incongruous bowler hat: Hedge recognised him as a man named Parely, a civil servant from Stormont. Hedge was relieved to see him since he might take some of the weight of responsibility.

The small man was in a state of excitement. He said breathlessly, "Mr Hedge- "

"Yes. What is it?"

The news was momentous and very welcome to Hedge. Parely said, "It's all over, Mr Hedge! All over! I've been sent by Stormont . . . the tunnel's been evacuated - "

"*Evacuated*? Peacefully? All the children?" Hedge gaped.

"Almost all, so I'm told, Mr Hedge. Word has just been released - they - "

"Good heavens!" Hedge mopped at his face. "Oh dear, *what* a blessed relief!"

"Yes, indeed, Mr Hedge, amen to that I say." Mr Parely paused. "And equally important - the remote control has been inhibited, deactivated."

204

"How, who by?"

"By Mr Shard – "

"Shard!"

"Yes. I'm afraid he's been injured, Mr Hedge, but – "

"Oh." Hedge turned to stare across at O'Carse and his grim-looking mob. Triumph welled in him: the ground had been cut from under Detachment X, their bargaining power had vanished now. Hedge turned again to Parely. "You're *absolutely certain* of all this?"

Parely nodded vigorously. "Oh yes, indeed yes. There are no doubts at all – "

"I can rely upon it, conduct negotiations – that is to say, bring this affair to an end – upon it?"

"Oh, most certainly, yes! The word came from Downing Street, Mr Hedge. It's unimpeachable."

"I see." Hedge cleared his throat pompously, then walked across for a whispered word with the Dublin contingent. Then, once again, he faced O'Carse. Fear was mixed with the triumph: O'Carse had that sub-machine-gun. But duty had, of course, to be done. Hedge stiffened himself, felt his stomach sink nevertheless; he licked at dry lips. His heart pumped and he felt a rush of blood to his head.

He called out to O'Carse.

He said, "I have word that the Blackwall Tunnel has been evacuated, O'Carse."

There was a laugh. "Bluff!"

"No bluff, O'Carse. There's nothing you can do now." Hedge poised himself for flight as O'Carse fingered his sub-machine-gun. "I – I advise surrender. I advise it most strongly."

O'Carse jeered. "I'll not be caught by bluff, English bluff! I tell you this: if you force me to, I'll transmit the signal to my remote control operator."

"By all means," Hedge said in an off-hand voice. He waved a hand in unconcern whilst sending up a prayer that Downing Street had known what it was talking about. The nonchalance was in fact very well done indeed. Hedge saw the reaction from O'Carse, the sudden tightening of the lips behind the beard, the wary look in the eyes. Hedge's stomach suffered a surge of

205

terror and he looked round for an escape route from the gunfire that he was sure must come. He moved backwards fast; he had seen the cornered-rat look in the bearded face. O'Carse turned this way and that. The Garda and the Irish troops began to close in behind their weapons. Suddenly O'Carse opened fire in a swinging arc. Hedge threw himself flat just in time, squirmed his limbs about as though burrowing into the ground like a lizard. Bullets smacked into two of the Irish soldiers and one man of the Garda. Then O'Carse fell, taken in the legs by a stream of return fire.

He was wanted alive, was O'Carse. There was a brotherhood among police officers that could transcend frontiers and the Irishmen knew all about the faked-up charges of bribery.

*   *   *

Hedge went home post-haste. The word had reached the province at large that O'Carse had been bowled out and the spirit had been taken out of the incipient rebellion, although sporadic fighting was still going on and there was the odd explosion and more men died, so it was too potentially dangerous, Hedge thought, to linger; and in any case he would be wanted back to make his full report as to how he had finally settled the trouble. And upon arrival in London he reported personally to the Permanent Under-Secretary.

"It was very tricky, Under-Secretary. A fine balance was needed throughout – very fine."

"And you maintained it?"

"Yes, Under-Secretary."

"Training will out, of course." The irony was well under control.

"Yes, indeed. Training . . . and a good deal of experience. One learns to read these people, you know. They're tremendously – er – *unsubtle*, Under-Secretary, if you follow."

"Unsubtle, yes, a good word, that. So you brought it off, Hedge. They caved in."

Hedge was unaware of any nuances. He said, "Yes, that is so, Under-Secretary." He passed a hand over his hair.

"Persistence is the key, it always is. Whilst – er – persisting I was, of course, most particular as to *discretion*. I managed, not without some difficulty, to commit nobody to anything."

Sir Edmund gave a grave inclination of his head, hiding the sardonic smile. "A true diplomat, my dear Hedge."

*　　*　　*

Detective Sergeant Farrow went later that day with Shard's own DI, Bob Orwin, to the Queen Elizabeth military hospital in Woolwich where Shard had been taken by ambulance. They were told that Shard had regained consciousness and they could go along for a few minutes. Shard had already been told that Beth was all right though currently under sedation – she was suffering from reaction but there was no cause for worry and she'd be along to see him as soon as she was allowed. Farrow gave Shard the rest of the story: it was simple enough. One of Shard's bullets had gone through the headphone earpiece and into the man's brain and another had smashed the remote control transmitter. There had been police casualties when the officers from the mobile had closed in; the remaining men of Detachment X had been taken alive and would be put through the grill.

Shard said, "So it's all over." He felt light-headed, and in a good deal of pain: his right shoulder was giving him hell and there was a bandage around his head, which felt as though it had been kicked by an elephant.

"Yes, sir. We were only just in time. I reckon they were about to transmit, maybe even without orders from O'Carse – "

"Because we'd gone in?"

"Probably, sir, yes."

Shard let out a long breath, a painful breath. "Where angels fear to tread . . . it was a bloody great risk, Farrow. But I suppose it paid off." He caught Bob Orwin's eye. "How did Hedge get on, Bob?"

Orwin told him.

"Is he preening?"

The DI grinned. "Well, sir, what do *you* think? He's in very good odour currently. He brought it off. I reckon he's thinking in terms of a knighthood."

Shard made a rude noise: a raspberry, in fact. Hedge was as ever Hedge and had to be accepted.